MARK L. WILLIAMS

ALBA IULIA

PRELUDE

ISBN 978-1-966540-84-7 (softcover)
ISBN 978-1-966540-85-4 (ebook)

Printed in the United States of America.

INK START MEDIA
265 Eastchester Dr Ste 133 #102
High Point NC 27262

For
Paul and Stella
Nicholas and Minda

PART THE FIRST

CHAPTER ONE

Once upon a time, I assumed life was linear—or relatively so. I left college early with a desire to see Europe. My modest monetary situation stood in the way. The line from campus to the Army recruiting office was not, strictly speaking, straight; nevertheless, the path was easily negotiated. Similarly, the recruiter presented me with various options. I was interested in only one: a European posting.

"That," burly Sargent First Class Morgan announced, "I can guaran (expletive deleted) tee."

To be sure, there were speed bumps. I endured weeks of training at Fort "Lost-in-the-Woods," Missouri and additional weeks of advanced training at Fort "Puke," Louisiana. Most of my fellow "trainees" disliked both the training and the venues—one even went over the hill. I, however, remained fixed on my goal. Without adequate funds, I could never travel to Europe. However, in exchange for playing in the dirt and doing things the Army way, I'd get European living quarters, *and* be paid for the privilege!

Mine was a four-year sentence. Knowing the exact, terminal date of my enlistment allowed planning. Save for weekend travel and expenses, I banked my pay. When my separation from service arrived, I'd be bucks up and ready to "vacation" in Europe for several months.

True, there were potholes. I had to put in for an extension of my tour. This was simply a paper shuffle. When my orders came for Fort Polk, I posted them on the squad bulletin board with a raffish, hand-drawn cartoon near the bottom. My extension superseded my PCS orders.

Fort Polk was forced to manage without me.

By the time my enlistment expired, I was the longest-serving person in both my company and the battalion. I'd earned my reward.

However, unexpected detours proved the best-laid plans are subject to amendments.

With eleven days left of my enlistment, I was dispatched by our Home Station Commander to proceed to England and pick up a deserter and return him for court martial. Because my battalion was training in Bavaria, the company billets were secured. My few personal items were stored in the basement of battalion HQ—under lock and key. For the duration of the training exercise, I reported for duty with the eight soldiers too sick, too lame or too lazy to train with the men. As the ranking NCO, I was acting Battalion Command Sergeant Major. My commanding officer was a martinet attached to S-1. Doubtless, he was selected to remain behind to watch the store by the colonel's staff who found his impersonation of General Patton both presumptuous and abrasive.

In the battalion conference room were stowed two changes of underwear, my shaving and hygienic needs and my class-A greens. For reasons only the Army understood, I had to be mustered out in dress uniform.

My TA-50 was inventoried and repossessed by the supply sergeant prior to the company's departure. Thus, I slept on the floor under the large, polished mahogany conference table. I used my arm for a pillow and a borrowed overcoat for a blanket.

My routine was to shave in the officer's latrine, go to chow, and report to Lt. Hardass. As the ranking NCO, my job was to supervise the eight enlisted men in the stay-behind activities. Lt. Pompous, however, insisted on deploying the troops himself. Thus, while his command scrubbed the latrine, polished floors and enjoyed lengthy smoke breaks, I reported to the base library and read boredom away—while getting paid.

Nearing twenty-five. I had two years of college under my belt. Unlike others in my unit, I was content with the peace-time Army, and pleased with Europe. I shot up the ranks like a Fourth-of-July rocket. Upon promotion to E-5, I slammed into the apathy wall. I could not motivate my troops and soon became weary of writing them up, bailing them out, or escorting them to and from punitive non-judicial and judicial proceedings.

My only remaining military objective was to become a civilian.

On my second day as battalion CSM, I presented my meal card at the brigade mess hall and enjoyed a leisurely breakfast. It was slightly past eight when I reported to Lt. Stalin. Had it been anyone else, I'd pop my head in the office door, bid a good morning and scamper off to slurp coffee in the snack bar until the library opened. *He*, alas, was not anyone else. Therefore, I knocked boldly on the door frame, entered the office, braced two paces before his desk and whipped off a basic-training salute.

"Sergeant Nelson reporting, sir."

That ginger-haired bastard hid behind a moustache which, if it didn't violate regulations, certainly stretched them to the limit. Of course, Lt. Piss-'em-off would not deign to recognize a subordinate with a proper salute—those were reserved for officers and, specifically, those whose asses he intended to kiss. Since I didn't rate an ass kiss, he leaned back in the boss's chair and gave me something resembling a Girl Scout salute. I was not too short to get thrown in the brig or I'd have propelled across that desk to rearrange his obnoxious cookie-duster. In the absence of witnesses, it would be my word and service record against his. The odds, however, were arrayed against me. There was a chance I'd cross paths with him after my discharge.

It was a slim chance, but I'd cling to it rather than splash blood over the Colonel's desk.

"Nelson," he drawled, "get your ass over Brigade S-1. You're leaving for England this afternoon to pick up a deserter."

"Yes, sir!"

I snapped off another salute and did an about face before he returned the salute—probably by picking his nose. Once out of his sight, I presented an additional gesture the Joint Chiefs would consider unmilitary—save, perhaps, in the presence of the enemy.

It's a blur, now.

Somehow, I acquired a set of orders and a sergeant from HHC of a tank battalion. I think we reported to the MP station for a pair of cuffs and instructions in how to use them. We were briefed on how to escort the prisoner from an Air Force base to the desk sergeant on duty at our post. Somewhere in our preparations, we were each issued .45s and a magazine of ammo.

Somehow, we were delivered to the Rhine-Main Airbase where, after presenting our orders, we were hurried onto a hospital plane, a military version of the DC-9.

We took off for SHAPE Belgium, but during final approach, the pilot announced there was unexpectedly early snow on the runway. We pulled up our gear and headed for Hamburg. We proceeded to Berlin, then to Ramstein before trying SHAPE once more. Finally, approximately seven hours after our initial ETA, we arrived at Minldenhall.

Arriving at the Air Force confinement facility, we discovered our prisoner buffing the tile floor. A more innocuous looking person I've never seen. He was haggard and wan. His clothes were tattered, his hair in a state of mutiny, and his face hadn't seen a razor in months. The tread-head sergeant and I tacitly agreed that the handcuffs were superfluous.

"Where've you been for six years?" I asked.

"Shakin' wif my girlfriend."

"Was it worth it?" my associate asked.

"Shiiiiit no, it waz't worf it!"

There'd be no return flight to Germany until the following afternoon. The Air Force cop tending our charge assured us that, after the floor was properly shined, the prisoner would be returned to his cell to await collection.

Somehow, we got into the transient billets. It cost us two dollars each, but we got a spacious apartment with two upstairs bedrooms and—most important—shaving gear and tooth-cleaning equipment.

Our planned eight-hour (linear) excursion turned into an overnighter. Between the blond sergeant and me, we pooled twenty-four dollars. We opted to walk to the NCO Club and satiate our growling stomachs.

We sat at a table for two covered with linen so white that it hurt our eyes; we ordered what we could afford. As we ate and conversed quietly, we were extremely self-conscious. We wore our class-A greens—still crisp despite our day-long Odyssey. No other patrons were uniformed. Enjoying a second cup of after-dinner coffee, the English waitress reluctantly made a journey to our table.

"Pardon me," the embarrassed woman began, "people are asking about your uniforms."

My partner and I exchanged an incredulous glance. Army personnel held the Air Force in low esteem, but we assumed a modicum of intelligence was required to fly and maintain aircraft.

"We're Army," my astute colleague replied, being the first to find his tongue.

"We're here to pick up a prisoner," I added, for want of something germane.

The waitress smiled and nodded. She proceeded to make the rounds and the atmosphere in the dining room relaxed.

"They figured us for SMLM," I whispered.

In military slang, we used the word *Smell 'em*. Unlike civilian bureaucrats, we enlisted men shied away from lengthy abbreviations.

Had we not, it would translate as *Sierra Mike Lima Mike*; hardly risk free for those of us who had yet to master correct spelling.

I'd seen uniformed members of the Soviet Military Liaison Mission twice in the Frankfurt PX, specifically in the *Stars and Stripes* bookstore. There were always two (the one on the left was watching the one on the right and vice-versa). On both occasions they were thumbing through the *Army Times*—the cheap bastards would never deign to buy a copy.

During the occupation, the four-powers required military personnel to maintain contact with various units and HQs to avoid confusion. I doubt if any of the allied powers continued relations, but the Soviets pretended to. They were, as with their diplomats, spies. They monitored our convoys to and from training areas, recording vehicle types and numbers. At other times, they paged through the *Army Times*, picking up little items to forward to Moscow. Who knows? They may have sent their bosses news of my promotion, though I doubt the *Times* ever bothered to print promotions of junior NCOs.

Neither of us understood how Air Force personnel failed to recognize a soldier in dress uniform. Everyone I knew could identify Navy, Marine, Coast Guard *and* Air Force uniforms *without* the aid of a British civilian.

Sometimes, I despair.

Too late, but in a sincere effort to provide brevity to this opening narrative, I will report that we caught a C-130 to Ramstein. The MPs arranged a "co-op" to get the three of us from one point on the map to another. We logged time in four police cruisers. Our last leg was interrupted. The Frankfurt MPs were diverted to provide backup at a rowdy night spot. With the prisoner sandwiched between us in the back of the cruiser, I half expected to see one of my enlisted subordinates dragged away in cuffs. Alas, to escape from a secure training area for a night in the Frankfurt sex plaza was beyond the wiles of the cerebrally indigent members of my unit.

Finally, we returned to station. The mess halls were shuttered. The snack bar was closed. At the MP station, I bid farewell to the prisoner and the tanker sergeant. I reported to the night window of the NCO Club and squandered my remaining assets on a bratwurst.

"Start at the beginning."

Easy advice by those who are never forced to assign a "beginning." A conspiratorial effort forced me to the word processor. One's friends can be brutal. When one's wife is among the conspirators, however, resistance is futile.

Regardless, there's method in the madness of the narrative thus far. In a very real sense, it constitutes a *beginning*, so innocuous and tenuous that it embarrasses me.

The battalion conference room had, tucked away in a corner, behind the stars and stripes, an ancient console radio. It contained a bevy of tubes, but—against all odds—it worked. In my barracks room I shared with a buck sergeant in the radar section, we listened to baseball on AFRTS. We'd drift off during the early innings, but it provided a relaxing background to blunt the "quiet-hours" noises of troops scuttling to the shower, latrine, and tending equipment in preparation for inspection.

The conference room was dead silent. It was unnatural and unnerving. The tube radio, left over from the occupation days, was too tempting. It might, still, be possible to drift off during a ball game.

Ah, bliss!

It was a multi-band set. It's presence in the battalion HQ was predicated on a spurious legend that it served in Ike's occupation headquarters. His office was in Frankfurt's I.G. Farben building. A more plausible explanation, whispered here and there by the less gullible, was that it came with the *Kasserne*. Prior to and during the war, the facility housed a tank hunter-killer unit. If the console radio was inherited from anyone, it was the local branch of the *Wehrmacht*.

To ward off boredom while awaiting bedtime, I explored the shortwave band. Within minutes, I found Radio Bucharest. For reasons unfathomable, I listened to most of the English-language broadcast. It pricked my funny bone to listen to Eastern propaganda. On the AM band, I garnered many laughs by tuning in Moscow. Radio Tirana, however, supplied the greatest comedy by far! I expected Radio Bucharest to be similarly riotous. Surprisingly, much of the broadcast dealt with the city of Alba Iulia and its history, beginning with the Roman days. There were a few, oblique, references to the superiority of Romanian socialism, but these didn't dampen my interest. After this feature, I enjoyed selections of Romanian folk music. I liked it. (I still do.)

Later, I fell asleep during a relay of an American League game. However, I dreamed of Romania.

I leave it to the shrinks to evaluate; my unprofessional opinion, however, is that this one-hour broadcast in English counts as a "beginning."

After my Army hitch, I became European tumbleweed.

It was never my intention to go anywhere near the mob gathering for the Olympics. Alas, in Prague, I fell in with a fellow *expat*. We found the cheap beer positively—you will excuse the expression—*intoxicating*.

The word *cheap* is inappropriate. True, by West German or American standards, the price of beer was sinful. There was, however, nothing wrong with its quality. It was the best I've experienced.

Matt was a well-heeled hippie. Disgusted when McGovern got buried in ballots, he took his bundle and left the States. Because he was a spoiled rich liberal, his attempt to look and act like a hippie was a failure. Aside from the fact that the hippie uniform had morphed into something more than the traditional battery-acid clothes and ugly sandals; it was passé. Matt's hair was rakish—clean but carelessly trimmed. His clothes were fashionable but not gaudy. His face was splattered with freckles and his attitude toward life was devil-may-care. He turned his back on politics and was just out for the ride.

"Let's crash the Olympics!" he said over his fourth beer.

"Not interested," I countered, still working—or, more accurately, *enjoying*—my third stein.

"C'mon! We can rub elbows with the posh bastards and really put their elevated noses out of joint. Hell, we might even sneak into a couple events."

"It's too cold to sleep on park benches," I reminded.

"I'll find us someplace."

I agreed because I was lubricated—and spiteful. I wanted to prove Matt wrong even if it earned me a case of frostbite.

Damn, if he didn't find us a place! True, it was a tiny room we shared with eight other people of both sexes. The only things we had in common were our relative youth, lack of inhibitions and the ability to brave an under-heated room by sharing body heat. There wasn't much room to practice proper hygiene though we made a brave effort. After two days, there wasn't much we didn't know (or see) of each other.

Matt and I marched around the skating pavilion and heckled ticket holders as they came in and went out. In truth, Matt did the heckling for us both. However, I managed to—um—*procure*—a pair of tickets. We were allowed inside to enjoy warm, circulating air. We unzipped our coats and relaxed.

It wasn't an event, *per se*. The women figure skaters worked out. At first, it was a general melee not unlike a medieval event but without lances and swords. Eventually, the ice was cleared, and contestants practiced their free skates while the judges looked impassively on.

Simone Albescu

It was the first I knew of her existence. She was not top tier and had no appreciable following. However, she was Romanian. That, alone, riveted my attention.

I recalled my bizarre sojourn in the battalion conference room a few weeks prior. Inexplicably, romantic notions were conjured by seeing a girl from an imprisoned nation. What were the chances she hailed from Alba Iulia? Mightn't she have traces of Roman blood?

Simone was cute—from a distance. Her hair was light (timid) brown and her bangs were strangely seductive. She was short. As she skated, she appeared to pout. Her leaps were low-altitude demonstrations of power, but her moves were exceedingly graceful and polished. When compared with the other skaters, her routine was, alas, insipid.

Leaving the ice, Simone sat in a reserved area to watch the others. I watched her watching. I sensed gears turning in her head. She must realize she had no chance for a medal, but she studied as if scouting the competition. She was sixteen. She had an Olympics or two in front of her, and she mightn't always be a cypher in the world rankings.

Matt was off creating a scene. Thankful to be alone, I paid more attention to Simone than to the performers. To say that I found her attractive would be a lie, but there was a quality of intelligence and determination that earned my instant admiration. The other competitors conferred with coaches, members of their retinue or—in rare instances—each other before heading to the changing room. Simone, however, never took her eyes off the ice. She absorbed everything in studied silence while her coach, a stocky bull of a man, sat several feet away.

I saw enough of the man's face to notice his lips move from time to time. Simone remained expressionless. Just as I imagined her coach was humming or speaking to himself, Simone nodded. He might be evaluating skaters, critiquing their performances or authoring skating tips. One observation, however, required no interpretation: when Hamill took to the ice, the coach remained silent.

Simone watched with the same stoic demeanor she maintained for all other competitors. When Dorothy skated off the ice and disappeared among a mob of people, Simone let out a huge sigh. That was the one expression she allowed herself.

Christine Errath was the reigning world champion—I think. Figure skating, hitherto, was not on my radar, but Errath was a favorite. I, however, joined Simone in sighing after Dorothy's practice performance. It was, literally, breath-taking.

On a subsequent day, chance led me outside the pavilion following a medal ceremony. The competitors, coaches and sundry personnel were being herded to—wherever they were being herded. Even the "free" athletes had security escorts, but the Iron-Curtain contestants were extra-carefully guarded.

I was one more rubber-necking goose milling around in swamp grass. I thought morbid thoughts and payed scant attention. Suddenly, my right hand was seized and gripped firmly in two smallish paws.

"Albescu, Simone!" A bold voice announced.

I looked down into the sparkling brown eyes of a young girl as she pumped my hand for all she was worth. There was a disturbance in the crowd and several shouted commands in a language I didn't recognize. When she released my hand, she was gathered up by a burly arm in a heavy coat and guided away. A second goon in equally bulky togs glared at me as if daring me to move.

My shock and perplexity were such that an air raid wouldn't register. All my attention was focused on the beef-faced goon glaring as if plotting my demise. How long he studied me, I know not, but my socks melted under the intensity of his hatred. The moment he lumbered away, dragging his knuckles, I was a celebrity.

Fellow by-standers fired questions in a dozen languages. Next, reporters were shunting people aside to take a crack. Who was I? Was I an Olympic skater's boyfriend? (They didn't know her name. It's a wonder they knew she was a contestant). What did she say? What did she want?

I muttered a few things in English, but it was soon obvious I was a person of no consequence. In a matter of seconds, I was transformed from the life of the party to the forgotten man. When the reporters evaporated, I was quarantined.

The next morning, Matt punched me in the arm and hooted. He had a copy of a local paper turned to my picture. It looked as if Simone and I were old pals.

A Romanian skater greets a fan after the skating finals.

That was the caption. A six-sentence article was appended. Even factoring in German compounds of twenty letters or more, it was insipid pap.

"It says you're Roland Young," Matt poked with a gloved finger.

After I shed confusion, I explained.

"Facts confuse reporters."

Obviously, he knew nothing of the *real* Roland Young. It was just as well I was caught off guard. Had I known I'd be assaulted; I'd have identified myself as William Boyd. The pseudonym pleased me. I'd give an arm and a leg to have his pipes!

Not until much later did I learn Simone Albescu was exercising one of her many spontaneous revolts against her authoritarian masters. Recalling the malevolent expression sent my way by the Romanian goon, I consider myself lucky my body wasn't left face down in the snow. The *Securitate*, likely, included Roland Young on their hit list. The *real* Roland Young was safe in his grave, and my refusal to identify myself may have saved my life. Though too petty for the big, bad security forces to expunge...

Progressing along life's road, I learned that a certain dictator was constantly in Simone Albescu's thoughts. She, in turn, woke each morning lusting for a printed obituary.

CHAPTER TWO

My parents went to their graves two years apart. Their end was, likely, accelerated by an insatiable smoking habit. My brother was dispatched by a freak bicycle accident that, I'm certain, contributed to my parents' early exit. Though orphaned, I was not without relations.

When money ran out, I was delivered, on the Army's dime, to Logansport. My childhood home no longer stood. My family no longer existed.

I caught the first bus out of town. I didn't tarry long enough for coffee.

I have an uncle with influence in Chicago. He's a great high mucky muck in a hotel conglomerate. After a few days in limbo, uncle helped me into a tiny apartment near a technical school. He aided me in landing a position at an up-scale hotel just off Michigan Avenue. I hesitate to use the archaic *house detective*, but it serves better than the modern, politically correct, far-less accurate title.

It was not very taxing, though it entailed considerable abuse. The more money and power guests have, the more they regard others as slaves. I put up with their bullying and their outrageous demands because, in a very real sense, a key part of my job was to provide a buffer between the ass holes and the worker bees who kept the place humming. I understood this and thought nothing of scraping and bowing to placate the implacable.

Still, it wasn't my idea of a job. As great a city as Chicago is, it was not my kind of town. I was never morose, but felicity never found me there.

When I wasn't working, I haunted Navy Pier, the museums, the library, theatres and two sedate coffee houses. In my introspective moments, I found myself thinking of Simone Albescu—not her grabbing me by the hand. Rather, I focused on the pensive expression she wore when watching her competitors.

My Chicago years predated the home-computer era, so I couldn't track Albescu through the internet. I searched for her in the library. Pictures were both rare and wide-angle. Information was blurred and scarce.

Entire weeks passed without a thought of her. Then, unexpectedly, something would trigger my memory. When she snuck into my remembrance, I experienced a stomach knot. It wasn't unpleasant, but it was bothersome. I never loitered over barracks pin-ups; I was well past that stage. Still, the thought of Simone initiated a curious longing.

Then, skaters descended upon Chicago.

As fate would have it, the Romanian women and their entourage joined the Japanese men and their support team at my hotel. I examined the dispersion list. Simone Albescu was assigned to a single room on the eighth floor.

She must have juice. East Europeans generally roomed in pairs, trios and quads. (All the better to keep an eye on you, my dears.) Perhaps, Simone was isolated from the others because of her "counter-revolutionary" tendencies. An independent spirit might constitute a bad influence on the other slaves.

I'm guessing, of course. Someday, I might inquire into the reasons behind Simone's single-room anomaly. In truth, I don't really care.

I recognized her from afar when the Romanian gang entered *en masse.* Two thugs, constituting the advance team, distributed room keys. Simone, unsmiling and engaged in thought, accepted her key and headed for the elevator. She picked up her little roller bag to clear the gap. She turned to face front with three others. Her eyes looked directly at me from several yards away. She didn't recognize me, but, then, why would she? I doubt she took any note of me. After a moment, she examined the object in her hand for her room number. The doors closed; she was gone.

Back in those good old days, my TV and VCR were connected. Since I couldn't witness the exhibition, I set my equipment to tape the event from a local cable channel. It was just as well since most of the coverage consisted of commercials.

One of life's great pleasures is fast-forwarding through pap.

The only time the cameras focused upon Simone was during her performances. As she was not a headliner, the media paid scant attention.

As she took the ice, she smiled—momentarily. It was as phony as a six-dollar bill. During her routine, she wore an expression worthy of a surgeon in E.R.

It was a different routine than her Olympic performance. It was, even to my untrained eye, more difficult than her Innsbruck effort. Nevertheless, it was graceful and technically proficient. Unfortunately, she lacked the boldness and daring do of the major players. Perhaps, she merely strove to get on the judges' radar. It seemed to me that she was ready to break out of the pack and make a lunge for a ranking. At eighteen or so, time was no longer an ally.

Much, much later, I discovered why Hamill's performance at Innsbruck earned that wistful sigh. A heavy favorite going in, Hamill's skills, technique and performance were considered by the Romanian skating autocrats as the base line for the "big push." As bureaucrats are wont to do, they imagined that the key to victory was to skate Dorothy's program better than Dorothy. Only people with blades on the ice understood reality. First, nobody could skate the Hamill program better than Hamill. Secondly, it would constitute a miracle if any Romanian could skate half the program half as well.

Thirdly, judges are unlikely to reward copycats. Fourth, the press was sure to invent a scandal. Fifth, there were only four years between games. That seems lengthy until one accounts for the time required to master the skills *and* the endless string of minutia that go into an Olympic performance.

Knowing they could be shot, the skating coaches met on the Q.T. to discuss the government's two-year plan. They concluded that individuals be schooled only in the Hamill techniques best suited to the individual's strengths. This mightn't keep the storm troopers at bay. The only remaining device was to kowtow and explain—as rapidly as possible—that it was better to attempt an imperfect routine than to embarrass "the Party." Dorothy-Hamill copycatting was certain to end with the Romanian contingent performing on their asses rather than their skates.

Trusting reason and rationality is risky strategy when under the thumb of an authoritarian regime. The coaches and choreographers crossed their fingers and kept their heads down.

Of all the slave-nation lady skaters approaching the Hamill mystique, Simone was the runaway best. She worked day in and day out on the layback spin, the delayed axel and a combination double flip and double toe loop. She was at a serious disadvantage, however; Dorothy could fly; Simone was a granite pillar.

Simone's coach and her choreographer made her do the jumps as best she could. They felt that graceful, expressive skating and polished gestures would earn higher marks. This strategy worked. Simone spent far less time in the air than any other participant, but her routine was polished to a fare-thee-well.

Still, the Chicago gig was *only* an exhibition. In the skating world, however, *everything* is competitive. Ergo, the ten nations, both the men and the women, were keen on performance results. The Romanian coaches were sitting on a stove. The Regime expected to see a Dorothy Hamill routine, right down to the haircut. It was impossible. Still, scores would be tabulated and the higher the scores, the fewer Romanians would be liquidated.

Circumstances were more favorable for Simone than in the skating years B.L. (Before Lynn). Prior to the seventies, the bulk of the competition rested with school figures. The disciplined Albescu was rock-solid in figures—that is, she was *very good*. Before Janet Lynn, however, one had to be *excellent* or better in schools to have any chance at a medal. After Janet Lynn, schools counted for less; therefore, Simone skated at the precise time when figures no longer eliminated her. Theoretically, if she held her own in the compulsory moves, spins and jumps, her programs would keep her in the hunt.

Theory, however, doesn't travel far in the skating world. The fact that Simone competed under the Romanian flag guaranteed obscurity. Had she come from a country with a skating tradition, she'd have a better shot.

In Chicago, according to information garnered years after the fact, Simone skated better than ever and collected the best scores of her career to that point. At the end of the day, however, Simone bested only six other skaters—two of them were teammates.

Two things caught my attention: First, Simone performed to an instrumental version of a Gershwin tune. The relaxed tempo matched her style. Second, following her performance, a junior pixie skated out to present her with a bouquet of Chicago flowers.

The little girl was not ten if that. She skated to Simone who acknowledged the crowd's tepid adulation with another forced smile. The child was required only to hand Simone the flowers and skate to a neutral corner. Simone, however, didn't accept the proffered tribute with the expected dismissal. Instead, she leaned over and conversed with the child. It was a violation of established protocol; the broadcasters were forced to fill unexpected time. I like to think the director wet his pants because the scheduled bank of commercials was delayed by six or seven seconds.

Then, I saw it. Simone's smile—not that hideous contortion she offered as a part of her performance, but her genuine, heartfelt smile. It was warm, radiant and engaging. Even the frightened girl, eager to flee for safety, was disarmed. She nodded twice and returned Simone's infectious smile with one of her own. Still, Simone refused the flowers until she hugged the cherub and kissed her on both cheeks.

This was Simone's Chicago revolt. Her handlers crapped cocoanuts because she always—*always*—engaged in some spontaneous demonstration. At Innsbruck, she broke her tether to introduce herself to some hapless schmuck. In Chicago, she disrupted a scripted event by chatting up a young skating hopeful. I'm left to imagine what she did at other public venues. She'd get away with a defiant gesture *once*. The stooges were alert for repeats, but they were helpless to predict Albescu's next exhibit.

In addition to hours of commercials, the programs featured a quartet of the world's top female skaters. I never gave them a glance. I watched only Simone's performance—several times. She had the personality of an oyster, stoic and aloof. Nevertheless, during her few seconds with a young girl and in front of the assembled multitude, Simone was warm—and very human.

The Romanians (eighth floor) and the Japanese (fifth floor) were our guests for six nights. Both teams were slated to depart the afternoon following the women's finals. Because a pair of *Securitate* goons was posted on each end of the eighth floor, problems were strictly prohibited. Since only Romanians were billeted on the eighth floor, the discomfort created by security apes was limited to the slaves. It was not, by official edict, our concern.

I left work shortly after six and passed several Japanese guests chatting in the lobby. They babbled away in two languages based upon the composition of their varied trios and quintets.

Not a single Romanian was ever seen in the lobby. They would mingle in the eighth-floor hallway or stay in their rooms. Their "security" contingent would allow no unauthorized congress. Doubtless, even confabs among teammates was closely monitored.

My phone rang just after three in the morning.

Instantly awake, I grabbed from memory.

"Nelson," I mumbled.

"Houston, we have a problem."

It was the first I'd heard the coded message beyond training seminars. After the chill ran up and down my spine, I threw back the covers. I reviewed my personal, pre-planned, emergency procedure. I turned on a light and called for a taxi. After a quick shave, I dressed speedily. The cab arrived moments after I opened the front door.

"The *Titanic* might be sinking in the lobby," the boss said, during a previous briefing. "Do nothing to feed panic or causes panic where none exists."

Just how one enters a downtown hotel at an ungodly hour and appear casual was not included in our seminars. No one thought to ask. I, certainly, hadn't.

I came in at a normal pace and nodded to the people minding the front desk. They nodded back, feigning boredom, but an electric undercurrent flowed through the lobby. A police cruiser was parked in front of the main entrance and the presence of two uniformed cops next to the revolving doors was as subtle as a train crash. Still, we were schooled to *appear* normal; I did my best.

I turned sharp left at the far end of the desk and headed for the manager's office. I opened the heavy wooden door without knocking and was nearly bowled over by cigarette smoke. There were a dozen men and two women crammed into the office. They were smoking like war factories.

"Dixie" Dixon, my immediate supervisor, slithered through the mass of blue incense. He pressed me against the closed door and spoke in low tones.

"One of the Romans copped a walk," he explained.

"Who?"

"Not sure. One of the coaches. 'Must've snuck out by fire escape after the team got back last night."

I couldn't imagine such a thing. Those goons posted in the halls were there to keep the slaves from escaping. Even a Romanian bully must know a fire escape was the second-best way to leave the eighth floor. The *Securitate* couldn't spring for an extra few bucks to post a goon in the alley behind the hotel?

"What's the score?" I asked.

"Damage control. The guy's downtown asking for asylum. The goons upstairs must know, but nobody else does—we hope. We're to stand by in case the shit hits the fan."

"It is a guy, then?"

Dixie shrugged.

"As far as we know."

I scanned a room filled with partially controlled panic.

"Mind if I lounge in the lobby?" I asked.

I was doing a lot of asking that morning. There was scant information, but I knew Dixie wouldn't hold out. If he didn't tell me, he didn't know. Meanwhile, the atmosphere in the crowded office was far too cozy.

"We don't want people getting the right idea," he objected.

"There's no one on the street, the residents are asleep, and there are two cops out front. What the hell difference does it make if some Joe snatches a snore in the lobby? This room is as suffocating as an Army orderly room."

I attribute Dixie's sudden obtuseness to the tension in the smog simulator. After I reviewed the facts, his head cleared.

"Okay," he nodded. "Don't wander off. If I need you, I won't have time to search."

I shot him with my finger pistol and got out of that room before I keeled over.

As I sprawled out on a couch, I was careful to keep my shoes off the upholstery. A feeling swept over me that there was something very, very wrong. In a major city during an international exhibition, there should be State Department flunkies tripping over each other. Despite the certainty that government bureaucrats don't drink breakfast before early afternoon, there should have been a phone in—some supercilious fool from Washington to instruct us about the animal sacrifice we were obligated to offer. Well, as a former member of the Federal Government, I knew full well that there would be a round of finger pointing and an excuse exchange before anyone dared consider a plan of action.

This could take months.

Visions of Simone Albescu danced in my head as I slumbered lightly. My dormant state lasted just over an hour before Dixie's voice roused me. I blinked awake in an instant.

"Anybody from State here yet?" I asked.

His contemptuous snort gave me both the answer and his personal evaluation.

"I think, it is about to hit the fan."

That was no news bulletin. This was *our* predicament from the first. That was no excuse to disturb my sleep.

"Take a step back," I pleaded. "You reek of cigarette smoke."

He accommodated me, much to my surprise.

"You want me to step to the plate?"

I was the new kid on the block. I knew the drill. If shit started rolling down hill, it was the newest junior nobodies who would take the brunt.

"The desk just got a frantic call from room 812," he began. "She no speak the English too good, but she wants into 815. She claims she left something in there; she wants it—now!"

"Let me guess the room number of the guy who bailed."

"Don't strain yourself," he countered. "I'd go with you, but we're sitting on top of an international incident here. You know how paranoid these punks get when confronted by any number greater than one. Speaking of which, could you poke out one of your eyes?"

I held out my hand.

"Give me the pass key."

It was done.

"I'm going to get fired, ain't I?"

He didn't reply. If the Romans pitched a fit, the State Department would demand somebody's head. I was on a suicide mission.

"Oh, well," I sighed, "I was getting tired of this town anyway."

When not in use, the three elevators automatically returned to the lobby. Therefore, I had my choice. I took the box on the left. It was closer to the room I was tasked to investigate. Also, I knew what awaited me.

Sure enough! As the doors slid back, I found myself facing a burly security goon. He was six three if an inch; his visage told me there was no trace of humor in his family tree.

"Private floor," he growled.

"Did you use the word *private*, comrade? I should report you to your superiors, if you knew who they are."

I took a step forward, but he wasn't buying.

"Private floor," he repeated.

He extended his hand to block me, but he was playing by the rules. He made certain not to touch me.

"Take it easy, Comrade Beria," I responded. "I was preaching socialist revolution in this town while you were trying to sound out the first word of the Communist Manifesto."

(It's A, by the way.)

I avoided his hand and side stepped past him. Before I could approach the figure in the hallway, the gorilla slid past me and blocked my path.

"Comrade, it is true that I work for Yankee, imperialist, war-mongering pigs, but it is both my job and my personal mission to help people—ALL the people. Who are you to prohibit me from carrying out my mission?"

His indoctrination did not include thinking on his feet; thus, he resorted to a well-reasoned argument.

"We do not need your help."

"You needed no help to lose a man last night, correct?"

That was a stunner. While he was struggling to get his teeth back in his mouth, I side stepped again and headed down the hall.

The figure was that of Simone. It was difficult to identify her at first. She wore flannel pajamas, was barefoot, and her hair, hastily done up in twin ponytails, hadn't seen a comb for ages. It was her set, stoic expression that gave her away.

She watched me approach with a goon on my heels but only for a moment. She turned her attention back to the door. She stood erect with her feet together and arms at her sides. Swiftly, she raised her right hand and pounded at the door with its heel. She spoke pleadingly but not so loud as to raise the alarm. I assume she was calling out the name of her coach and begging him to respond.

The second goon, stationed at the far end of the hall, issued commands; Simone paid not the slightest attention.

"Are you the woman who called the front desk?" I asked.

I was sweating bullets. There was a goon I couldn't see behind me. I didn't think he had balls enough to whack me over the head, but I'm frightened most by things I cannot monitor.

"I—something in this room—forgot," she stammered.

Logic dictated that I ask what she *forgot had*. It was a blind. She wanted to talk to a person she suspected was no longer on the other side of that door. There was no time to follow established practices. Sooner or later, one or both goons would employ another blocking gambit. I wasn't confident I'd succeed in keeping them off balance.

I brought out the key and rapped sharply on the door. All four people in that hallway knew there would be no response. I inserted the key and opened the door. Simone's trembling fingers fumbled for the light and turned it on. She stepped inside with me close behind. The goons didn't dare follow. Should they leave their patrol area, the geese would stampede putting them in greater trouble than they already were. This did not, however, keep them from issuing sharp commands. They may as well have barked at the moon.

Simone checked the bathroom and stared at the toilet articles, abandoned where they lay. She sniffed the air as if attempting to gain a scent before stepping further into the room. I kept station just off her right shoulder.

We ignored the hyenas in the hall.

The bed was undisturbed. The defector returned to his room only long enough to open the window and cling to the ledge and shuffle to the fire escape. I wondered why he took the time and effort to close the window behind him.

Simone studied the bed and the suitcase which lay open in the space provided. Clothes hung in the recess. She studied every detail as if memorizing the scene. Finally, she turned. I saw her full face for the first time since entering. Her familiar, frozen stoic expression remained but her face glistened in the refracted light. Tears streamed, uninhibited.

"Thank you."

Her voice was soft and even. This English phrase, at least, was impeccably enunciated.

She walked to the door frame and exchanged glances with the bookends. They no longer barked orders. I suspect, buried deep in hearts of lead, some flicker of pathos stirred.

After vacating the room, I pulled the door closed and made certain it latched. The noise made by this operation created so little noise I barely heard a sound. Simone, however, started as if a bomb exploded. She spun about, drew a deep breath through her nose and glared at the door. The tears continued to flood her eyes and ran in torrents down her face.

The door barred her life's path. She was condemned to traverse rocky detours.

"You should drink some water," I advised, fearing dehydration.

"You dare to speak to a Romanian citizen?" the second ape demanded.

I figured that my employment was ended; a temptation to take aim at his bulbous nose swelled. Discretion, however, prevailed.

"We demand your name," the first goon growled.

He should have asked first thing, but I'd been too clever. In fact, I suspected nearly everyone was too clever for him. Had I a banana, I'd offer it.

"Miles Nelson," I informed. "Recording-secretary for the Chicago cell of The Marxist Revolutionary League—look it up in the FBI list of subversive organizations."

Normally, I fell back on my long-established joke "Miles from Logansport." In this instance, I decided I'd yank chains. These clowns couldn't look up each other's rectums; there was no way they'd chase down FBI records—that required cerebral activity. It didn't help that I made it all up. I was confident they'd honor the habit of a lifetime and remain ignorant.

Because their barking didn't reduce me to a blubbering, prostrate blob, they turned to someone they could flay. I don't know what they said to Simone, but their snotty tone irritated me. I recalled the indignation of being mistaken for a Soviet spy in an Air Force NCO Club. The memory grated.

"Soviet bastards!"

"We are not Soviet!"

Touchy, touchy! I wasn't the only one with thin skin.

"Then stop behaving like it," I bellowed, not giving a damn if I woke up the entire city.

Until that moment, I never appreciated the phrase *pregnant pause*. Suddenly, I was in the middle of one. It was Simone who broke the still-life moment. She turned silently about, disappeared into her room and closed the door quietly behind her. I didn't like being sandwiched between two brainless apes, so I slid adroitly past them.

"If you need anything, call the desk," I said over my shoulder.

I daren't wait for the elevator. I dashed down the stairwell. When I had three floors between me and Romania, I called for a mobile living room. As I waited, I wiped the sweat from my brow and caught my breath. I wasn't concerned for myself, but my heart bled for Simone.

Later, after State arrived to kiss Romanian ass and bully the hotel staff, I wasn't in a charitable mood. They, of course, had to *debrief* me on my encounter with representatives of our foreign *guests*. I was terse in answering. Further, I answered only direct queries. When they presented a leading question, I impersonated a sphinx.

Most of the interview consisted of the diplomatic ins and outs of sucking up to primates, thus promoting harmony between nations. It was bad enough to take guff from the *Securitate*. Being fed bullshit by employees of my own government was intolerable. There remained a slim chance that I was still employed; I didn't want to blow it. Moreover, the State Department appeared more infuriated by my silence than my caustic comments, so I spoke sparingly.

When they finished, I retreated to the lobby and pouted in an easy chair. After an hour or so, a somber herd of Romanians came down. They were corralled in the lobby until the entire mob was assembled. Only then did they board the chartered bus for O'Hare.

The eighth-floor goons spied me on the far end of the lobby. They did not speak, but their warning glares and their facial expressions communicated volumes.

Finally, they filed out. Stoic Simone walked slowly between two towering men. I don't know if they were *Securitate* or team staff, but I recognized the technique. I and a fellow sergeant once employed the same method when escorting a deserter to a holding cell.

Simone kept her hands in the pockets of her winter jacket. I saw her cast a furtive glance in my direction. I knew she saw me, but she made no sign. Similarly, I didn't risk a nod. The young woman's head was up and her back ramrod straight, but there was no bounce in her step. My heart bled anew.

The moment the bus pulled away, I elevated to the eighth floor with the pass key.

As expected, her toilet articles remained in the bathroom—symbolic empathy for her departed comrade. Among these was a white brush containing several strands of hair. This I pocketed.

I glanced at the waste basket below the sink. There were the tattered remains of an American candy wrapper and an empty box of wafer-thin cardboard. I knew no Romanian, but I didn't have to. Eastern Europeans are not very creative with packaging; there was no need. Suffice it to say that the larger letters on the side of the box told me Simone's emotions were tapped at precisely the worst time of the month.

The bed was a shamble. Either she tossed and turned something wonderful or she writhed upon it with tears in her eyes and sorrow in her heart. There was a hair ribbon on the nightstand.

On the dresser, in a vase provided by the staff, was a profusion of flowers. They were presented to her following her final performance. They remained fresh; beautifully and (I suspect) lovingly arranged. Alas, in the cold empty room, they were reduced to a symbol of insufferable mockery. It would pain me if the cleaning girls tossed them. I hoped that they'd be salvaged and provide someone with a modicum of enjoyment.

The only other item was the roller bag Simone wheeled in during her arrival.

I sat at the end of the bed and unzipped it. There were several knick-knacks, but the bulk of the space was taken up by a pair of figure skates.

Was she announcing her retirement?

I zipped up the bag and left it standing at the end of the bed. The maid would report it, and, between the front office and the Department of State, the lost luggage would eventually catch up with her. Were I not afraid of the consequences, I'd have slipped in a note. Brushing aside the fact that I knew not what to write, I figured a message, in English, would be all the *Securitate* required to fit Simone's neck with a noose. It was, after all, her coach who skipped. The authorities were sure to insist Simone knew of his plan. Her failure to turn stoolie would keep her in deep doo-doo. She'd require no assistance from me.

CHAPTER THREE

I wasn't fired. Dixie went to bat for me. I could confide in him. I refused to confide in the diplomatic service inquisitors. He talked to the boss. Later, the top man, a balding sexagenarian addicted to pungent, imported cigars, called me in for a chat during the Christmas bustle. He was satisfied I'd represented the interests of the hotel with adroitness during an explosive situation. However, he suggested that I take a vacation until the snoops at State found another sandbox. They insisted I be "sternly disciplined." The boss, though he couldn't afford to antagonize a powerful arm of the government, insisted that he, *not* the State Department, ran the hotel.

My *vacation* was the push I needed. Chicago is—possibly— the tax capital of the world. My wages provoked envy among the ignorant. In Chi town, however, I existed barely above subsistence level. Confronted with nothing to do until after the New Year, I charted a different path. My GI Bill would lapse if I failed to take advantage. Therefore, I decided it was time to finish college.

The FBI, likely, kept a file on me. I'd stood up to Romanian thugs and was, therefore, a security risk and a threat to world peace.

Had I the morals of a congressman, I'd build on this reputation until I was a wealthy celebrity. Sadly, I have standards.

I left with a few clothes, a dozen books and a box of VHS tapes. I rented a car and set off, a nameless unknown, on a journey to the unknown.

I found myself in Cedar Falls, Iowa. Since Uncle Sugar would pay my tuition, I had hundreds of universities available. I was propelled to Iowa by a work-study job and the vague promise of additional off-campus opportunities.

In the few days before the start of the spring semester, I located a "studio" perched above a matronly widow's garage. A man of simple means, I required little space and few amenities.

My landlady, her gray hair snared meticulously in a tight little bun on the crown of her head, invited me to a get-acquainted tea. My display of manners and dexterity in tea-and-scones conversation passed inspection. As a reward, she referred me to an Iowa State Trooper who moonlighted in his own workshop, repairing and refurbishing VWs.

Two days later, I was puttering around the snow and slush-laden streets in my own vehicle. It had been "totaled." The trooper cum shade-tree mechanic scarfed up the remains for a song and rebuilt it so only he, me and the insurance company would ever know. The engine was brand, spanking new. Though there were eighty thousand miles on the odometer, the engine—for all practical purposes—had zero.

The VW motor and I made an even start on the next linear segment of my life.

For no reason, I opted for U.S. History as my major. I had no idea what I'd do with a degree. Since the Army footed the bill, I was determined to study something compelling. Perhaps, I harbored a subliminal hope that my rich uncle would join his ancestors and leave me a bundle. In the meantime, I'd hope for some viable means of making a living despite my accumulation of historical lore.

Trapped in the pre-word-processor age, I remained ignorant of the few who had both programs and printers. We peons made do with typewriters and ribbons. Nevertheless, essay composition was my forte. I established myself as the department word merchant. Because of my age, I was called *pops* and *gramps*. It was, of course, assumed that I was eccentric as well. This reputation was acceptable enough for me to promote it.

My life consists of chance encounters. I introduced supporting evidence in the preceding pages. There are several other instances which shall remain unrecorded, but my life in Cedar Falls was a combination of my uncanny ability to be in the right place at the right time, a benevolent uncle of means, and my selection of compatriots.

After obtaining wheels, I expressed my desire for a good cup of coffee. While ambulatory, I would adjourn to a nearby Gulp-and-Vomit. It was pleasant enough. I paged through newspapers while sipping coffee from a paper cup. With the increased range of my VW, I sought something better than fast-food joe.

"Molly's Tea Bar," my grandmotherly landlady suggested. "Don't let the name fool you. They serve great coffee."

They did not, however, have complementary newspapers. Thus, I puttered around with a history book on the seat beside me. Once on the premises, I sipped coffee from a bone-china cup while absorbing either historical narrative or critical essays of same.

Alas, my worship of Clio was shattered by a distractive element. The young lady who took my order and delivered my coffee was the personification of *cute*. Indeed, when I publish the Nelson Dictionary (to set right the glaring omissions of Mr. Webster), I shall illustrate the word *cute* with a miniature portrait of my waitress.

She was five three or four and her light-brown hair was a meticulous copy of the Dorothy Hamill style. She wore an imitation pearl in the pierced lobe of each ear. Save for a light coating of blue shadow, she wore no discernible makeup—nor did she need any. She had an attractive visage highlighted by a pug nose which blended perfectly with her other features. Her legs, what I could see of them, were shapely and functional—quite a contrast to the toothpicks so trendy in Chicago (I was always nervous when spying a woman in shorts parading along Michigan Avenue showing off a pair of gams too fragile to support a body). Moreover, "cutie's" figure was shapely—but *not* gaudy.

Try as I might to digest Allen Nevins or Richard Hofstadter, I broke off whenever the young waitress whisked by. Had I any nerve, I would have spoken to her. Alas, I am to women what Marcel Marceau is to radio. Better, I concluded, to admire from a distance than to prove a fool. Such a cute and classy young woman was certain to expose me as a crushing bore.

I made mention of the attractive waitress to my landlady. After describing her, I was not particularly amazed to learn that she was the woman's relation. Such coincidences are a reoccurring feature of my life. Still, not even I was prepared for what followed.

My first class at UNI was Diplomatic History of the United States. For reasons herein recorded, I am no fan of diplomats or their methodology. Consequently, I entered the room in a mood decidedly *not* felicitous. As I leafed through the assigned text, a co-ed in jeans and tennis shoes settled into the desk beside me. This was bizarre. There were thirty or so desks in the room and only eighteen enrolled in the class. I chalked it up to some local oddity and continued my survey.

There is little need to relate who sat next to me.

"I'm Miles Nelson," I blurted, involuntarily.

"Ellen Good," she smiled charmingly.

"You work at Molly's Tea Bar," I announced.

"You drink black coffee," she replied, equally informative.

She was a twenty-year old sophomore and had switched majors from sociology to history. It was her goal to become a teacher. Ellen figured that her rudimentary foundation in sociology would lend itself to teaching history.

"There are so many interesting American people, aren't there? So many cultures and so many blends—and so many juicy ironies! What scriptwriter would dare punch out a screenplay with a character named Eisenhower heading up the invasion of Germany?"

"No studio would go for that," I agreed.

"They would insist that the name be changed, of course. Smith maybe—"

"Or Nelson," I suggested.

"Or Good!"

I made a face.

"That would make it an allegory."

She thought a moment before agreeing.

Ellen was not merely a farmer's daughter; she was a farmer's granddaughter and a farmer's great-granddaughter. She came from a sod-busting family, favoring sons. As the only female among five children, she was the bubbly, vivacious one who turned the tedious grind of a family reunion into a long-remembered experience. It was her goal to become the first college graduate in her family—ever!

She lusted after a teaching post in a rural school. However, she refused to be daunted by long odds.

"My brothers are sure to have large families," she prophesized. "I'll teach them."

"How about you?" I had to ask. "Will you have a large family?"

She paused again.

"I haven't given it much thought," she confessed. "I don't see a husband yet. Maybe, somewhere on the distant horizon—"

"What are you doing after class?"

I must have asked. I recognized my voice.

"Oh, I couldn't possibly marry you before Thursday," she shot back instantly. "I'd have to gather my trousseau."

"Thursday, it is," I agreed. "How about coffee after class?"

"If we go Dutch."

"You're too easy."

She laughed.

In truth, Ellen dedicated much time to laughter. She had, what I consider, an exceptional sense of humor. Unlike me, she did not recall or invent gags; she just injected little jests into the conversation. There were no knee-slappers and no vulgarities. Her humor was subtle, clean and—dare I say?—down home.

I fell in love with her instantly. That was a sure sign she was spoken for. Alas, she was free as the air. With Ellen, however, it was first things first: college, graduation, teaching and then, maybe, connubial bliss.

I was on the road once more. This one, however, contained not only detours, but the proverbial fork. Unbeknownst to me, I would select the path least likely.

We started at the union over coffee. We made study dates for the library. We compared notes, shared ideas and debated over interpretative matters. Interspaced with our collegiate activities, we shared brief verbal snapshots of our lives. No matter what we did or where we went, her perpetual smile and her captivating laugh remained a staple.

She worked three hours on Mondays and Wednesdays and Fridays at the USO (Ellen-speak for Molly's Tea Bar). Additionally, she worked Saturday mornings and Sunday afternoons. Between a straight salary and tips, she never asked her family for expenses. Her father, bursting with pride over his co-ed daughter, salted money away for years to cover the lion's share of tuition. Even her brothers—that most dreaded of creatures—pitched in a few bucks from time to time. They were as proud of Ellen as their patriarch.

After my second weekend on campus, Ellen invited me to dinner with the family. I picked her up at the tea shop in my gray ghost just after noon. She lived just beyond Waverly, an easy drive.

The family surname is *Good*, but it could well have been *Squeaky-Clean*. They were the quintessential Midwestern farm family. They read the Bible, went to church, and worked their asses off with never a discouraging or off-color word. They made the Waltons look like barbarian brigands.

Ellen's two elder brothers were away: one doing a hitch in the Navy and the other in partnership with two other bachelors in a pig-raising operation in the western part of the state. Her two younger brothers were scrubbed, neatly groomed and so polite and well-mannered they'd make a favorable impression at a state dinner in Buckingham Palace.

The dinner itself was something out of Norman Rockwell. The home-made biscuits melted on my tongue, and the vegetables were fresh. (In January??? There is no way to credit this, but I assure you, I *know* fresh vegetables.) The potatoes were whipped by hand (Ellen and her brothers contributing) and, for dessert: apple pie, of course, but homemade and nothing like any other apple pie this side of the grave.

The proud patriarch is a bull of a man who speaks with a resonant yet reserved voice. His greatest boast was that he never raised a hand against his children. There was no need. The tutelage of their mother was so loving and wise that they knew right from wrong. Much more, they knew what was appropriate and what was inappropriate. They behaved because they honored and respected mater and pater.

It was not *exactly* true. There was a wooden paddle in the room which, I later learned, found occasional employment. Though I'd never be so bold to accuse Mr. Good of saying false, I concede his memory may be selective.

Academically, the siblings ran the gamut. Ellen was clearly the scholar, but she shared the highest grades with her sailor brother. The others were either average or slightly below, but none suffered a disappointing grade for want of effort.

Most importantly, however, the family unit ticked like a delicate Swiss watch. Everyone pitched in with the chores, often without being reminded, and always without complaint or resentment.

In summary, then, I enjoyed a dinner with a family created by Walt Disney. Save for my personal experience, I'd never believe such families existed. Life, however, is surprising. Alistair Cooke, during World War II, found the embodiment of democracy—the concept for which we were fighting—behind the barbed wire of a Japanese internment camp. Similarly, I discovered the embodiment of a harmonious, functioning family atop the black soil of an Iowa farm.

Such examples provide this curmudgeon with a reason to have faith.

We enjoyed the traditional Sunday pot roast made in accordance with Mrs. Good's special technique. This was a once-a-month treat and my being there to share it implied that I was, likewise, special. Normal Sunday dinners consisted of pork chops or round steak.

The alert reader will doubtless realize I'm recording the events of a Saturday afternoon. Because Ellen worked Sunday after church, the family adjusted. A Sunday dinner at the Good's consisted of the entire family—save absent sons. Thus, the *official* Sunday dinner was predicated on Ellen's presence. Once, a Sunday dinner fell on a Wednesday, prior to the eldest son's departure for Navy boot camp.

Regardless of the chronology, I respected family tradition. As the savory pot roast delighted my tongue, I suggested that Mrs. Good deserved a place in the cooking-god pantheon.

Alas, a truly enjoyable meal and delightful society must terminate. It was my duty to get Ellen home at a decent hour; she required a proper night's sleep before church. That I had the trust of the Family Good to ferry their precious to and fro was both the ultimate compliment and a weighty responsibility.

Once underway, we reviewed features of the Clayton-Bulwer Treaty. This was but one of many historical landmarks I considered highly pedestrian and of minimal consequence. However, our quizzes and exams were demanding. We discovered that the more detailed an answer, the higher our score.

Suddenly, during a discussion of President Tyler's foreign policy, I was arrested in mid-sentence.

"What is it?" Ellen demanded.

Something triggered a memory. The image of Simone Albescu's wet face shunted aside everything. Naturally, I was obligated to explain. This resulted in an impromptu mini lecture on the checkered career of Miles Nelson. Ellen listened with heroic patience and asked astute questions.

She had to wonder what I was to Simone or what Simone was to me. She did not, however, pry. If ever there was a person who understood my deep concern for a near stranger, it was Ellen Good.

"Is that Romanian woman a skier?" she asked, days later, before class.

"Skater," I reminded.

There was something ominous in the way she said "oh." I refrained from comment, but Ellen read my expression.

"I think I heard—before Christmas break—a Romanian skater tried to kill herself."

I swallowed but kept silent.

"I didn't pay attention to the name," she admitted.

Why should she?

"*Tried?*" I asked.

She nodded.

Why should I care? Likely, it hadn't been Simone. Romania was, after all, under an acutely repressive government. Suicide might be the leading industry. Besides, there must be hundreds of skaters.

Hell! Who was I kidding? The entire competitive figure-skating contingent of Romania wouldn't fill our history classroom. Then, there were speed skaters—their numbers might lessen the odds. Still, I could not dismiss the image of Simone in tears. Despite her stoic expression, those tears communicated horrific pain.

It was spring.

After twenty-three dreary days of below-freezing temperatures, there appeared tiny puddles of water at the edge of sidewalks. People who'd been bundled up like Eskimos for weeks were striding about gloveless and with coats unzipped. Students and faculty were positively giddy.

Ellen and I were growing closer. She captured my hand one afternoon while we studied in the union. I gave it a squeeze and realized our feelings were cresting a wave. When, a couple hours later, I slid my arm around her without resistance, I reveled in the notion that our relationship was headed somewhere. Twice, I declined the opportunity to kiss her. I knew she wanted me to. Still, I couldn't break through my inhibitions.

I wasn't worthy of her. Until I considered myself free of my shady past, I didn't want to risk despoiling her. Yes, I know that a kiss is perfectly innocuous, but recall my verbal portrait of the Family Good. I was a product of a corrupt and promiscuous age while the Goods, in a very important sense, were stuck in the morality of the early nineteenth century. To impose my will and my standards upon her (and them) constituted profanation.

Ellen, I knew, did not share her family's standards of propriety. She'd not cry foul if we grew apart after a few rounds of smooching. I, however, would feel I'd taken unfair advantage. Until I was satisfied with my motives and conduct, I refrained from besmirching her innocence—even a little. If I learned anything from Nate Hawthorne, it is that a fastidious conscience can be destructive.

Because Ellen is Ellen, I didn't hesitate to share my concerns. Because Ellen is Ellen—and despite how trite it sounds—she understood. Because Ellen is Ellen, there was no subject under the sun we couldn't discuss. She insisted my reasoning was silly and expressed disappointment in my "prudery." Nevertheless, she respected my views.

She beamed and planted a smacker on my cheek.

Revelation: there was nothing wrong with kissing her on the cheek! *Ergo*, I adopted the Romanian custom of greeting her with a kiss on each one whenever we met. This was, also, our accepted means of saying *au revoir*.

This appears excessively prim, I know. Nevertheless, my sincerity and motives were genuine. Because Ellen is Ellen, she tolerated my eccentricity.

Because Ellen is Ellen, I had an extra pair of eyes and ears. Little escaped her.

We enjoyed a few extra minutes in the balmy spring weather. After an endless winter, forty-degree temperatures were intoxicating. Every few minutes, the gray clouds would part long enough for us to experience blessed sunlight. Exam scores skyrocketed. No matter how fussy the prof, the first days of moderate temperatures brought about a marked, albeit temporary, relaxation in grading standards. The world was good; life was sweet.

Reluctantly, Ellen and I forced ourselves into the library. I reviewed my notes and attempted to get a handle on Jackson's bank war before drafting an assigned essay. Ellen sat across from me, reviewing a chapter in her econ book. After several minutes, she excused herself.

Ellen didn't need my permission to go to the bathroom, get a sip of water, page through magazines or browse through the stacks. Similarly, I didn't demand to know her exact location. We were secure in our relationship. Thus, when she failed to return after the bulk of an hour, I wasn't concerned.

I wrote my thoughts in rapid longhand on a yellow legal pad. I sensed Ellen's presence but was too engaged in my train of thought to break off. Ellen recognized this and waited patiently behind my chair. Only when I put down my pen did she come within my line of sight. She held a copy of the Waterloo paper.

"Simone's coach," she began tentatively. "The one who defected, do you remember his name?"

I accessed my memory.

"I'm not certain I ever knew. Why?"

"Well," she lay the paper before me, "I found this."

The paper was open to page 4, section C. It was folded so only a quarter of the page was presented. My eyes zeroed in on the only headline within my ken. It concerned the Waterloo Ice arena—the *center of ice hockey* and other winter sports for Northeastern Iowa. There was a new member of the figure skating faculty.

Former Olympic skating coach, Ion Lupei, the article stated, *is the latest addition to the figure skating instructors on our excellent staff—* and blah, blah, blah.

"It doesn't mention anything about a defection," I noted.

"It doesn't say anything about Romania either," she added. "Still, Ion is Romanian, isn't it?"

"East European for sure," I commented, searching further. "One of the many variations of *John*—as common as the hydrogen atom."

I examined the entire article. It was a pitch for skating classes and youth hockey.

"I hate journalists," I moaned.

"Well," Ellen concluded. "I thought you'd be interested. The chances are pretty slim, I guess, but how many former Olympic coaches, named Ion, are running loose?"

A point well taken.

"They provide a phone number," I noticed. "I'll give them a call."

"Or," she suggested, "We could drive over tomorrow afternoon."

I eyed her suspiciously. She grinned.

"If we happen to end up at the mall—"

Yes, of course. Ellen was on the lookout for winter clothing mark-downs. She had some dollars in reserve; I had wheels.

"It will cut into study time," I warned.

She shrugged.

"So, I'll study longer at night."

"Easy for you," I observed, "but I need my beauty sleep."

She laughed softly as only Ellen Good can laugh. Coupled with the welcome heat wave, her laugh was a balm.

Ion Lupei was a burly, balding, round-faced man whom I judged was in his early fifties. Instantly, I realized he was not the man I sought. There was no way a person with his bulk could shuffle fifty feet along an eighth-floor ledge to a fire escape. Still, we were in the warmth of the rink's lobby. Moreover, it would be rude to march out.

"This is Ellen Good," I began. "I'm Miles Nelson."

"Yes, please," he acknowledged without extending his hand. "I have class twenty minutes is starting."

His accent was as thick as Mrs. Good's gravy—and as delightful.

"Were you in Chicago four months ago?"

He didn't move a muscle, but I noticed his eyes changed color. I suspect I'd have achieved a similar reaction had I clubbed him with a snowshoe. Moments later, he cocked his head to one side.

"You are re-porters?"

The peculiar pronunciation swathed his final word in suspicion. It communicated dislike.

"We are university students," I assured. "However, I was employed by a certain Chicago hotel when a certain Romanian coach left through a window."

For several seconds, he didn't blink. I wasn't certain he breathed.

"Why you ask me with these question?"

That settled it. Ion Lupei was the man. His reticence was understandable. Doubtless, he insisted certain items be quashed in the rink's press release. As if living in Romania weren't hellish enough, he endured hours, if not days, being grilled by Government chuckleheads.

"I was sent upstairs early in the morning because Simone called the desk. She was very upset. I found her standing in front of your door. She was desperate."

He gulped, averted his eyes and let out with a doleful sigh.

"Ah, ZEE-mo-NAH!"

That was all. Four quietly enunciated syllables dripping with pathos.

I glanced at Ellen. She felt the impact and choked back a sob.

"Did she know?" I whispered.

He shook his head, once, slowly.

"I could not put with up another day—another hour. Not another minute! I had to get out. I feel so badly for Simone, but—if she know, I think she go crazy and both be punish. My heart cry much for Simone, but—but I cannot do. Not even for Simone can I take one more minute! No one more minute."

"She left her skates in her room," I informed.

He snorted. He intended a laugh, but it wouldn't come.

"She always losing her skates," he confirmed. "She always make with the problem."

"Why?"

This was Ellen. Her single word came out with an impossible elongation. She was on the verge of tears. I, also, was wrapped in pity over the sight of this poor man struggling with his composure.

He couldn't answer immediately. He rubbed his eyes—twice. He swallowed a huge lump before he dared speak.

"She has the good talent. She love to skate. Fun is it. Then, she is took from her family and placed in special school. She is made to skate. She skate and skate and skate until her feet bleed. Soon, she is come to hate the skating. Big surprise, no? But is trapped. If she quit, her family suffer."

I looked at Ellen. We both wanted to get out of there, but— there was no window to crawl through. Poor Ion Lupei was within an inch of breaking down. He could no more be left alone than we could abandon him. Either Ellen or I might need to phone for help.

"A thousand times I want Simone to say to me what she feel. I know she in pain, but she never say. She keep it inside. I try to—help. I am only person she talk to, but she never tell me what she feel. Never! Her quiet—it frighten me."

"I know," I couldn't keep silent. "When she realized you were gone, she never made a sound—not a sound. She just stood there like a statue with tears running down her face."

He buried his head in his hands and let out a sob and gulped for several seconds.

"Yes," he confirmed, coming up for air, "This is Simone. I hate to leave her alone, but I cannot stay one more minute! For myself, I can—I can—go on—maybe. Maybe. But—I cannot look at Simone and know—This I can no do. No more."

That was all I could take. Had I dared, I'd have put a comforting hand on his shoulder. Somehow, I suspected he was emotionally beyond reach.

"Mr. Lupei, forgive us for bothering you. We should not have come."

He nodded his head as he wrung his hands and stared at the floor.

"Is okay," he assured.

Bullshit! I should never have told him about Simone's reaction. It was cruel. Now, I suffered.

Ellen being Ellen couldn't slink away. As I turned to leave, she grabbed the sleeve of my coat so firmly, I feared for my arm. With strength only farm work produces, she forced me to remain. As she held me fast with one hand; she extended the other to rest, reassuringly, against Ion's arm.

"Mr.—sir," she began.

Atop all else, Ellen did not want to further injure the man by bungling the pronunciation of his name. He responded to her touch by gazing into her angelic face. He wiped his swollen eyes.

"If there is anything we can do," she continued with perfect enunciation, "you call us. Do you understand?"

He nodded, but it wasn't convincing.

"Miles, give him your number."

She'd left her purse in the Bug. I, however, carried a pen and a small notebook in my shirt pocket—a holdover from Army days.

Under Ellen's demanding gaze, I printed my name and phone number. Only then did Ellen release my arm. She added her name and number, tore the page from the notepad. Ion accepted it with trembling fingers.

"Anything," she reminded. "If you wake up in the night and need a blanket, call us. If you crave a pizza, call us. Do you understand? Anything."

This time he was more convincing.

"Thank you," he said, gulping once more. "Thank you very much."

"Anything," Ellen reminded once more as we turned to leave.

I looked over my shoulder to witness him mouth a final, inaudible *thank you.*

There was a blast of cold air greeting us. I doubt Ellen noticed. She was experiencing her first major catharsis, and I wasn't lagging far behind. Someone needed to say something.

"*If you need a blanket?*" I asked, incredulously.

For once, Ellen was not her bubbly, vivacious self. The Walt Disney creation was never subjected to such a pathetic scene. It was a hundred times more powerful than a movie experience. She was bruised. Shaken to the core, Ellen remained true to her family values.

"Anything!" she insisted.

There was no bargain hunting that day. We sat silent in the car until the chill became annoying. I revved up the engine, put the Bug in gear, and drove. I aimed the Gray Ghost in the general direction of Cedar Falls but turned off at a watering hole residing under a garish sign.

"I need a drink," I announced.

"I can't go in there," Ellen said.

Damn!

I opened the door only to slam it closed.

"When's your birthday?"

"April twenty-first."

There was a gag there, but I let it go. Ellen enjoyed a good laugh and my most labored joke set her off. In the circumstances, however, any attempt at levity deserved condemnation.

Simone was top on our list of suicide candidates.

Oh, hell! If we camped in the library and examined every microfiche roll of major newspapers for the past year, we might—just maybe, perhaps—find a shred of evidence. Simone Albescu was not of a reputation demanding media attention. Even if she was a star, she lived on the wrong side of a fence. Anything written about her would contain more fiction than *Gone with the Wind*. Nevertheless, Ellen and I went to the university library; perhaps, on the off chance that we'd find Simone Albescu sitting at a study carrel.

CHAPTER FOUR

Ellen discovered that Simone came from Sibiu, roughly twenty-five miles southeast of Alba Iulia. Both cities are in Transylvania. She was born on—wait for it—April 21. Yep, the coincidences kept rolling along. Of course, the Romanian press was even less reliable than American dissemblers, but there is little reason to lie about such rudimentary information.

After meeting Ion and experiencing his melt down, Ellen's heart was his forever. She invited him to the farm for one of the family's Saturday-night Sunday dinners. He, to my great surprise, accepted. I was not invited, but that caused no pain. I did not own Ellen and had no ambition to manage her life. In fact, I allowed her the use of the Gray Ghost for the occasion.

Ion didn't last in Waterloo. His ability to discover and nurture skating talent was uncanny. His reputation grew until he was snatched up by a school in Kansas City. Eventually, he coached a young man who, many agreed, had Olympic possibilities. Ion, who anglicized his name to *John Wolf*, balked at additional Olympic appearances. He'd develop talent and hand it over to more ambitious trainers.

I kept tabs on him. We exchanged Christmas cards and appended brief notes about our respective careers. His reluctance to re-enter the

Big Time kept him away from big money. He lived within his means, modest by American standards. A Romanian divorce, years before his defection, left him reluctant to try again. It, also, shaved expenditures.

I made an egregious mistake in not chasing Ellen with all the ardor of Apollo's pursuit of Daphne. Alas—

I couldn't help being attracted to her. Aside from her infectious personality, I was infatuated with her looks. She seldom wore anything but jeans, summer or winter. I loved the way they tapered—particularly, over those portions of Ellen which did not taper. During the Holiday Season, she'd wear dresses, skirts and boots. One hot summer day, she appeared in a sun dress. Never having seen so much of her legs, I didn't immediately recognize her. Perhaps, according to the standards of the time, she was less than a stunner; I, however, never thought of her as anything but.

I not only fell in love, I convinced myself I was worthy. We never argued and seldom disagreed. Her personality made her more charitable about my flaws and failings than I deserved. In short, I couldn't imagine myself being happy with anyone else.

It was merely a matter of time before I proposed. There were always reasons for delay. A shrink might insist I feared commitment.

I suspect the real reason resides with the Nelson knack for adhering to the dictates of fate and the accompanying potholes.

I became a pedestrian with increasing frequency. I don't recall Ellen ever *asking* for the loan of my Bug. I'd never deny it. Her essential obligation was her weekly family visit. Employing the Gray Ghost freed her from restrictive bus schedules. Moreover, despite my being welcome in the Good home any time, I felt taking frequent advantage of Mrs. Good's cooking constituted trespass. Just as I had an open invitation to a *Good Sunday Dinner*, so, also, Ellen had an open invitation to borrow my car. I provided her with a second set of keys.

The event which indefinitely postponed my speaking to her father was innocuous. We celebrated her twenty-first birthday at the proverbial tavern in the town. We were hardly seated before a waitress in white blouse and dark slacks appeared. She asked for Ellen's ID. This formality concluded, we ordered Shirley Temples and toasted her coming of age.

The waitress did *not* ask for my identification.

I was used to students teasing me about my age. Even Ellen, frequently, called me *Pops*. Nary a feather was ruffled. Indeed, I felt the break in my education resulted in a more mature attitude toward learning. When I didn't get carded, I viewed the years between us as an insurmountable gulf—it was both foolish and unfair to subject a young and vivacious girl to a life chained to an ancient albatross.

By contemporary standards, age gaps aren't worthy of attention. However, a significant part of my life was behind me; Ellen had yet to clear the launch pad. I could never hope to find a better woman. Ellen, however, could do far better.

Symbolic of our relationship, I went to the graduation ceremony. I sat with her family in the bleachers and watched with pride to match theirs as Ellen shook the university president's hand and accepted the first ever degree in Good-family history. Since I didn't participate, my parchment arrived in the mail a week later.

Simone won silver in the '76 Romanian skating singles. In '77 and '78 she captured gold. In the European community, this counted for nothing. It was the equivalent of winning an award as the smartest kid in the remedial class. If she brought all her gold medals into the union cafeteria, she could buy a cup of coffee—if she had exact change.

She did not place in '79. It's possible she didn't participate. Perhaps, she *had* attempted suicide. Of course, retirement—an Iron-Curtain euphemism for a stretch in a state prison or, worse, *treatment* in the People's Mental Hospital—were, also, possibilities.

Simone returned in 1980, winning her third Romanian gold and finishing somewhere in the middle in Europeans at Dortmund. The Europeans were an anti-climax; I imagine she suffered from a case of *what-the-hells*. My first interview with John Wolf confirmed

Simone's status as a state slave. Joy and excitement were beaten out of her. Protecting her family was her only motivation.

Between winning the Romanian crown and competing in the Europeans was an amusing little interlude in Lake Placid. I know nothing about the politics involved in becoming an Olympic competitor. A casual observer cannot divine the process by which Simone became the only Romanian singles skater in New York. I suspect Ceausescu took hostages or threatened war or used some other devious method to get his athletes into Olympic competition despite lackluster performances. Most likely, it was the fruit of some corrupt bargain with the IOC. This, I emphasize, is pure supposition and devoid of any supporting evidence. However, I, and the rest of the world, could not fail to notice that Romania sent a team to the Summer Games in '84. Led by the Soviet Union, there was a boycott, and Romania, alone of all the slave states, attended. Hardly evidence that would stand up in court, but appearances remain highly suspicious.

Regardless, Simone was there. Her coach was a woman who resembled a professional wrestler and had a face to make a clock run backwards. Looking at her made me shudder. I can only imagine how she and her performing monkey got along.

The big story—for most Americans, the *only* story—was the hockey team putting an end to a long-running Soviet win streak. It was one of the greatest David-and-Goliath stories in Olympic history.

Of little note was a second David-and-Goliath result. Since an American was not the subject of the story, few were ever aware. Of those, only three Americans cared—John Wolf (not yet naturalized), Ellen Good and Miles Nelson.

There were twenty-four woman-singles skaters at Lake Placid. Simone, by universal acclamation, was the overwhelming favorite to finish last. As a result, very few beyond the arena saw her performance. I wonder if the Romanians saw it, even on film. Simone's skate was selected by the media to air a cartload of commercials. Therefore, John and I swore at the TV while Ellen eyed us disapprovingly. She, perhaps, shared our low opinion of the sport coverage, but it's more likely her dour expression was prompted by John's Romanian and my English pejoratives.

When the ice crystals settled, and the numbers were run, Simone Albescu finished twelfth. Granted, this is light years from a medal, but. considering initial expectations, it remains a miraculous finish. For years, she skated in obscurity—outside of Romania that is. Suddenly, she was the stone-faced giant-killer. At twenty years of age, she had an Olympics left in her, not to mention additional World Championships.

I didn't attend the games, either as a spectator or groupie bum. I had no idea what Simone did to twist the tails of the *Securitate*; indeed, I never heard so much as a rumor. Still, I'm certain she set teeth grinding.

John Wolf didn't attend. As badly as he wanted to see his former pupil, he couldn't take the chance she'd see him. More importantly, however, he seldom thought of her without courting clinical depression. This did not prohibit him from keeping a keen eye on her scores.

She skated early in the rotation.

"Is good score," John said. "Is *very* good score!"

For Simone Albescu, it was a personal best.

As the contest continued, other girls scored higher; BUT, not *all* the girls!

"Good, good," John said. "She is not to be last."

Then, incredibly, Simone's numbers withstood a second contestant. John clapped his hands. When another skater failed to match Simone, John got to his feet and began pacing. Then another and another and another failed to surpass Simone's aggregate.

Soon, Ellen and I were catching his enthusiasm. We bit our lips and wrung our hands when competitors climbed over her, but we cheered unabashedly when Simone survived an assault.

However, behind my cheering and applause, I conjured Simone in my imagination. She'd watch every routine. Distractions would not be tolerated. Through it all, her facial expression wouldn't change an iota. If her gorgon coach was near to keep her informed of the standings, Simone, likely, was too absorbed to hear. If she did hear, she'd care not.

I wondered, should she win a medal, would she smile? Would she react as a normal person? Or, would she remain morose and unmoved?

Behind my glee over John's antics and the satisfaction of seeing Simone climb higher and higher out of the cellar, I felt pangs of sorrow. No matter how well or poorly Simone did, it would merely be the preface to additional long, dreary days of tedium and drudgery.

Only when we were alone and away from John's radar-like ears did Ellen ask me the question which burned inside for the entire evening.

"Do you think Simone will—make a break?"

I shook my head.

"They're on her like red on an apple," I was certain. "They probably won't allow her to be alone in the bathroom."

Ellen shuddered at that.

"She'd stand a better chance of getting out of Romania," I concluded. "Because there are several layers of prison guards at home, they're more careless. The people detailed to watch Simone here know what will happen if she gets away."

After Simone's remarkable Olympic performance, there was talk that she'd be in the hunt at Dortmund. Her marked improvement was not ignored. She got another coach and a novel form of motivation.

The Boss wanted someone at the Winter Games to set off the jewel, Nadia, in the Summer Games. It became an obsession. Nadia captured the hearts of the world and the Boss used her to focus attention on his country—that is, of course, on Ceausescu. The front-runner to succeed Nadia (in winter sports) was Simone, but she was truculent and somber. Even Nadia smiled occasionally, but Simone remained as lugubrious as a hanging judge.

When Simone's coach was sent to the ugly farm, two were dispatched to take her place. The skating coach was given the task of challenging her. Albescu wasn't getting any younger. The complexity of her program and the level of difficulty were increased.

The second coach was presented with a greater task: it was her job to paste a smile on the sphinx.

The Boss—or whatever underling was tasked with Project Gold Medal—enlisted the service of an established choreographer to provide an artistic context for Simone's leaps and spins. Since he was not Romanian, his services remained a state secret. Thus, in 1981, the new and improved Simone skated to her fourth Romanian title. She beamed and even laughed, but the sparkle of her smile was as phony as the gold in her medal.

Her performance in Innsbruck at Europeans was spectacular. The press began asking about the Romanian *wunderkind* who unexpectedly challenged established skaters. She was bright, cheery and her skating was described as both *dynamic* and *inspired.* The press exhausted adjectives in praising the winning personality who captured the hearts of the crowd. The photographers couldn't keep lenses off her. They wanted a photographic record of Simone Albescu having the time of her life while striking fear into her competitors.

Simone became the media's wet dream. Because she came from behind the curtain, and because they had no access; she was *tabula rasa.* Expertly, the press sculpted a creation by burying the stoic and unflattering photos in favor of those which supported *their* image of a carefree, enthusiastic young woman attending her first ball. As with all works of fiction, problems arose. Whenever, for example, she appeared in a group photo, with other skaters or with her adoring public, Simone looked sullen and uncomfortable. When she did flash a smile, she looked as if suffering from acute constipation.

You can take someone with no personality and make them dance the conga, but you can't make them have a good time. If they aren't having a good time, it shows.

After placing sixth in a superlative field, there was buzz. The authorities were quick to spirit away their little darling before any of the successfully manipulated media dupes got the right idea. Even inside the publicity black hole of Romania, Simone was kept under wraps. She made staged personal appearances, but these were limited to no more than a quarter of an hour.

There followed another year of training. Simone was awarded gold in the national competition—as usual. After subjecting the little darling to twenty months of torture, someone decided she needed a boost. Thus, she appeared with the Boss and members of his gang. Music blared, flags flew, speeches were made, and Simone Albescu was sent off to the Europeans in style. This, everyone knew, was *her* year!

France remains in harmony with the Romania's socialist agenda. As with anyone admired from afar, the French didn't know what a hell hole the shining (red) star of Eastern Europe really was. Presumably, they didn't care. The country was in love with the socialist façade and didn't give a damn about the suffering and degradation of the slaves propping it up. No matter what the motives and feelings, the Romanians felt secure enough with the French nation to allow them a share in the security arrangements.

Simone stepped off the plane in Lyon and posed for the cameras. Her smile was infectious. Why not? For the first time, Simone was a force. A half-dozen favorites looked over their shoulders while hopefuls realized they must leap-frog over her to have a chance.

She waved imperially as she stepped out of the airport and into a black Limo.

Three days later, haggard, rumpled and unsmiling, she appeared in Geneva.

PART THE SECOND

CHAPTER ONE

It wasn't planned. Simone had no confederates, no money, no transportation and no knowledge of her itinerary. Through a felicitous series of circumstances, not the least of which was sloppy security, she walked across the hotel lobby and through a door. Before the goons regained their limited senses, she was in an alley clinging to the darkness and shuttling from shadow to shadow.

Without money or papers, she relied upon the kindness of strangers.

There are, at least, five written accounts of Simone's three-day flight. All were punched out by journalists; ergo, there is no reason to believe any version was fact-based. The only common thread was the *Securitate* bungled—again!

Simone never spoke of her escape save for what she shared with Ellen. Her adventure was another act of rebellion; this one went tragically wrong. Her object was to prove to her leeches that she was in better condition by racing them up the stairs. Instead of the stairwell door, she pushed through an exit.

"It's a capital offense to leave hotels," she reported mournfully.

She could have turned about immediately and begged for mercy. Alas, Romanian mercy, particularly for a chronic pain-in-the-ass, is problematic.

She ran, literally, for her life. In the company of a Swiss-Catholic prelate, Simone realized her thoughtless, unplanned flight was her family's death sentence. This, then, was the epiphany that germinated into years of nocturnal horror.

John Wolf was in Kansas City. Ellen attended seminary in Dubuque. I worked for a title company in Allen County, Ohio. It was my job to research and update property abstracts. In addition to earning a living, I was researching local history with an eye toward writing a modest treatise about the history of the area, from the first settlers, through the French and Indian War and concluding with Ohio statehood. Toward this end, abstracts were a valuable resource.

Because Simone was hardly a household name, I missed reports of her defection. I knew she'd gone to Lyon and wondered why her name failed to appear in wire service results. Not until I exchanged Christmas greetings with John did I discover that Simone was living with him.

John was the only person Simone knew outside Romania. Somehow, they found each other. Three months after leaving Switzerland, she reunited with her coach. Through him, she improved her starter English. Additionally, she learned to live without having her mail confiscated, being shadowed in public, and playing bobble head whenever an officious bully ordered her about. She learned to shop and pay bills. She learned to drive. She got a license. She learned to cook.

She suffered over her family's demise.

In truth, there was no reliable word. Reports stated that the Sibiu Albescus were *taken care of.* Even in Romania (*especially* in Romania), such items don't make news. John insisted it was likely Simone's parents and brother were interrogated to a fare-thee-well and sent to prison. When the Boss's embarrassment ebbed, they'd be set free—sort of. Since these imagined alternatives were better than being "taken care of," Simone held them close. There was no way to get news, and any attempt to contact them would only exacerbate her family's plight.

Simone grieved. No matter what, it was unlikely she'd ever see or hear of her family again. This left her alone, save for John and the emptiness of hope.

John invited me to visit. He was anxious to have me meet Simone and insisted that she meet me. He, also, invited Ellen. This led to three-pronged communications. Since neither Ellen nor I was anxious to meet Simone alone, we planned a joint expedition in early June.

Before leaving Cedar Falls, I signed the Gray Ghost over to Ellen. She drove it down to Keokuk where we met up. We then took turns driving my blue Ford, a repo dubbed *Old Blue*. It was roomier than the Ghost and managed the miles to Kansas City in reasonable time and comfort.

I had to call John for directions. He neglected to inform me of his move to Shawnee Mission. I had to stop for directions in Kansas twice.

Twenty minutes beyond the state line, I slowed to a crawl in an aging, modest but well-maintained residential area. John and Simone lived on a cul-de-sac. With only seven houses to choose from, numbers were superfluous. John sat in a lounge chair on his modest porch. He leapt up and pulled my car door open before I came to a stop.

Yes, he was happy to see us, but he was more eager to introduce me to his former pupil. He called to her before assaulting Old Blue, but Simone preferred to keep under cover. When we entered the aging home, Simone was in the kitchen. She claimed she'd been making coffee. In truth, she was hiding. One sip of coffee told me that it had been brooding for some while.

She was shorter than I remembered, but there was no mistaking that implacable facial expression. Having completely discarded forced smiles, she shook hands with us while muttering a timid "nice to meet you." For my money, she really didn't care to meet anyone.

"Nice to see you under better circumstances," I said, shaking her limp hand.

She made a special effort to avoid eye contact, but my comment piqued her curiosity. The name Miles Nelson didn't mean anything. My face, however, rang the proverbial bell.

"Chicago," she nodded.

She looked over her shoulder at John to reassure herself he hadn't fled. Naturally, she was concerned. Since she saw me in the company of two *Securitate* stooges, it was only natural to consider me hostile.

John remained smiling and relaxed. He would never assume such an attitude in the proximity of a lethal weapon. Taking relief in his composure, Simone relaxed and looked at me with timidity.

"I remember," she whispered. "That was—very—bad—night."

It was a general announcement. I got the feeling that she was addressing John. If she intended her comment as a rebuke, it fell flat.

We sat down and sipped stale coffee. There were only three people conversing, however. Simone sat and listened and kept a sharp eye on John. The great stone face moderated slightly when Ellen narrated her experiences at school and her post-seminary plans.

Though disappointed by Simone's aloofness, I inwardly rejoiced in detecting a glimmer of emotion from time to time.

"Let's eat!" John insisted, slapping his knees and standing.

I was ready. Though Ellen would never announce it publicly, I knew she was famished.

John picked up his cordless phone.

"Simone is shy about going out in public," he reported. "So— pizza? Chicken? Chinese?"

Tacitly, and in unison, Ellen and I insisted Simone chose. With considerable hesitation and palpable discomfort over deciding something for herself, Simone selected pizza. She limited her speech to that one word and inflected it to form a question. John punched in the number without a memory aid. That spoke volumes.

"How is your English?" Ellen asked point blank.

Simone jumped as if stabbed. She realized a verbal response was expected.

"Is better than before now," she replied haltingly. "Ion is best teacher. When he teach to me English, he refuse to listen to Romanian. I must always say to him in English."

"I think you speak well," Ellen replied without perjuring herself over much.

Simone knew Ellen was being polite and clearly appreciated the gesture. Though difficult to detect, a timid little smile came Ellen's way.

"Simone starts work on Monday," John announced, waiting for the pizza palace to pick up.

"Wow!" Ellen enthused. "What is your job?"

"Ion help me with getting job at small store by here. I put things on shelves, put out price signs, maybe, too, sweep floor."

Nobody ever assumed Simone would be asked to head up a Wall Street brokerage firm, but stocking shelves in a mom-and-pop store didn't strike me as particularly fulfilling. Simone, however, thought enough of it to compose her first unsolicited comment.

"It first time I ever have the work," she stated with reserved but unmistakable pride. "Soon, I have my own money and pay Ion rent."

He was busy ordering a pair of pizzas, but his energetic sign language rejected her comment. Obviously, they'd argued over this.

"I want to make money so someday I can take care of me," she continued.

Once she got started there was no shutting her up!

I'm being facetious, of course. I was thrilled that stone face was secure enough to join the conversation without being coerced.

John briefed me by phone. I took notes. On the drive down, I reviewed the rules with Ellen. No matter what, we were not to ask about either defection. Additionally, questions about Romania and Simone's family were strictly *verboten*. If Simone wanted to talk about these things, fine. Otherwise, we were to avoid butting in where our butts were unwelcome.

Above all else: no talk about skating! None! Don't even allude to it!

As a result, our conversation was strained. Everyone was so nervous, any vocalization, figuratively, made the room tremble. Ellen never attended an Olympic venue and pumped me repeatedly about my Innsbruck experience. Similarly, she'd never met an Olympic athlete; she lusted for the opportunity to interview one. It was difficult for her to endure the prolonged silences. She burned to ask Simone questions. I expected to see blood from biting her tongue.

The pizzas arrived.

Simone became a blur. She rummaged through the kitchen cupboards. John, a man of simple tastes and needs, was caught with one plate, a knife and spoon, a cup and a plastic tumbler. The moment Simone moved in, they acquired additional equipment. They were frugal—as only people who experienced a command economy can be frugal. As a result, the table settings for our pizza pig-out were garage-sale gatherings.

John gave me a plastic Winnie the Pooh plate to host my slices of grease, but Simone snatched it away. She blushed as she slid a plain, white porcelain dish in front of me.

"My favorite," she explained with embarrassment.

Ellen and I exchanged a surreptitious look. We exchanged a second look moments later when Simone crammed an enormous amount of pizza into her gaping maw. When chewing, she resembled a baseball player nursing a pound of chaw. Simone realized we were watching. She did her best to smile despite the tonnage in her mouth. Much more interesting, however, her brown eyes positively danced.

The Winnie the Pooh plate was strictly for her aesthetic enjoyment. She never allowed any slice to leave her hand. She ate so fast and so powerfully that I feared she might ingest the tips of her fingers. She desperately wanted to speak; perhaps, she wished to excuse or explain her impersonation of Attila the Hun at his wedding feast. Alas, she had manners enough to spare us the trauma of spraying food over us.

John offered to put us up for the night, but that wouldn't do. Ellen was on a tight budget and was persuaded to sleep over. John wanted her to take his bed while he parked on the couch. Ellen was adamant; she would sleep on the couch or on the floor. John yielded. I adjourned to an economy motel several blocks away.

We met up at a small café for breakfast. It was difficult for Simone. No matter how relaxed she appeared, she jumped at every sudden noise or motion. She ate all her food only after picking and fussing with it. Not surprisingly, she didn't smile. The only thing she appeared to enjoy was the tea. She put away three cups.

Simone spoke very little. When she did, she leaned across the table and spoke in hushed tones. Despite her precautions, she ended every conversational burst with a search for anyone who might have come within earshot.

Ellen was equally quiet. She spoke when spoken to; her responses were terse. Her smile was forced, and her appetite miniscule. John tried to carry the conversational load. It was obvious that he felt the pall and made a superior effort to feign normalcy. The air was not, exactly, tense, but it was decidedly uncomfortable.

Finally, we said our good-byes and promised to see each other again.

Ellen radiated a calmness I failed to appreciate until later. Among her numerous talents, she is a consummate actress. How she maintained her poise, I shall never understand. All the while, she suffered. She didn't break down and cry in deference to Simone's xenophobia.

When I left late the previous afternoon, Simone excused herself and retired to her room "for a nap."

"She isn't sleeping," John whispered while turning a radio on to a modest volume. "She is very nervous around strangers. She needs to be alone for a while."

Ellen was instantly guilty and insisted that she leave at once. John refused her request. Simone, better than anyone, realized her fears were irrational. She labored hard to overcome them, but it was a work in progress. Two months prior, she'd hide in her room whenever anyone came to the door.

During Simone's "nap," John produced a carefully folded sheet of paper kept in his American-English dictionary. Though written in Romanian, Ellen recognized fourteen quatrains in what, she presumed, were either pentameter or hexameter. As she studied the artful cursive lettering, John explained; Simone presented him the poem on his birthday.

He refused to translate but provided a narrative that inspired Simone's composition.

Young athletes in Romania are routinely beaten, the lazy and the recalcitrant more so. The only ones not beaten were those lacking talent; they were sent home. Presumably, the talent scouts who brought in dross were disciplined or reassigned for wasting state food, money and resources on non-starters.

Simone was frequently switched on the back of the legs. When her trainer was particularly miffed, he would do his best to strike her repeatedly on the same spot. The pain would, thus, become unbearable. When Simone needed special "motivation," she'd get ten strokes down the back of her thighs and calves.

One day, when Simone's mother was allowed a rare visit, she noticed the marks on her precious daughter's legs and boiled over. At great risk to the entire family, the mother verbally tore into the trainer. Any attempt to explain or excuse was drowned out in the shrill vitriol of an implacable mother. Finally, the man's temper was up. He swore at her and threatened to beat her as well—in Hungarian.

Only Simone witnessed the scene. At the first opportunity, she informed one of the goons that her coach swore at her mother in a forbidden language. The next day, Simone had a new trainer.

Word spread. Switching Simone became a public event. The trainer made certain there was one or more goons nearby when administering punishment. Even then, Simone would often complain about Hungarian tongue-lashings during those rare occasions when there were no witnesses. The goons assumed she lied, but they might get in deep trouble should they fail to question the accused.

When Simone turned fifteen, the bulk of her beatings were over. Still, she knew when to expect *motivation*. She got three tries to execute a skill. After the third failure, she'd turn away, and be "motivated." The coaches weren't eager to discipline Simone; she was a sneak. Should Simone suspect unjust switching, she'd subversively retaliate. The greatest fear among coaches and goons was that she'd encourage others to copy her passive resistance.

When John was assigned, Simone was the best teen on the ice. They worked hard. Sometimes, her performance lagged; John would shout and yell and swear, but Simone was too old for traditional "motivation."

John explained how figure skaters develop a large *anchor*—his euphemism. It took a while for Ellen to understand; he utilized effective sign language.

One day, barely a month after John was assigned, Simone fell while attempting a double axel. John swore. She could do that jump. In fact, Simone was highly accomplished in that skill.

A few minutes later, she fell again. John swore again. After her third fall, Simone reacted instinctively. She skated toward John, pulling up the legs of her sweats. She turned obediently away and, inexplicably, bent over. There were two goons milling about. Once Simone assumed the position, they'd expect discipline. Indeed, because Simone was such a sneak and a chronic pain, the goons would demand strokes.

John reached for the switch and presented Simone with three of his best.

Simone skated around until the pain subsided and the tears no longer clouded her vision.

The poem Simone wrote was a tribute to John's mercy.

He didn't swat her bare legs; instead, he brought his strokes down on her sweatpants *and* her natural padding. It was their first meaningful communication. He didn't want to hurt her. Three lashes on her legs would have stung excruciatingly and would leave wicked marks. Applied to her ass, however, the pain subsided within seconds and left no appreciable welts.

Simone's poem was a celebration of a coach who desired her success. Previous trainers enjoyed torturing her.

Ellen was incredulous. How could Simone author a poem lauding her abuser? There was no way to decipher the Romanian script, but the tears in John's eyes told her what she needed to know. Life behind the Curtain sucked! It was coarse, emphatic and brutal. Nevertheless, when one discovered a true comrade, even state-supported punishment became endurable.

"I tell Simone, if she want rid of me, she has only to say. I promise to swear in Hungarian at her in front of witnesses."

John wiped the corner of his eye.

It would be years before Ellen told me either of these poignant anecdotes.

"This time, I need a drink," the seminary student announced.

"Kansas is dry," I reminded. "You'll have to wait."

We had just breakfasted. It wasn't yet noon. Ignorant of what got under Ellen's skin, I reverted to the Simone rules. If she wanted to talk about it, I'd listen. Meanwhile, I'd mind my own business.

In Missouri, we discovered a restaurant and lounge open for those who drank breakfast. It was a dive. There was sawdust on the floor and the smell of stale beer was so pungent it could—unaided—put me over the blood/alcohol limit. There were two alkies at the bar hunched over drinks. Neither Ellen nor I was anxious to get close to the disheveled bar flies, so, we picked the cleanest dirty table and made the barman come to us.

I ordered a coffee, knowing full well the chance I took. Ellen demanded a vodka martini.

"Don't tell me that's the communion drink at your school!"

Ellen was in no joking mood. I suspected she spent the night taking blank-expression lessons from Simone. Rather than converse, Ellen held out her right hand. It took a moment to adjust to the dimness, but I noticed the proffered appendage trembled.

"I'm a mess," she confessed.

After her "nap," Simone relaxed slightly. She even smiled once or twice. Ellen was quick to explain these were not what we considered smiles. They were, however, enough to indicate Simone possessed more than one emotion.

Simone accepted Ellen's assistance in making a light dinner. As they enjoyed a closely guarded conversation in the kitchen, John took the opportunity to visit the necessary. At that point, and without any announcement, Simone took the skillet off the heat and—spatula in hand—wandered idly into the living room. When John returned and resumed reading the paper, Simone went back to the stove.

"It was as if she blacked out for two or three minutes," Ellen whispered. "She took up our conversation right where we left off—like there was no interruption."

Spooky, I concluded. That, however, was only the start.

John and Simone's bedrooms were across the hall from each other. After the lights were out, there was perfect silence—as one had a right to expect in a secluded neighborhood.

Suddenly, Ellen awakened.

She heard a noise—a rustling. It wasn't worthy of attention, so she rolled over and attempted a return to dreamland. The rustling, however, increased until it became thrashing. She heard John creep out of his room and across the hall. He spoke softly; Simone responded, in Romanian. After a few seconds, John went back to bed.

"This happened three times," Ellen said as her drink arrived.

Highly disturbing, I concluded, but hardly worthy of a vodka martini.

"Simone looked like the creature from the Black Lagoon this morning," Ellen went on, taking a sip. "I caught her coming out of the bathroom. She had on a sleeveless t-shirt. I was close enough to see the inside of her arms. Two long scars, Miles! Angry, ugly, brutal scars."

She covered her mouth with her hand and struggled to stifle tears. A moment later she removed the hand from her mouth and held it over the table. With the opposite hand, she indicated a spot above her wrist. Slowly, she traced an invisible line up her arm to within an inch of the bend. Once the task was completed, she helped herself to a good, old-fashioned, down-home gulp of martini.

"I nearly screamed," she added, catching her breath.

I was stunned.

"The reports of her attempted suicide were not exaggerated," I concluded.

"I'm a seminary student," she said with pronounced self-loathing. "I should be able to cope. I was completely rattled. That's not right; I was frightened out of my wits! What makes me think I can minister?"

She started to take another drink, thought better of it and put down the glass.

"I may not be cut out for this, Miles. I want to help people, but—I was shaking. I didn't have a clue what to say or what to do. That poor woman can't sleep nights, can't exist unless John is in her line of sight, and—and this was no cry for help, Miles. She intended to kill herself! Why couldn't I do something?—say something?"

I cleared my throat. It was my turn to cultivate a craving for drink. The coffee sat in front of me. It looked like crank-case oil. I made no attempt to find out.

"Right now, she's comfortable with John. Maybe, that's what she needs—that and time."

"And what did I do for John?" she demanded. "This must take a lot out of him. He was up half the night. He isn't getting much sleep, and he supports them both. I've been racking my brain. I stood like a great lump and was frightened out of my skin."

She sucked in another long pull from her glass. There wasn't much remaining when she set it down. I watched her look at the glass in disbelief. Next, I watched her hold her hand over the table to inspect it. It was rock steady.

Ellen looked at me with terror in her eyes. She was no Polly Prude, but I'd wager she'd never dispatched a vodka martini in record time. Nevertheless, she remained rattled. To be found wanting was against the family-Bible tradition; having to rely on alcohol to steady her nerves was blasphemy.

I waited.

Finally, she averted her eyes in shame and swallowed hard.

"You have a great advantage over me," I said at long, overdue, last. "You are a believer; I'm a skeptic."

She rested her head on her fist and stared at the tabletop.

"So, what?" she taunted.

It was half snarl and half resignation.

"Well, let's play in your court," I reasoned. "If you were expected to help Simone or John—or, for that matter, both, He wouldn't let you to stand there with your teeth in your mouth, would He?"

She sat up with a jerk. She studied me with her back as straight as a West Point plebe.

"No," she whispered in agreement.

I extended my arms to display the palms of my hands.

Nothing up my sleeve.

"When He wants you to pitch in, He'll let you know."

She took a while to digest this.

"If we play in your court," she demanded, "what's your take?"

I shrugged.

"Skeptics, by definition, don't have answers," I reminded. "If you're asking for an opinion, I submit that John and Simone know far better what they're up against. They like and respect each other; they'll figure it out. Together, they can cope."

She leaned forward and rested her arms on the table. She stared at what little remained of her drink. After a long bout of rumination, she stirred.

"You'd be a good seminary student," she concluded.

"Only if the lights are low, there's a lot of soft jazz, and the beer is on tap," I responded. "Now, can we pay up and get out of here? This place gives me the creeps."

CHAPTER TWO

I visited John and Simone twice more. Once was in Cincinnati when John brought his star pupil to a competition. Simone came along for the ride but refused to go into the arena. Consequently, I didn't either. Instead, Simone and went out for dinner and a show. She'd put on weight. Her language was much improved. Also, she was far less aloof than our first meeting.

The rules that applied in Shawnee Mission were observed in Cincinnati. I found myself talking a lot about the history I was writing. In truth, it wouldn't qualify as a proper book. It might run a hundred pages and would likely be printed as a pamphlet. Still, it constituted a milestone in my decidedly pedestrian life.

Simone acted interested. Perhaps, she was being polite, but she asked several questions, indicating she paid attention. Though hardly a conversationalist, Simone participated in brief exchanges. Her eyes remained alert. Occasionally, she smiled politely at my labored jokes.

During the stage performance, she occasionally squirmed in her seat when her attention lagged. Her facial expression never changed.

It was hardly an evening for the memory book, but it was pleasant. The fact that we spoke freely was a relief. Our exchanges in

Kansas were so strained that Ellen and I were left mentally exhausted. Not so in Cincinnati.

John sent a family photo at Christmas. They posed in their living room. John stood behind the couch with Simone seated in front of him. It looked as if she'd shed weight. Most impressive, however, was the smile on her face. I saw teeth!

Ellen and I frequently speculated about the precise nature of the relationship between John and his ward. Though a romance might qualify as eccentric, it wouldn't be unseemly. It appeared platonic enough in Kansas, and nothing at Cincinnati prompted revision. Simone called John *Papa*; that satisfied me.

My second visit with Papa and Simone was in Altoona, Iowa. Papa wanted a week away from the grind, and Adventureland promised succor. He invited Ellen, but she could manage only one day away, and that was reserved for a long overdue Sunday dinner. Since everyone else, including Ellen's two new sisters-in-law, would be on hand, she excused herself—reluctantly, I should add.

I continued my work with abstracts but, lacking a pension plan, I took a second job.

A former Marine and I shared a drink one afternoon. He waited table at a posh Lima feed bag. They needed part-time help; he offered to put in a good word.

I made money enough for rent and food. The royalties from my booklet averaged twenty-seven dollars a month, due, almost exclusively, from area schools buying up classroom sets. What the hell? If a barrel-chested, ramrod straight ex-Jarhead could wait table, so could a broken-down former Army buck sergeant.

The wages were nominal, but the tips piled up until I found myself playing Silas Marner two evenings a month. I worked from five to midnight on weekends and from six to eleven on Tuesdays and Wednesdays. It took a while to get used to being on my feet for lengthy periods, but I was padding my bank account. It occupied otherwise idle hours.

I enjoyed two brief romances. The first was with a divorcee who, though slightly older, was nearly perfect in every way. She was a professional woman, an RN, cultured and intelligent. The failure of her first marriage, alas, made her wary and wise.

Lois and I got along swimmingly. I even met her ex-husband who was never anything less than civil to me. In fact, he, his business associates, and his girlfriend frequently dined at the restaurant.

Just as I thought Lois and I had a relationship headed for a happy end, I was confronted by the fact that, ultimately, her alimony was more attractive than I. No fault there. Miles Nelson is no prize.

Cindy was younger and had the most spectacular, natural blond hair on the planet. Normally, I preferred brunettes, but Cindy made blonde look good. We got along well. She loved me because I never failed to make her laugh—and, by the way, her laugh had all the pleasing textures of a Brahms adagio.

Eventually, however, I realized I hadn't ambition enough to be a funny man for the rest of my life. Our romance, which started as a raging torrent, gradually diminished to a babbling brook. Eventually, it became a stagnant pool.

Truth to tell, I remained angry over not wooing Ellen when I had the opportunity. Occasionally, I'd fool myself into thinking that I still had a chance—which was true enough. Unfortunately, feelings of inadequacy would wash over me, and I'd drown my conceits in booze. I might coerce Ellen up the aisle; I might even make her think she was happy. Regardless, she remained light years out of my league. More importantly, I'd be little more than a pet, providing perpetual disappointment. Groveling to make up for transgressions and failures would wear thin.

I'd love Ellen more if she enjoyed partnership with someone worthy.

Ellen, meanwhile, didn't reside in her seminary like some cloistered nun. She was moved by her first encounter with Simone and kept track of her (and John) with the doggedness of a Pinkerton operative. She called frequently. After some weeks, she and Simone exchanged lengthy missives, lyric and philosophic.

Before long, Ellen was Simone's confidant. Ellen was privy to matters that Simone was hesitant to share with Papa.

Ahm—Adventureland, I remember now.

I could shake free for a Friday, but I must be back in harness Saturday evening to scarf up those substantial tips on the busiest evening of the week. My absence from the title company would not be missed. I left Wednesday and spent the night in an Illinois pest-house motel.

John reserved a room for me at their Altoona motel, which was fine, but I insisted on paying my way. I arrived around noonish. John was there to meet me.

"Where's Simone?"

"In the park, waiting for us."

Simone, of course, was weaned prior to Cincinnati. She felt secure enough to allow Papa out of her sight. There were additional pleasant surprises.

After stowing my junk in my assigned room, John closed the door behind us.

"I want you to see something," he said, reaching for his wallet.

I don't care for secrets. Even more, I was uncomfortable being locked in the room with someone between me and the door. It wasn't that I didn't trust John; it's one of my many traits which qualify me for a padded cell.

He worried a photograph from his billfold and presented it to me. It was slightly contoured from being sat on repeatedly but was otherwise sharp if pitifully small.

It was a picture of Simone, kneeling behind a young boy. Her arms were around him in a loving hug. They were laughing. Yes, Simone was laughing! That, however, was nothing compared with the ice skates! One pair was adult sized; the other was clearly those of a child.

"God!"

That's all I could manage. The image was so unexpected—indeed, impossible—that I was stunned.

"She works with me now," he explained. "She takes care of the children while I work with the teens. She's good. She's like a mother to the little ones."

"How—" I gulped, struggling to find my tongue, "How did you get her inside?"

"She must borrow the car one day to run errands," John began excitedly. "She parked outside and waited. The little ones came out with their parents. She asked about them."

I attempted to memorize the photograph.

"For two days, she asked about the children. She couldn't believe young boys and girls *wanted* to skate. That was great revelation: nobody forced them! She started coming inside to watch. After twenty minutes, she is leaning over the barrier offering tips. Before long, she is giving instructions."

I swallowed that with joy and relief.

"Now, she works there—with children; only with children. She does not yell, she does not swear, she does not smack them or shove them—she love them, Miles. If skating makes them happy, then helping them makes Simone happy."

I cleared the lump out of my throat.

"Somehow, I got the impression that her shelf-stocking days were numbered," I said.

John laughed.

"Can I have this?" I asked.

He snatched it back before I could react.

"I promise to send you a copy," he assured. "A bigger copy."

This earned my profound thanks.

We had no problems locating Simone. She was addicted to the roller coaster. As luck would have it, she was screaming and laughing and having a great time. When she freed herself of the restraints, she rushed to us with pure giddiness.

She hugged Papa for all she was worth. Then, she gave me the same treatment. Bystanders must have mistaken me for her long-lost best friend the way she grabbed me and held me and kissed me on both cheeks, Romanian style.

"Take me on the waterlog," she insisted, grabbing my hand.

I hadn't time to speak. She has one hell of a grip and her legs, as expected, were all muscle and sinew. I resisted only to prevent entry into warp speed and, thus, endangering others. It required more strength than expected.

Waiting in line, she talked a mile a minute about everything she and Papa did, saw and ate during their stay. They had separate rooms, but she'd sit with Papa evenings to watch TV or play a game originally intended as an English vocabulary builder.

"I like teddy bears," the Winnie-the-Pooh fan revealed. "When we filled in the items for the letter t, I put in Tiber for the river, Treasure Island for the book, Texas for the land, Tirana for the city and—" she giggled, "teddy-bear seller for the occupation."

She thought this hilarious. I laughed at her laughter rather than the anemic punch line.

Simone was twenty-four or five, but she acted like a ten-year old. How a person could maintain such excitement after four days was beyond my understanding. Still, she was burning calories at an amazing rate. She was getting six to eight hours of uninterrupted sleep. She promised to visit Papa if she experienced difficulties during sleep hours. John assured me, Simone had, yet, to bother him. Exhaustion, apparently, stifled horror.

"I ride in front!" she squealed, jumping into the imitation dugout. Straddling the upholstered bench running through the long axis of our craft, she leaned against me as if to assuage her fears that I might abandon ship.

The first part of the ride was tranquil.

"There's a camera up there," she advised. "Smile and look happy."

Simone Albescu, the same woman whose facial expression was tailored for skating to a funeral dirge, was telling *me* to smile and look happy.

We splashed down the final ramp, getting our jeans and shirts moderately soaked. We went by the photo booth where I saw our image on public display.

Simone waved and hooted merrily while I saluted with one hand and held her fast with the other. I had smiled—or I thought I had. Compared with Simone's expression, however, I looked like Calvin Coolidge. Still, there was no way I could not plop down three dollars for a copy of the picture.

I have it still—and I won't accept a million dollars for it.

Our clothing dried in a matter of minutes under the sun's warming rays. John, mildly hydrophobic, eschewed the ride. However, the log aced the roller-coaster as Simone's favorite. Owing to her xenophobia, she held me captive for much of the afternoon.

I learned that the sun's drying rays were blunted by repeated drenching. Nevertheless, Simone's enjoyment was so acute, complete emersion couldn't have deterred me. I became Boo Radley; my delight was predicated entirely on Simone's palpable expressions of *bucurie*.

You are amazed at my Latin vocabulary? Rest assured, I came by it honestly and without ulterior motives. Shortly after the Innsbruck incident, I engaged research. Among a myriad of trivialities, I hit upon one possible origin of the name *Bucharest*. Beyond *E Pluribus Unum*, the Roman tongue remains Greek to me, but it provided a welcome insight into *Dacia*.

CHAPTER THREE

In my modest apartment, there was a modest, third-hand desk. Made by a friend, an apprentice or a disinterested amateur, the device was nearly useless. The drawers did not function, and the legs were uneven. Nevertheless, there were two pigeonholes on each side and a flat surface upon which to write. It cost me next to nothing. Should it prove non-functional, I'd chop it up, sell it for scrap and, probably, come out ahead.

I placed a lamp and the telephone on the desktop. When a bill arrived, I kept it in one of the pigeonholes until I had an excuse to sit down and write a check.

A wooden chair standing sentry at this monument to mediocrity looked as uncomfortable as the desk appeared useless. It was, however, so comfortable that I used it when reading. Similarly, with any incoming call, I'd sit down before lifting the receiver.

As luck would have it, I sat at the desk re-reading *A Distant Mirror* when the phone rang. I continued to the end of a paragraph and made a pencil tick to mark my place.

"Nelson."

"Do you remember Noah, Ellen's kid brother?"

I was startled. The Noah I knew was a rosy-cheeked whirlwind with thick but disheveled hair who spoke in an excited soprano. The voice which crackled across the miles was a pleasing baritone.

"No Good, of course I remember you," I replied. "It's been a while."

Ellen, a.k.a. *La Goodo* around the hearth, addressed her littlest brother as Noah Good. She, however, can do Italian dialect. My Italian accent sounds the same as my Irish brogue; therefore, on those rare occasions when I desired his attention, I fell back on *No Good*.

"It's been a long time," he agreed.

"How's your sister?"

"Annoying."

I laughed. I'd witnessed the interactions of the Good siblings. As previously recorded, theirs is a highly efficient, functioning family. The word *annoying* was devoid of context.

"I assume you didn't call me up to complain about Ellen."

"Not quite. I got scholarship offers from both Heidelberg and Wooster."

"Whoa!"

I was pleased and amazed.

"Your sister started something, didn't she? Now, everybody wants to go to college."

He hesitated.

"Not really. I'm not sure I want to go."

"They're both good schools," I sidestepped.

In truth, I knew almost nothing of either. However, if one, or both, had a bad reputation, I'd heard nothing of it.

"Dad's loaning me a car to look them over and, maybe, talk to people."

"You need a place to crash," I concluded.

He cleared his throat.

"Well, I *am* on a budget," he confessed.

"Noah, *any* brother of Ellen's is welcome here. When can I expect you? I'll be sure to have a good meal ready, not near as good as your mother's, but nobody's died from my baked ham."

"That would be nice," he admitted.

We chatted for a while.

After hanging up, I ruminated.

The entire process was surreal. Based upon subsequent events, one might assume that I'm clairvoyant. I disagree, but there is no logical explanation for my train of thought.

I looked up the number, picked up the phone and dialed my fairy godfather.

"I'm over thirty and I haven't started a pension fund," I explained. "I wondered if you could advise me."

"Well, I know that a couple of the better hotels are head hunting—not like what you were doing before."

He was quick to add the qualifier.

"Chicago holds no appeal," I stated. "I'd rather be in a place where the tax collectors don't camp on the front stoop."

A baby is produced in less time than it took to clear taxes in Chi Town. Hyperbole, perhaps, but no one ever called me on it.

"Anything particular?" he asked.

"Well, I can load and fire both a ninety millimeter and a one-oh-six recoilless."

"Hmmmm. Don't know there are any tank threats in the private sector, but I'll shake some trees."

"Don't make this a priority," I pleaded. "Between my job and moonlighting, I'm aces high. Still, there'll come a time when a pension will come in handy."

"Understood," he replied. "Give me a couple weeks or three."

"Wilco, and thanks."

Noah is tall and lithe, not at all as I remembered him. He was taller than I! Under that slender exterior was probably enough strength to shred a telephone book. As with all Goods, he didn't boast or engage in meaningless demonstrations. His grip was sure. That was good enough for me.

I expected—nay, *hoped*—the Gray Ghost would crunch the gravel of my driveway; that Noah and Ellen would both step out.

Alas—

"Have trouble finding the place?"

Noah smiled and shook his head.

"Cridersville is pretty small," he grinned. "It's hard to get lost."

"How was your trip?"

"Interesting. Ellen sends her love."

I was pleased.

"Take mine back with you."

"I shall," he promised.

True to my word, I had baked ham at the ready. There was no way I could compete with mashed potatoes a *la Good*, so, we had baked. It isn't the done thing, but Noah didn't complain. I had three different flavors of ice cream for afters, but Noah declined. Instead, he paid me the supreme complement.

"Could I have just another little slice of that ham?"

Ham for dessert! Well, the guest is always right.

"Let me help with the cleaning up," Noah insisted, as I knew he would.

"Let it sit for a while. I've got coffee on if you like."

He claimed to be fine with that, but I detected feigned politeness. After a bit of thrust and parry, he admitted he was partial to tea. I had sun tea on hand, but he hankered for hot. Unhesitatingly, I made him a steaming mug. I could offer nothing except bag variety, but he expressed no reservations. He added a dash of sugar so niggardly it was hardly worth the effort.

"I have no TV and only the one bedroom where you will sleep—"

"That couch out there will do fine," he insisted.

I grumbled a bit, but he remained adamant. It was, probably, a Good family tradition.

"I really need a place with a second bedroom," I mused.

"Why?" he asked.

I had no answer. My statement might be construed as additional evidence of clairvoyance. I was ill equipped to rationalize my need for a guest room. Noah was so bone-crushingly logical, I should have dismissed the notion completely.

"Why don't you have a TV?" he eventually asked.

I had to think.

"I watched Super Bowl I," I advanced. "I watched Super Bowl II. I was still quite young, but I decided I'd exceeded my limit on commercials. TV has no allure. I'd rather curl up with a good book."

"A good book?" he asked.

Perhaps, he was hinting that I should curl up with *the* Good Book. Perhaps, he was chasing a pun.

"I hate bad books," I confided.

He laughed. It was subdued and, as ever, polite.

He took a sip of tea and leaned back. He began to quote "The Love Song of J. Alfred Prufrock." He went on, from memory, for some while.

"Go on," I encouraged.

T. S. Eliot qualifies as entertainment.

"My memory is a little hazy," he admitted. "I'd better not."

"*I have measured out my life with coffee spoons,*" I quoted.

He grinned. I knew that, somewhere, there was a cultured young woman just waiting to melt under that infectious grin.

"Maybe, *you* should go on," he urged.

I shook my head.

"That's all the Prufrock I know."

"Interesting."

I didn't much care for the way he said that. He wasn't snide or sinister, but there was an implication which grated. Sure enough, a few minutes later, he brought up *the* subject.

"Why didn't you ask Ellen to marry you?"

I stared at him.

"She was pretty excited, once," he continued. "She was certain you'd propose. It's none of my business, of course, but I can't avoid being curious."

I thought for some while.

"For this, for everything, we are out of tune,"

"English," he surmised. "Not Tennyson."

"Assuredly not!"

"I've read that line. One doesn't forget something like that."

"Pretty smart cookie for a high school student," I nodded admiringly. "It's Wordsworth, actually."

"Ah, of course." he said, defensively. "How are you out of tune?"

"I want Ellen to be happy. I don't think I can contribute to that end."

"Don't you think Ellen is the better judge of that?"

"No."

He let it go. I was glad.

"Cedar Falls isn't good enough for you?"

"If I go to college," he began, relieved by the subject change, "that's probably where I'll go. Ellen thinks I'd be foolish not to check out these schools. Their offers will defray expenses. Since she's the only family collegian, Dad backed her. He didn't make me come here—not in so many words, but his feelings are clear."

I didn't like the idea of a cursory examination of two potential schools. My suggestion was that he spend a day in Tiffin and another in Wooster. That wasn't much time, but it was better than an hour or two of stepping off the campus. He, again, referred to his budget.

"We can stop by the ATM. My treat. You can owe me; no interest charges."

He was visibly moved.

"Thanks."

That was all he said. Coupled with the expression on his face, it was enough.

The following morning, after hotcakes and recycled ham, I saw the handsome young man out to his car. He shook my hand and asked if he could sleep over on his way back. I replied, truthfully, that I'd be delighted.

"One more thing, No," I began.

This got his attention.

"This thing with me and your sister: Ellen is going to make a mark someday. I don't want to mess it up."

For a moment, he looked as if I spoke in Braille. I cleared my throat and shifted tack.

"If Abe Lincoln accepted the governorship of the Oregon Territory, would he have become President? Understand what I'm saying?"

He's a very perceptive young man, Mr. No Good. He nodded—and *not* out of politeness.

CHAPTER FOUR

"What do you know about computers?" my fairy godfather asked. "If I take off my shoes, I can count to twenty." He wasn't receptive to my humor.

"Are you willing to learn?"

"That depends. What is my motivation?"

"There's a company that will start supplying computers to high schools. They need somebody to handle instillation, networking and demonstrate systems."

"I can't get my radio to work half the time," I reported, my heart sinking.

"The company has trained people for that stuff. If you can boot and reboot, they'll train you."

Boot? Reboot? I hadn't a clue.

"Sure. Who doesn't know how to *boot?*"

He sounded skeptical, but he arranged a meeting with a corporate rep the following week, in Chicago (of course). I thought it was worth a shot, so I arranged for three days off work and two nights away from the restaurant. This latter was tough. On a good night, I could scarf up a hundred balloons. Still, if I could trade instant gratification for a more secure future, I was game.

I found someone to show me how to *boot.*

The personnel manager was interested, and I was excited about the job as he described it. I felt comfortable enough to confide that I really didn't care to work in Illinois. That, he assured me, was not an obstacle.

"You can, probably, stay in Ohio," he assured.

Who, I wondered, wants to *stay* in Ohio? Well, the company had nation-wide aspirations. If I did well in training, I'd have a say in where I'd be posted. The job, if I got it, would keep me on the road; where I kept my pelf was hardly a priority. Where I paid taxes concerned me more.

I managed to find a co-op in Chicago where I'd sleep during the six-weeks of training. There were six of us in residence. We shared the cleaning chores, and each was tasked with supplying an evening meal once a week; I drew Thursday. We fended for ourselves on Sunday.

Because I can find my way around the kitchen rather well, my once-a-week meal wasn't a problem. Two of the others, college students who couldn't boil water, treated us to pizza or Chinese take-away.

Once again, I was *Pops.* That diminutive helped motivate me. I realized my chance at a career was rapidly dwindling and, if I didn't get this job, I'd be in a pickle.

It was like living in a dormitory. In addition to the college kids, there was an Argentinean ex-pat prepping for missionary work, a waitress trying to cut expenses while studying for her Mrs. degree, and a mechanic who constantly smelled of Diesel and grease. We got along very well because we seldom saw each other.

My room was just off the kitchen, at the terminus of the rear steps. As a result, I got to monitor all the nocturnal comings and goings. Thankfully, I was the greatest possible distance from the TV room, but one of the college kids liked to practice guitar just outside the kitchen—usually during my study periods.

I got used to sleeping in a loft above my desk. I got used to leaning over my tiny desk squinting at texts punched out by Martians. I got used to being blown into the kitchen when I sneezed. It was like being stuffed in one of those Apollo command modules—but not as roomy.

There were compensations, however. Chief among these came on Saturdays when we trainees were dismissed at noon. This gave me a chance to tie up with Dixie and a few of my other chums from the bad old days. We'd shoot an afternoon in fun and frolic and, perhaps, a splash of fire water. These outing never got too wild since I had to return to my cocoon and study zeroes and ones.

On Sundays, I seldom bothered to shave or even dress. I'd sit and go over my materials again and again until I had most of the stuff in my head. None of us had a computer, so I couldn't do any hands-on work until just before the training day started. Normally, kick-off was eight-thirty. I arrived before six to practice.

Underneath our cramped and populated apartment was a lawyer's office. She had a computer. I spent two profitable evenings with the lady lawyer and her assistant. Their coaching proved valuable.

We were like trainees in one of those World War II outfits. Twice a week, three dozen candidates would elbow their way to the scores posted on a bulletin board. For two days, I was number one. This irked the few candidates with prior computer experience. I think my inexperience helped me. I didn't have to compare what I learned with what I'd learned previously. I didn't have to overcome bad habits. In short, I confronted confusion in small, bite-sized chunks.

When the dust settled, I was number six in a class of thirty-three (three people dropped out). I was interviewed by my instructor and someone from the company S-1.

(Please excuse my parlance; corporate organization remains a hopeless puzzle. It is much easier to equate positions through Army organizational tables.)

Following our chat, I was awarded a hearty handshake. I, also, got a modest stipend to cover a portion of my expenses incurred while living in a space capsule. Most importantly, I left the room with an employment application.

I was asked to list, in order of preference, the five states to which I was willing to re-locate. Because taxes were at the top of my concerns, I wrote down in bold, block letters TEXAS. Below this, I listed other tax-friendly states.

A week later, I got a letter congratulating me on my acceptance; I was to report to Dallas in two months. For this country boy, Dallas was Chicago where citizens wore big hats. I hoped I wouldn't be captive to schools in the D/FW area. There were, I knew, many wide-open spaces down yon, and, partner, I was hankerin' to find me such a place for to live.

I was running on hope, the refuge of the powerless. My rush of excitement was tempered by the prospect of being pinned down in another population center. My desire for an old-age pension waned. To trade city life for the promise of a few ducats years beyond didn't appeal. I might not survive a stifling cauldron.

Ambivalence perched on my shoulder and influenced my every activity, both personal and professional. Heaving a sigh, I opened my suitcases and began the traditional weeding-out process. I'd acquired a pile of books which I couldn't afford to ship.

I called the Goods and offered to leave them a small library if they were interested. The patriarch was amenable. Such a legacy was certain to reach Ellen and Noah anon. I doubted that the elder Goods would have much use for my eclectic collection. They were partial to religious tracts.

The phone rang shortly after I got off the line. I suspected Mr. Good had second thoughts. It wasn't in keeping with his rural code: a deal struck is a deal kept. Still, things weren't running true to form.

It was the man who shook my hand and, in a very real sense, hired me. He was miffed. He and my fairy godfather were very thick;

he demanded—*demanded*, mind you—to know why I hadn't mentioned my relationship to him.

Another rush came over me. Was this guy petty enough to fire me over the phone? For a thrilling second, I hoped that he'd do exactly that.

I told him, truthfully, that I'd tapped my fairy godfather twice; I wasn't eager to impose upon—or abuse—his benevolence further. Poor specimen that I was, it was never my intention to slide through life on nepotism. My fairy godfather was a friend and relation, not a magic wand to brandish about.

He accepted that. He became civil. He then asked if I really wanted to go to Dallas. Still half-hoping to be fired, I confessed that big cities caused my skin to crawl. Much to my surprise, he laughed.

"What if I were to tell you that you don't have to go to Dallas?"

"If I get the sack, that would be a good excuse."

He snorted. It was a grand-champion snort. I switched the receiver to the ear which was not temporarily impaired.

Fairy godfather was a big cog in the hotel and motel industry. The internet was relatively new, but certain hostelries were interested in computers as a means of storing information, handling billing and—gasp—accepting and facilitating reservations between corporate stables.

"Your job will be to train the staff in the use of our products," Mr. Huff and Puff went on. "We're launching a new computer line soon, much more sophisticated. You'll be properly trained, of course. Then you can train hotel staff."

"I don't have to go to Dallas?"

"Not unless your heart is set on it."

"Where, then?"

"For the time being, you don't have to go anywhere. We're in the pioneer stage. We have a contract with a Midwestern group. We start in three months in the Ohio-Indiana area, near the lakes. If it works out, we'll go national, the same as we're doing with the school-lease program."

"I'm not trained in LAN," I reminded.

"We have geeks for that. That's behind-the-baseboard stuff. We need people like you out front."

"I'm game."

Three more months of hundred-plus dollar evenings. Three more months of the abstract business (my mad money). Above everything else, no Dallas and, with luck, no more Chi Town!

I was on the company roster, but my checks wouldn't start for several weeks.

Close enough.

Ohio is, alas, Ohio. It is an unsatisfactory mix between corporate and agricultural America. Even a local farmer I knew worked at an auto-plant. Still, Cridersville was my little oasis. It was near enough industry and urban life, but it remained a quiet suburb. True, it abutted the Interstate, but transients seldom bothered to wander away from the gas pumps and hash houses. One daren't blink when driving through downtown, or it would pass unnoticed. I was happy there. It was a twenty-minute drive to work and thirty minutes from the snooty restaurant where I mined gold.

Being, almost, gainfully employed, I visited a real estate office.

For months, I passed a brick house settled placidly behind a *For Sale* sign. I was not interested in buying, but there was no law against asking about rental possibilities. As I suspected, the agent was happy to get a nibble after several weeks of bupkis. She drove me out to inspect the place.

Unlike a Hudson, you had to step *up* to get into it, by either the front or the side entrance. It featured a large basement the former owners used as a living area during blistering summer days. It was prone to flooding during wet weather, but a pump was installed to allay that problem. The place was so ancient that the floor squeaked and popped when one walked across it. There was, however, a nice wall-to-wall carpet in the living room. The bathroom was small but functional. A door off the living room hid a very nice wooden staircase leading up to the attic where one found only slats and billowy piles of insulation.

In the late 1920s, it was an ultra-modern masterpiece. By the mid-1980s, it was reduced to cozy. Most importantly, for me, were two bedrooms. The well-water, so insipid as to be drinkable only when chilled, and the lack of air conditioning were minor annoyances.

Why the bedrooms were a deal maker remains beyond the bounds of my limited intellect.

I leave all philosophical questions to Ellen Good.

CHAPTER FIVE

Max McGee was, at the time, a rakish young man with brown hair trimmed to military standards. He is thin and muscular. He got interested in computers when they were used only for Packman and Lunar landings. The devices themselves were nice for playing around, but Max had a vision. When the idea of linking one computer to another was introduced, he knew what he wanted.

Max wore dark-rimmed glasses and used a pocket protector. Nevertheless, he was hardly a geek. He was literate, witty and congenial to a fault, but not beyond. I took a liking to him instantly.

"I saw you in the Super Bowl," I said when introduced. "Great catch!"

He grinned.

Max grew up hearing endless variations on the Super Bowl theme. His grin did not fool me. I realized that further Max McGee jokes would prove as flat as stale beer.

The company delivered eight computers to a hotel conference room in Van Wert, Ohio. True to the project's conception, the suits began modestly. In fact, our efforts were called, informally, Project Mercury. It was a walk-before-we-run scheme, and we all learned as we took each modest step.

I unpacked and positioned the computers on four conference tables. Max began linking them and connecting the entire network to our Fred Flintstone printer.

We checked each station individually before locking the room, whereupon we adjourned to a nearby watering hole. Strangely, we talked of computers only briefly.

Max had a myriad of interests. Foremost among these was his desire to become the Grand High Pooh-Bah of networking. He wanted every computer in the solar system connected with every other. Being hands-on, Max quickly tired of talking about it; he'd rather get on with the job. Similarly, though trained in computers, I regarded them teeth-achingly pedestrian, save for word processing. I fancied that the hotel staff would find them useful and fun, but they, probably, did not care to become slaves to them. That was my focus from the start, and it served me well. Computer addicts don't need me. As does Max, they learn by doing and don't want some egg head droning on about systems, procedures and flow charts.

I should insert here that I had an Apple GS II until the CPU, after thousands and thousands of hours, flat lined. Yes, I kept up with the products which made my poor Apple look like a prehistoric, flint tool, but word processing was my only computer obsession. Ergo, my little toy and its floppy discs made me very happy.

When my GS II died, I'd have bought another. Alas, working GS IIs are as rare as hen's teeth (and priced accordingly).

Max sat quietly in the back of the room while I conducted training. I'm sure I bungled from time to time, but Max kept his oar out.

"If I screw up," I told him over a beer, "I expect you to set me straight."

"You stay away from my networking and I'll stay away from your computers," he replied. "I'm no kibitzer."

I didn't care for his attitude at first, but we got along so well that I didn't want to rock the boat. At another post-seminar conference (over suds) he pointed out that programs were changing so quickly, it was impossible for our *run-Spot-run* seminars to be of lasting value.

"When you memorize the times tables, you're set," he pontificated. "When you memorize a computer program, you can get screwed by an upgrade. You adjust. It's learning, learning and learning."

"People want to be able to run a program the most efficient way," I objected.

"So, they do what you and I do; they ask questions."

"Or read the manual," I added.

He gave me a smug grin.

"Tell me the last operator's manual you read."

"For computers?"

"For anything."

He had me there.

Rule number one in computer class: Do. Don't watch.

It was difficult to keep my hands off the keys. I could sit down and do in three minutes what most of the trainees struggled with for fifteen. It was useless. Even the brightest student can watch you do something fifty times and get hopelessly muddled when venturing out on his own. Conversely, the most obtuse person can learn if you just talk them through it three or four times.

In Fort Wayne one day, Max caught my eye during a session. He gestured with the nod of his head. I discovered some white-haired grandmother with her forehead touching the monitor and her right hand extended to the maximum. The mouse was at the very edge of the table.

"What's the problem?" I asked.

"I can't get that arrow any higher," she moaned.

Rule number two in computer class: Do not laugh or make fun of neophytes.

In this instance, poor granny had no point of reference. She grew up, raised a family and took a job late in life. Computers were hardly her trusty Hotpoint.

We laughed later over suds, but not because we thought her stupid (*blond*, I guess is the pejorative *de jure*). We laughed because of her incredible posture.

"Robert E. Lee was a really smart guy," I assured, "but I wonder what would happen if I tried to teach him to drive my car."

Max laughed merrily. I'm satisfied that the image of the stately General sitting behind the wheel of my Tub-of-a-thousand-leaks was funnier, even, than watching him struggle with the clutch.

After every training seminar, the suits wanted to know all. I give sincere plaudits for the gang of six who ran Project Mercury. As with the namesake, they wanted to learn from experience. Before they went nation-wide, they wanted to ensure that we were razor-sharp and as perfect as possible. Max and I crashed a couple times due to unforeseen problems. After experiencing a major gaff, it was no longer unforeseen; we'd avoid it in future.

It was slow and tedious work. Nevertheless, we made strides. Despite the setbacks and disasters, the gang of six remained supportive.

Eight months into our project, the bosses were confident enough to begin Project Gemini. They'd send out four teams simultaneously. Since Max and I were the veterans, it was our job to train the trainers. This took longer than we expected, but the gang didn't push. They wanted us to do it *right*, even if it cost time and money. They figured, correctly, that any financial losses at the front end would reap larger rewards at the other end.

I managed to sleep in my house only two or three times a week. I tried to get home for the weekends, but there were times when it wasn't possible. Max, who lives near Warsaw, Indiana, averaged slightly more time at home than I did, but we didn't make it a contest.

I managed to get a throw rug in each bedroom, but mine was the only bed for a long while. I purchased a nice double bed on wishful thinking rather than practicality. My vision was for a single bed or twins for the second bedroom. Alas, a used double proved cheaper.

During the summer, it was better to sleep in the basement. Not only was it cooler, but a tornado warning in the wee-small wouldn't send me scurrying. Thus, I purchased a cot from an Army-surplus store and found it unexpectedly comfortable.

My fridge was a near antique and fitted the interior well. The stove also came with the house and, I suspect, was designed by Edison. For underground living, I had a small table, a hot plate and a food storage cupboard.

Most weekends at home were spent catching up on my reading. Nevertheless, I assigned myself one home improvement per visit. Little by little, therefore, the house got an interior paint job. Little by little, house furnishings accumulated. I looked forward to coming home and always felt a touch of sorrow when leaving.

There was a recessed two-car garage. I thought the greatest feature of my rented home was seeing the garage from my bedroom window. If I forgot to turn out the bell light over the twin doors, I needn't trundle back to the side entry off the kitchen. There was a second switch in the bedroom. Similarly, if I suspected unwanted nocturnal visitors—either bipeds or quadrupeds—I had only to flip on the garage light for a minute, and all was well.

As my income proved steady and reasonable, my bank account swelled. The greatest feature of my job, however, was the expense account. In a way, it was tantamount to getting paid twice. As a rule, the hotels which benefited from our training were happy to give us rooms at reduced rates. We also got breakfast and lunch on the company dime. Max and I tended to drink our dinners since bar snacks were enough to see us through. If we had any additional cravings, we tended to douse them with drive-through gut bombs.

Max and I did not live like senators. We paid out of our pocket and were reimbursed upon submission of our swindle sheets. As a further incentive, we got a few dollars extra if we kept our monthly expenses below a certain amount. Therefore, we were seldom tempted to act like a couple of swells.

In Ohio I made progress toward a goal I set for myself. Though not in any field I ever envisioned, I carved out a niche and experienced relative comfort. Similarly, Simone progressed. She established herself in a sport she learned to hate. In America, she stocked shelves and, as her English improved, worked a register.

She was determined eschew the ice. Gradually, however, she was drawn back by the laughter and excitement of children. They wanted to learn, and Simone could teach so many things she was forced into doing. Moreover, she needn't employ swat motivation. Then, of course, there was her experience. Even the best coaching in the world is no substitute for experience, and Simone Albescu had experience to the gills. Two Olympics and four European competitions constituted a career for most people, but Simone *retired* with her best days, presumably, ahead.

Shortly after taking to the ice in the service of children less than half her age, she re-discovered the fun in skating. She cheered every triumph, no matter how modest, because it stoked the student's pride and enthusiasm. More importantly, the great stone face learned the pathos of life.

John had one particularly talented student. He stayed with the young man from start to finish precisely because there were no Olympic ambitions. He liked to do well and could have become a force in the sport, but he prized a less demanding life. He won several medals on the lower rungs and impressed many on the regional level, *but*—a very important word—he did not want to move away from home, sacrifice his social life, or leave his school. He didn't have the fire.

When John suggested his young talent round out his skills with a professionally choreographed routine, the young man turned to Simone. She laughed. However, the skating phenom was deadly serious. Simone protested that she lacked the qualifications. John's student shrugged his shoulders, dropped the idea, and went back to developing his own program.

John worked on her. He did not drive, neither did he nag. It was not his way; furthermore, Simone never responded well to pressure.

She respected Papa, however. Thus, when he dropped subtle little hints and made comments here and there, she reconsidered.

She spent countless hours sitting mute and unmoving while others performed. She evaluated each routine by her own standards and catalogued hundreds of performance items. More than once, even with medal-winning routines, Simone believed certain things could (and *should*) have been done differently.

Over the course of several days, she sorted through her capacious memory. She played a game with herself. What, she asked, would she include? The program must match the talent by highlighting strengths and masking weaknesses.

Three weeks after rejecting the offer, Simone sat stoically, as was her wont, watching the skater as Papa talked him through his routine. Halfway through the workout, Simone watched him land a double axel. She was dissatisfied with his exit. She thought he should go directly into a spread eagle.

She stood up.

"I'll do it!" she shouted.

What, after all, was the risk? By his own insistence, the skater had no intention to move up. If she worked out a program, and it turned to dust, what harm would result? Meanwhile, she had definite ideas. She considered music options as well.

Two days later, she presented her work. The young man went out and won a competition with his long program. No one was happier than Simone.

"At last," she said to her mentor, "I've accomplished something."

Ion sent a summary of Simone's laudatory choreography.

She makes me so very, very happy. I am so proud of her.

Additionally, Simone was "very, very happy."

I shot off a letter to each, pleased as anyone at Simone's latest accomplishment. I suggested to John, facetiously, that he commission a statue of her. We'd have interminable fun inventing tributes to place on the pedestal.

It was enough for me to know that John, Simone and their reluctant skating phenom were all proud and happy. What I was told later underscored the magnitude of the group effort: Though John and Simone trained a young man with no international aspirations; he finished ahead of four skaters who did. Of these, one eventually secured a place on the U.S. Olympic team.

My home-improvement campaign officially concluded when I sold my sway-back couch and replaced it with a more comfortable one. It was a hideous burgundy color and I had to dust-bust it three times to free it from an alarming compilation of cat hair. The monster took up so much of the windowless wall of the living room that I had to make my end table into a nightstand. However, for all its faults, the couch was so supremely comfortable that I dare not recline upon it. Any violation of this rule would result prolonged imprisonment by Morpheus. Sitting on the end, leaning on the arm, however, became my preferred reading venue.

I banished my unsightly reading table to the master bedroom and set my GS II upon it. There was no internet connection, of course. In fact, it took an entire decade before I contemplated such a thing. As a result, I was never distracted or tempted to surf during word processing or creating my spread sheets.

I was, at last, open for business. My failure to put twin beds in the guest room was nullified by my palace-of-comfort couch. I could now host two guests in comfort and have no worries about the sleeping arrangements.

Not a second too soon.

We had an afternoon seminar in Marion. Max came by Sunday evening and spent the night in the guest room. He pronounced it most satisfactory. While he took his turn in the bathroom, I fried a nice breakfast.

Our equipment was sent ahead and secured by the hotel staff. This was one of the improvements in Project Gemini. Rather than our toting the computers, the company hired a professional service. The project also called for day-before delivery owing to an unfortunate breakdown in the early days of Mercury.

Max, graciously, offered me a ride in his modish and reliable sedan. I finished the breakfast dishes and the rest of the morning coffee. Since Marion was an easy commute for me, we decided to return to my pad that evening rather than remain on site. The company would appreciate our trimming expenses. We'd grown tired of motel rooms anyway. Sleeping in a real house was a heady prospect.

The phone rang. I assumed it was another pitch for aluminum siding. I was ready with a rude speech I'd composed and practiced mentally to strike exactly the right note. Before I picked up the receiver, I reviewed my memorized text.

"Nelson," I said with perfect calm.

I was assaulted by full-fledged hysteria.

"Ellen!" she screamed. "I must talk to Ellen—but—how? I—I have to talk to Ellen!"

"Simone?"

It was only a guess. I'd never heard her unhinged. She blasted me for a few seconds in, I assume, Romanian. The diatribe ended with a blood-curdling "Ellen!"

"Ellen is in Costa Rica," I reminded.

"Oh, God-oh-God-oh-God! What do I do? How—what—? Oh-God-oh-God!"

"Simone!" I gripped the phone until my knuckles blanched. "Breathe! Tell me! What is it?"

"Papa! It's Papa—oh-God-oh-God! He's dead!"

"What?"

The perennial stupid question number one was all I could muster.

"He did—not come to breakfast," she stammered. "I think he sleeps late. I call him and call him—oh-God-oh-God!"

Stupid question number two was on the tip of my tongue; I strangled it.

"Simone, have you called an ambulance?"

"What? No, I—oh-God-oh-God! Miles, Papa is dead!"

"Simone, listen. Listen!"

"Oh-God-oh-God!"

"LISTEN!"

Silence.

"Are you listening?"

"Oh-God-oh-God!"

Well, at least she'd stopped screaming.

"Call for an ambulance. That's all. Call the operator. Give your name and your address. Can you do it?"

"Oh-God-oh-God!"

"Simone, hang up now. Dial zero. Give your name and your address. Ask for an ambulance. Do you understand?"

"Yes. Yes. I do."

Click.

Quickly, I jotted down John's phone number and stuffed it in my pocket.

"What's wrong?" Max asked when I staggered out to his car.

"Trouble," I replied. "Simone; big trouble. I've never heard someone so shook up."

"Simone?"

I was sure I'd mentioned her. Still, since Simone is reluctant to review her past, I seldom spoke much about her except to people who knew of her.

We stopped in Kenton and I called the Shawnee Mission number. There was no answer. That could mean anything, but, of course, I assumed the worst. When we hit the Marion city limits, I called again.

No answer.

When we arrived on station, I used a hotel phone.

No answer.

How I managed to get through the training is anyone's guess. I don't recall a thing. Max assured me that I talked a little slower, but I got through without making major gaffs. Prior to starting back, I called again.

"Papa's dead," she moaned in a sad, timid voice.

She did not say *hello or who the hell are you*? If a siding salesman called her number, that's the greeting he'd get.

"Simone, are you okay?"

That was, (what?), stupid question six through nine. Still, my retarded brain couldn't quite cope.

"Papa's dead," she repeated.

"Are you alone?"

"No, no. Some of Papa's friends are here."

"Will you be alone tonight?"

"No, no. Papa's friends are here."

"I'm leaving for home. I will call you in a couple hours, okay."

"Yes. Yes."

That pairing of words I knew very well. That's what people said whenever they didn't understand—or care. It was the language of resignation. A woman with angry scars on her arms was not a person I wanted left alone.

"Simone, let me talk to one of John's friends."

Nothing.

Nothing.

Nothing.

"Hello."

It was a subdued and decidedly male voice.

"What happened?"

I avoided stupid question number twelve. *Who are you*? It wasn't a priority.

"Heart attack. John had problems, but—he took his meds. The doctor thinks it was very sudden. He didn't suffer."

"Please, don't leave Simone alone. She was hysterical this morning."

"The doctor doped her up. She's calm, now. No, we have no intention of leaving her alone."

"Good. Very good. I'm Miles Nelson, by the way."

"I kind of thought so. Simone said she called."

He, also, gave me his name. I haven't a clue. Simone wasn't the only one who shut down.

"I'm leaving for home now. I will call back within the next two hours."

"We're not going anywhere."

"Has she eaten?"

"Mr. Nelson, we are not going to let anything happen to Simone. She's in shock, but she's sedated. We'll take care of her."

"Thanks."

Damn! Of all the times for Ellen to be at some mission school in the boondocks, it had to be when John left. If I sent her a note right away, she might get it by the weekend. What, however, was the point? There was nothing she could do from another planet. Still, she'd want to know.

"Hello, Miles."

Her voice was very calm. It was far too calm. I didn't need to see her to know that stone face had returned.

"Feel better?"

"No."

She did not elaborate.

"Are they looking after you?"

"Yes. We just had a pizza."

Stone Face and Miss Automaton—together again!

"Let me know when the funeral is," I groped after a long pause. "I'll try to be there, but I can't promise."

"I know you're busy."

"Not too busy for you, Simone. Not ever."

It was her turn to meditate.

"What do I do, Miles? I can't stay in this house—it's just too—I can't stay here."

I took a breath.

"I want you to come here. I have an extra bedroom waiting for you. Until you figure things out, you can live here."

"Okay. Thanks. I'll let you know."

She might as well have driven a stake through my heart. If I had any respect for myself, I would be on my way to Kansas City at that very moment.

"Simone,"

"Yes."

"I need you here."

The telephone was not the proper medium for transmitting silent question marks. Nevertheless, there were hundreds leaking from the phone that evening; they piled up around my ankles.

"You need *me?*" she asked, incredulously.

"Don't let me down."

Several more seconds ticked by.

"I'll talk to you later," she promised.

Max sat silently on the couch next to me. I'd given him an abbreviated biography of both Ion and Simone during our travels. During my phone exchange, however, he never spoke. He just sat with one leg crossed over the other and one hand holding onto the opposite wrist. He looked at me through his glasses.

"Yes," I concluded, hanging up, "you heard right."

I need you here. Where did that come from? It wasn't premeditated, but it burst in my head with force. I hadn't approached a fork in the road; I had created one. Would I travel down this new path? How far?

PART THE THIRD

CHAPTER ONE

Project Gemini terminated. Max and I initiated a follow-up survey. The company was anxious to learn how many clients were using the equipment, how much and how effectively. Of interest, however, was the extent the participants made use of the LAN. Once the clients were comfortable with information exchanges within their offices and stations, they'd be more apt to make use of an expanded network of twenty-eight hotels thus far equipped.

Max and I continued as a team and were never far afield. Our sector included Toledo, Marion, Lima, Van Wert and Findley. Save for Toledo, we seldom remained overnight. Rather than commute back and forth from Warsaw, I offered Max a room, at company expense, in a Lima hotel. He, however, was willing to bunk with me for the projected six-week follow through. This made the company happy.

I, however, was ambivalent.

Simone arrived after settling John's affairs in Shawnee Mission. I picked her up at the Dayton Airport and drove her home. As expected, she was taciturn and expressionless. She remained so when she met Max over a meal on my garage-sale dining-room table and chairs.

I showed her to her bedroom. She studied it in silence.

"It's very nice," she concluded.

She was, however, reticent about the living room. I promised to get a television if she desired one.

"No," she said blandly, "it's fine."

I did not kid myself into thinking this would be easy. I was, after all, the scrub team. Simone had pleaded for Ellen's help. Had my former girlfriend been available, Simone would, likely, have roomed with her until the panic attacks subsided. Then, the Romanian expat would secure a job and look after herself.

Ellen and Simone were near strangers. Still, there was some mysterious aura which lured the young Romanian into Ellen's orbit. Simone never broke free of it, as if she wished to. Their copious and lengthy letters cemented a bond which could not be broken.

The therapeutic powers of Ellen Good were exactly what I lacked. Rather than attempting to protect her from harm (and to prevent her from harming herself), there was little I could do to aid her recovery. It might take considerable time, and expense, before the former Olympian was mended enough to leave the nest. Still, I'd do my best and hope for some miraculous intervention.

Hope: how I hate the word. When one is so powerless as to be reduced to *hope*, it is a sign of undiluted desperation. I needed control, no matter how feeble. To hurtle through space and time on *hope*...

She began by examining my books. The collection was sparse. The lion's share had been dispatched to the Good's. What remained was banished to a squat, unfinished, bookcase which contained eighteen volumes I refused to ship for selfish reasons.

Simone would take up a volume, leaf through the pages, and replace it. Finally, she settled on *A Distant Mirror*. It was the copy I secured at UNI. It was all the rage in the history department, particularly among grad students. My copy passed to me through several hands. I added several highlights and annotations to those left by previous readers. If Simone found the marks and scribbles a distraction, she made no complaint. Likely, Simone would, as in her skating days, keep criticisms to herself; in Romania, it was a survival skill.

When she curled up on the couch, I realized she was a goner.

Max and I settled down to a game of Scrabble. A quarter of an hour into the contest, we heard snoring. It was subdued and feminine, to be sure, but Simone was out for the count.

Max had his back to the large archway dividing the kitchen from the living room. He looked over his shoulder to satisfy himself that Simone was not pretending.

"How did you ever tie up with her?" he asked. "My shoes have more personality."

"It's a long story."

That's all he needed to know. In any case, it was all he'd get that evening.

I caught glimpses of the real, down-deep Simone. I knew her to be witty, effervescent and gregarious. Through John, I learned of her exceptional intelligence. My hope was that Simone would re-emerge after her mourning period.

I need hardly record my worst fear.

She woke when I bid her to retire. She yawned and stretched before announcing that Max should have the bed. I was hurt. I put time, effort and expense into making her room ready. I purchased a nice, new throw rug and a dresser. Atop the dresser were a mirror and decorative ornaments to make it homier.

Simone remained adamant.

"Max is your friend," she insisted.

That burned me! It was as if I'd taken in a street urchin. The only thing keeping a lid on my temper was the knowledge that Simone Albescu might be unstable.

Max was coming out of the bathroom when I redirected him to Simone's room.

"I like sleeping on the couch," he said loud enough to be heard in Lima.

He spoke truth. As with Simone (and me), Max was unable to resist the seductive comfort of my prized furnishing. He insisted on sleeping there before the guest bedroom was spoken for.

"You have a job," Simone reminded. "You should have a bed."

My fists were clinched. I pantomimed a murder which prompted Max to counter with silent though frantic gestures. While he fetched his overnight case from the side-door recess, I brought out bedclothes from my closet.

Simone was bent over. She grabbed her ankles and stretched awakening limbs. This allowed me to spread out a sheet and toss a pillow in that place where her head recently rested.

"Thank you, Mr. Nelson."

That was all I could handle.

"Don't ever call me that again."

She shot to attention at the tone of my voice.

"Sorry," she whimpered.

"You may stay here as long as you like, Simone. I promised you. Please, don't make this difficult."

Her eyes locked onto mine. She nodded.

I left my door half open to be alert for the thrashing that, once, terrorized Ellen. If she started suffering from night horses, I'd rush to action before Max got spooked and phoned a SWAT team.

Light from the living room slithered into the bedroom. I could hear pages turning. After her nap, Simone resumed reading. I drifted off.

My alarm clock was a wind-up model with a feature that magnified its value a hundred-fold. Rather than rattle away with a clanging intended to wake the dead, it began with a single stroke against a muffled bell. After five strokes at three second intervals, it would clang like a claxon.

Though a sound sleeper, the alarm never had a chance to strike more than twice. With guests in the house, I considered it the ultimate insult to send everyone scrambling for a bomb shelter with a clamorous alarm.

Secure in the knowledge that I'd be first in the bathroom, I threw back my covers and swung my feet onto the floor. At that exact moment, a light went on in the living room. Realizing I had a competitor, I dashed into the bathroom and shut the door.

Max stirred when he heard water running. Ever the gentleman, he insisted that Simone go next while he lounged on the bed.

"That was quick," he complained when she vacated the facility in record time.

"I shave very quickly," she replied.

I was putting my shoes on when she made this announcement. I *hoped* (how I hate that abominable word), she intended humor.

My Army habit of making a bunk never abandoned me. It was more bother with a double bed, but my speed was not appreciably hindered. Perhaps, a quarter might not bounce on the counterpane, but any surprise inspection by a top sergeant would be a surprise indeed.

Passing through the living room, I found Simone's bedclothes neatly folded at one end of the couch under a recently fluffed pillow. Slightly off balance, I turned through the archway into the kitchen to find the coffee on and Simone, barefoot in her flannel pajamas, standing at the stove.

She did not see me, so I slunk back into the living room and sat on the vacant end of the couch. *A Distant Mirror* lay on the floor near my feet. I noticed she used my historical pamphlet as a bookmark. It was amazing how much reading she'd completed since the previous evening.

Max left the bathroom to dress. I stood in the hall and waited for him. He was mildly startled to find me blocking his path.

"She's making oatmeal," I whispered quietly. "Just go along. We can stop at a slop kitchen on the way out of town."

Max, who hates oatmeal, nodded.

Simone paid no attention when we entered. I pulled three mugs out of the cupboard and poured coffee into two of them. Max, diplomatically, sat in the same chair he occupied during Scrabble and waited.

"Do you have oatmeal in Romania?" he asked, unable to endure the silence.

"We don't have breakfast in Romania," she replied.

Max and I exchanged looks.

Later, I asked Max to back the car out of the garage. If he drove, we'd stop for a breakfast sandwich at the place of his choice. I tarried.

Simone sat quietly at the table. There was a bowl of oatmeal before her, a steaming cup of coffee to her right and next to that a small glass a third full of milk. She put a spoon full of goo in her mouth before noticing me.

"Will you be okay alone?"

"I'll be fine."

"Promise me you won't do anything—drastic."

She eyed me suspiciously.

"What do you mean?"

Slowly, so as not to alarm her, I reached down and took her free hand. I turned it until the palm was up; with a finger, I traced the length of the scar. She followed the progress without any detectable emotion. Finally, she looked me in the eyes.

"I promise," she said quietly.

I was not familiar enough with the woman to gauge her veracity. There was nothing more I could do except take her word. Somehow, I doubted she planned to join Papa. John would not approve, as she well knew. Still, I had many visions during the day about returning to a blood-smeared kitchen.

When we arrived after six that evening, we found the table set for three. The morning dishes were cleaned and put away. The coffee pot was clean. The counters and the table were wiped.

I was impressed.

Max once expressed incredulity that I'd rent a place without a dishwasher. I was tempted to mention that the dishwasher slept on the couch, but I didn't want to push my luck.

"I would have something on, if I knew when you'd be back," she announced from the living room.

I found her curled up on the couch, the bed clothes still on the opposite end. She was well into *Mirror* and had dispatched my pamphlet. In its place were two more books—Hamilton's *Greek* Way and the paperback, volume one of Morrison's *Oxford History of the American People*. Judging by the bookmarks, she was well advanced in both.

"Have you been reading all day?"

"I walked around for an hour," she replied. "I stopped at the store and bought some apples. Is that okay?"

I sighed.

"You may come and go as you please," I assured her. "You don't need permission."

"May I borrow your car tomorrow?"

"You have a license?"

She nodded.

"It's a Kansas license. I used it in Missouri. I guess it is good here too."

I nodded again.

"I'd like to drive out to Fort Amanda. Do you mind?"

She'd read my pamphlet. I hadn't expected her to find it interesting.

"There's nothing there," I warned.

She shrugged.

"I can walk around, can't I?"

"You may use the car."

Max put his horse in the stable prior to entering the house. When he saw Simone with her stack of books, he was amazed.

"Don't they have books in Romania?" he asked, stupidly.

"Reading for pleasure was never encouraged," she responded dryly.

I made a mental note to speak to Max. He didn't intend to be contentious, but he was being unaccountably obtuse. With Simone in her emotionless state, there was no way to know if his questions bothered her. Until we could establish what she felt, I wanted our conversations to remain bland. Questions, particularly the *wrong* questions, risked igniting a four-alarm fire.

Later, I woke to thrashing.

I padded silently out to the living room. The floor, of course, creaked. The noise woke Simone who, caught in mid-thrash, sat bolt upright and gasped.

"It's okay," I whispered soothingly. "It's Miles."

She heaved a sigh of relief.

"Papa's dead," she whispered.

I was bold enough to sit down at the end of the couch. She drew up her feet and made a fortress wall with her knees. It might have been perfectly innocent. Conversely, she may have felt threatened. With only the refracted light of a distant streetlamp, it was difficult to examine her expression. In her full stoic mode, a dearth of light was moot.

"I know he meant a lot to you. I hope you don't think I'm trying to take his place. Still, if there is anything I can do to get you back on your feet, you have only to ask."

She sat still and silent for a while. I expected that, so it caused no concern.

"Why?" she asked. "Why do you be so nice to me?"

"That's a difficult question. From the first, you made quite an impression."

"In Chicago—on that awful, terrible night," she mused softly. "I was a baby."

Did she mean this figuratively, or was she referring to her copious tears?

"That wasn't the first," I informed.

She made a dismissive sound.

"If you watched me skate—big deal; I was nothing compared to the others."

"Do you remember the Innsbruck Olympics? You were leaving after the free skate. You broke away from your guards and grabbed the hand of some poor schmuck and introduced yourself."

She was silent for a long, long while.

"That was you."

It wasn't a question.

"Since that day, I've taken keen interest in you. I saw you skate in Chicago—I recorded the TV broadcast. That and your practice at Innsbruck were the only times I saw you skate, but that isn't why

I followed your activities. You struck me as a quiet, intense person who—how should I put it? I thought that behind that hard exterior of yours, there was a vibrant person wanting to break out."

"*Vibrant?*"

"Let's discuss English vocabulary later," I suggested. "Are you feeling better?"

"Yes, much. Thank you."

"I'm just in the other room," I reminded. "Good night."

"Good night."

Before I turned away, I brought up another concern.

"You don't have to sit here reading books."

"I like to read," she insisted.

"Let's get you a library card."

"You can do that?"

The concept amazed her.

"Why me? You can probably handle it yourself. We'll check out the requirements this weekend."

"Okay."

I couldn't read her expression, but I sensed Santa had come early.

There'd be no mention of this nocturnal exchange in Max's presence. Undoubtedly, he'd want to know if there was a Romanian Santa.

The following morning, I found the couch and the bedclothes in pristine order. The aroma filtering throughout the house announced that oatmeal was *not* on the menu.

Sure enough, Simone, barefoot and in her flannel p.j.s, presided over a skillet of bacon sizzling over low heat. The table was, once again, arrayed perfectly for three with paper napkins folded into triangles on each plate. In addition, there was a serving platter crowded with seven pancakes, a pitcher of syrup and an entire stick of butter sliced evenly into single servings.

"I woke up a little earlier this morning," she said in her patented monotone.

I headed directly for the coffee maker to empty the grounds—too late.

"Simone, you're a guest here," I reminded. "You're not a live-in cook and maid."

One-thing-at-a-time Simone refused to divert her attention from the bacon.

"This is America, right? People do what they want, right? Papa always let me fix breakfast. I like being nice to people who are nice to me."

It was impossible to keep my eyes open under her flat, tedious tone. I reached for the nearest of the three mugs on the counter and filled it with Aurora's aromatic ambrosia. There was no milk on the table. Max always drank coffee white. I started for the fridge but hung fire. If I brought out the carton and put it on the table, Simone would interpret it as a criticism. Additionally, she'd fetch our remaining pitcher, fill it half-full and return the carton to the fridge. If I performed these simple tasks on my own, Simone might feel she'd failed us.

Resigned to my fate, I sat at my place and nursed my coffee. I considered doing my Henry VIII routine and demand bacon that instant. I suppressed the temptation. It was one thing to resign to fate but dangerous to taunt it.

My back to the stove, I couldn't see Simone's every move. When the bacon was placed on the table, there was no trace of grease.

She helped herself to coffee and took her place. She used the boarder-house reach to snatch a single slice of bacon and nibbled tentatively. Max charged around the corner and came to an instant stop.

"Wow!"

There'd be no gulp-it-down, fast-food indigestion that morning.

As he pulled out his chair and set aside his napkin, Max remembered his manners.

"Thank-you, Simone."

Stone face remained intact, but she lifted the remnants of her bacon strip in a salute of acknowledgement.

Max and I talked shop, as interesting to Simone as her monotone was to me. She coped, however. After finishing her bacon, she stabbed a pancake. From the pitcher, she poured out enough syrup to feed a fly or two. At this point, she chipped off tiny bites with her fork as if intending to swallow *sans* mastication.

There are only four Romanian athletes known to me. There was Simone Albescu, of course, Nadia (known to the universe), Szabo and Păucă. Albescu, Comaneci and Szabo shared the same stoic demeanor. Simona Păucă, however, looked and acted like an American; she smiled and talked and not a moment existed when you failed to read her emotions. She sparkled on the victory stand and dropped out of sight. Were I suspicious, I'd attribute her disappearance to her un-Romanian personality.

Simone was in full Romanian growl at the breakfast table. I tried to keep Max occupied with business for fear he would leap into any hesitation with a comment or observation to or about Simone which might provoke a scene. When confronted with a fatal pause, I pounced.

"Do you know how to get to Fort Amanda?" I asked.

There was a map in my modest monograph showing its location and modern roads access. Only a fool could fail to find the place. Simone was no fool.

She eyed me suspiciously and shrugged.

"I drive up Shawnee Road and turn left at Fort Amanda Road," she explained with undue patience. "I think I can manage."

Quickly, I returned to Max and began with something equally fatuous. Despite my efforts, however, the conversation reached a cul-de-sac. Before I could invent something, Max stole a march.

"Simone," he began, much to my dread, "may I ask a question?"

There was no preventative measure open now. *Alea iacta est*, to quote Big Julie.

Simone glared at Max trying to decide if she'd ever heard a more preposterous request.

"Ask me another," she dared.

Max didn't understand. I did. I promised myself to chuckle over it later.

"When you spin around at a hundred miles an hour, how do you keep from getting dizzy and falling over?"

Simone's English had advanced in proficiency by this juncture. Max's syntax, however, was not on par with her late, loved and lamented Papa, so she took a moment to think it through.

"I just think about baseball."

Max and I were too stunned to laugh. Just as well. If Simone's visage provided a clue, she was in no mood for chuckles. Likely, she'd assume she was being laughed at. This would not promote a wholesome atmosphere.

When the initial shock wore off, I made a last trip to my bedroom before we headed out. Max was in the passenger seat. Though it was his car, we took turns.

He cackled softly.

"It would be funnier if *she* thought it was funny."

"She's difficult to like," I agreed.

"Then, why do you mess with her? I mean, she isn't even good looking—well, not very. It's like living with the Wicked Witch of the North. Flying monkeys scare me."

What it's like to live with an alcoholic? Once off the juice, a person might be congenial and fun. If he or she slips and goes on a bender, it'd take time for things to settle. That made me wonder further; how long would Simone's rehabilitation continue?

Before I buckled in, I slipped the cardboard photo folder in Max's lap. He opened it without interrogating. As I backed out, he studied the picture of Simone and me on the waterlog. After I turned north on Shawnee Road, Max closed the folder and twisted around until he could place it, carefully, on the back seat.

"Her face doesn't break," he concluded.

When we returned home, the table was set, and she had a casserole in the oven. Lamb casserole; John's favorite dish.

"Enjoy the fort?" I asked.

"Very nice. Did you know there was a cemetery?"

"Yes, I did. Why?"

She shrugged her shoulders and renewed moping around the kitchen.

On my way to "powder my nose," I noted three books stacked on the floor at the head of her "bed." It looked like *Mirror* was on its last legs. Morrison must be more laborious based on the progress indicated by her bookmark. Under that was *War and Peace*. I wondered if John influenced her veracious reading habit. He either had his nose in a book or carried one at the ready. Many people took a snack or smoke break; John took reading breaks. Perhaps a lifetime in a country where reading and reading materials were closely monitored creates an appetite. Still, devouring three thick books at once—?

I kept an ear out for nocturnal disturbances. I nearly panicked the first time; I was fearful of what I might see. I was unnerved by my inability to provide succor. In the movies, they always slapped sense into hysterical women. I would employ that tactic only if there was clear danger to life. That left me with only my wits.

What a *hope!*

Somehow, my slumber was uncharacteristically deep. Despite the creaking floor, I did not wake until the toilet flushed. This triggered no alarm; I rolled over onto my side to resume slumber. The water in the sink ran for a few seconds, but no one came out.

I rolled onto my back and stared into the darkness. Fully awake, I maintained a listening watch.

Only after the toilet reservoir refilled and silence returned did I hear the bathroom door open. The floor moaned moderately. Max's weight would produce more noise. I vowed to wait until the muffled sounds confirmed that Simone was once more sedate. The footfalls stopped way too soon. Just barely, I heard my door swing wider.

Frightened, I swung my feet out of bed to sit on the edge. The light from the streetlamp bounced around corners; the darkness was well defined. Nevertheless, I could make out a silhouette framed in the doorway.

"Are you okay?" I asked in a hoarse whisper.

"It's my time," she whispered her reply.

"I really don't need to know that."

She'd not allow her voice to disturb Max, but her tone was as subtle as a train wreck.

"Oh, and you're too stupid to figure it out!"

Something was very wrong. Not knowing frightened me. I went to her.

"Simone, this is not the Army. I'm not your commanding officer. You don't report to me."

There followed one of those truly despondent silences.

"Papa's dead," she moaned.

I wanted to put my arm around her and get her back to the couch. That, however, would imply that I was anxious to be rid of her. The alternative was to bring her into the room where we could talk without creating a disturbance. Not knowing how she would interpret my action, I drew her in far enough to close the door.

"Sit down. Let's talk."

There was only one place to sit. To my surprise, she did. This was a good sign. However, I could not bring myself to sit beside her. That might send an unintended message. Still, I wasn't going to stand like a bewildered loon. I put my back against the door and slid slowly to a sitting position.

"My family is dead."

"We don't *know* that," I insisted.

"I killed them," she continued.

I was wondering when she'd confess. I spent days planning a response.

"Simone, you're no more responsible than I am. That decision was made—if it was made—by people whose power is so complete they're never responsible for anything. They're afraid, though. They're, likely, insomniacs. The possibility that there is one person on the planet free to live his own life is an anathema to them. They hate freedom. In their world, there are two classes of people: slaves and slave owners. You escaped. They hate not owning you anymore."

I didn't dare continue. It sounded preachy. Moreover, it was better to assume her family had not been liquidated. It was a slim *hope*—damn the word—but within the bounds of probability.

"If you feel guilty about what *might* have happened, you're a slave still."

Even in the absence of light, I sensed she wanted to purge herself.

When the silence dragged on sufficiently, I dared change the subject.

"There's an ice rink in Ft. Wayne. Why don't we drive over there Saturday? You can skate a couple laps?"

"I don't have skates," she replied.

"John told me you were always losing them," I recalled. "There's no need. No one will force you to skate."

"I gave them to a girl who *will* use them," she snapped.

I wouldn't be baited.

"They rent skates."

Pause.

"There are rinks in Columbus, too," she reminded.

"I wouldn't go to Columbus to see pigs fly," I responded. "I'm an Indiana boy. You don't have to skate—but I told you that. Still, we can have a look. You'll be on your feet in a few days or a few weeks. You'll want a place and a job of your own."

She thought that over. I let her.

"Meanwhile, you can teach me Romanian."

"Why?"

She didn't have to think about that. I did. It took a moment.

"Someday, I want to meet your father. When I do, I want to be able to ask his permission to marry you."

Pause.

"Are you crazy? We don't know each other—much."

"I never said that I *would* ask. I said I want to be *able* to ask."

"You speak German?"

"Not enough to hurt me."

"You can ask in German."

Now, it was my turn to think.

"How's that?" I asked.

"Sibiu is a Saxon city. Many people still speak German. I have an aunt who speaks German—and a couple cousins who speak Hungarian—most of the time."

"Interesting," I concluded. "Still, I'd like to learn Romanian."

She made a noise which, in many circles, is not considered polite.

"Do you want to sleep in here?" I asked because silence had reigned long enough.

"I like the couch."

I got up, not without effort, and opened the door. She padded through in her bare feet. I followed.

"I'm glad we had a talk," I whispered as she pulled the covers over her. "If there is anything you need or want, you know where I am."

"Thank you," she said, reassuringly.

"Noapte bună."

"We never say that in my family," she corrected.

"What do you say?"

"I will teach you," she promised.

That was good enough for me.

CHAPTER TWO

The following morning. Max and I both beat Simone out of bed. It was a hollow victory. She woke lethargic and with a monster headache. Perhaps, I was expected to believe that her condition was the result of *her time*. It may well have been, but there was a much greater likelihood that her malady was stress related. As one who knew all too well the discomfort of a head throb, my heart bled for her.

She managed to steal a few winks before Max and I completed the morning cacophony. I asked if I should take her to a doctor, but she declined. I asked if I should stay home and play nurse. This she flatly rejected.

Before I left, I brought her some dry toast and a cup of hot tea. As I set these on the coffee table inches from her, she came to some semblance of life. She thanked me, assured me that she would be fine and wished us a safe trip.

Max and I ate on the road; we were concerned. When we returned, I discovered Simone had inaugurated my new washing machine. Most of the wash flapped merrily from the back-yard line; the intimate attire dangled from a rope stretched across the basement.

There was an earthenware container, partly filled with water, sitting beside the coffee maker. Simone explained that the tea I left her prompted a toilet aria. When she felt better, she canvased the neighborhood with a rinsed-out cider jug in search of city water. Eventually, she returned with a gallon and enjoyed a belated, medicinal cup of tea.

I pictured the episode: a strange woman with a foreign accent and the personality of concrete terrorizing people by asking to "borrow" water. I was tempted to send back a gallon of our soft water. If anyone tasted it, however, it might promote a neighborhood insurgence.

I discussed my qualms with Max. I feared that Simone was becoming a drudge. She cooked, cleaned and scrubbed. It was, I assumed, her method of paying rent. Though her efforts were appreciated, they were unnecessary. How, I asked, could I convince her that she was my guest, not my servant?

He ruminated through the day. On our way home, he offered his anemic conclusion.

"If you forbid her to do housework, we'll come home some night and find her shingling the roof."

He correctly assessed Simone's character, but it didn't assuage my concern.

On Max's final morning as my guest, he came into the kitchen and, somehow, caught Simone by surprise.

"O, hell!" she said. "Sorry, I mean *hell-o.*"

I thought it hilarious when Max told me. He, however, did not find it so.

"If she showed any expression, I might have laughed," he contended.

She remained in mourning. I knew from John's accounts that it took Simone weeks with him before she acquired appreciable animation. However, her sense of humor, the window on her soul, erupted within her first few hours of reuniting with her beloved Ion. In former times, John relied upon understated quips to gauge her feelings. If she went a day without authoring a humorous or sardonic comment, he knew she was on the edge and required kid gloves. It was a mode of expression the regime couldn't suppress. So long as she remained deadpan, Simone got away with near treason. If she cracked wise with a smile on her face, punishment would result.

My Romanian languished in rudimentary stages. I'd bet a tidy sum, however, that the "O, hell" malapropism had a Romanian equivalent. I pictured her greeting one of her *Securitate* goons thus. If she didn't smile, the Securitate would assume she was stupid. It is a matter of self-esteem for bullies to think of themselves as intellectually superior to the bullied.

On our Saturday drive to Ft. Wayne, Simone was irritatingly noisy. She insisted on relating certain salient points of *A Distant Mirror*. It was flattering to realize that I remembered most of the details she recounted. It was more important for her to talk than for me to listen, but she asked me about Indiana. I recounted anecdotes of my youth. These verbal snapshots were silently filed away in her capacious memory.

"I have a question."

Over time these four words made me quake. It wasn't enough for her to ask a question, she had to preface each query with a string of subjective remarks. Though I valued verbalization of her feelings, I was disturbed by her toxicity. If anyone earned the right to carry a chip on her shoulder, it was Simone. Nevertheless, I feared she needed professional help. Many of her observations weren't healthy.

"What was the difference between the Puritans and the Pilgrims?"

"Is this important?" I asked in turn.

"You don't know."

She was downright snotty.

How dare me not to have a mountain of information in my head!

I was caught in a mine field. Had I been bold enough, I'd have led her on just for practice. However, I'm more coward than paladin—particularly when dealing with women.

I began with Henry VIII's break with the Church and chuntered on for some while. Simone appeared to hang on every syllable. I expected her to cut me off and encourage me to give her the *Reader's*

Digest response. Gradually, I realized she *really wanted to know*; she wasn't reading history books merely to fill idle hours.

"So," she began tentatively, "the Puritans wanted to purify the Church of England while the Pilgrims—ah, Separatists—thought it was hopeless. They wanted to start a new church. Is that the only difference?"

What the hell kind of question was that? After a good twenty-minute lecture, she wanted an opinion?

"The Puritans killed the Indians because they weren't Christians," I added. "The Pilgrims tried to convert the Indians—then, they killed them."

This was both glib and unfair, but I was too taxed to spend the morning with Puritans and Pilgrims.

"Oh," I added, "the Puritans outnumbered the Pilgrims about a thousand to one."

I'd have felt better had I the opportunity to review my texts and notes, but Simone demanded instant satisfaction. She'd check up on me. I expected her to scold me for any errors. Meantime, I kept her from hating me for not indulging her.

Growing up in Logansport, I listened to WOWO frequently. Over the years, it changed format. Nevertheless, I continue to refer to Fort Wayne as "Wowo Willage" a la Arthur Q. "I'll-get-that-waskly-wabbit" Bryan. Max and I sans Simone used the term *Wowo Willage* frequently. Eventually, we pared it down to Wowo.

I was bound to slip sooner or later, ergo: I explained my use of Wowo. Simone, not surprisingly, was devoid of my extensive knowledge of Arthur Q. Bryan. She did, however, know Elmer Fudd. Next to Winnie the Pooh, Elmer was her personal favorite. Without any trauma or the need for extensive indoctrination, Simone adopted Wowo Willage into her ever-expanding use of American slang and colloquialisms.

This harmless coup lightened our mood considerably.

I refused to force Simone onto the ice. I made a vow: If she declined, I'd call it a day. However, I assumed Simone wore loose-fitting shorts for a reason.

Sure enough, she stood silently by and pouted while I secured skates. When I held them up in front of her face, she looked at them before looking at me. There was no trace of felicity, but there was fire in her eyes.

"Just take them for a spin," I suggested. "Do whatever you want or just stand there and frown at me for twenty minutes. Either way, you'll feel better for it."

She sighed. She wanted to, but she carried a load of accumulated and distasteful memories.

"I'll try," she promised.

Simone Albescu is the world's worst actress. She could frown with the worst of them, but she could not mask the life in her eyes.

After a few minutes of stretching, she strapped on the skates. There were three couples and two teens gliding about. The kids were struggling to navigate, but they were having the time of their lives. They laughed and squealed even while taking bum busters. The couples were experimenting with ice-dancing. They were far more advanced than the kids, but they, also, tested unfamiliar waters.

Simone glided around for a while watching the toes of her boots as if they'd betray her. Arms akimbo, she pushed off to maintain steerageway. Then, she twisted and skated backwards. She looked over her shoulder for traffic and kept this up for some while. At last, she went into a spin—slowly at first but she brought her arms in until she was a blur.

"What's she doing?" a small child asked, pointing at the whirling Romanian.

I'm a worse actor than Simone, but I recognized a cue when I heard one.

"She's thinking about baseball."

Child and parents surveyed me before moving off. I didn't care. I had a story. When time, place (and companions) were right, I'd share.

She broke off the spin and pushed for the exit. It wasn't much of a performance, but her attitude suggested that it was therapeutic. I moved toward her to lend a hand in the unlikely event she needed one.

Two pairs decided to call it a day and blocked Simone's egress. I read her thoughts—since she had time to idle, she may as well fill it. She was halfway around the rink when she opted for an axel. She landed and went into a spread eagle. She repeated the combination. Skating past the exit, she picked up steam and did the combination a third time. Then, she built up more speed and tried a double axel. She wobbled on her two-footed landing and nearly fell.

For the first time since leaving John's place, I noted marked emotion. She was pissed! Never mind that she hadn't practiced in months. She knew she could do that move; she refused to settle for failure.

She charged around that rink as if on fire. She needn't avoid other skaters; they kept clear of the Romanian bullet. They moved to the edge and watched. Perhaps, they'd learn something or, at least, witness a crash.

Simone didn't re-try the double axel immediately. I suspect she was lashing down her temper. Perhaps, she was boosting her confidence. Regardless, she did a lutz, a layback spin and a flying camel. By this time, she had an audience.

"Hot shit!" The man next to me exclaimed. "Who the hell is that?"

This time, I was the one who moved away.

I saw it coming. I saw it on her face. She was approaching freeway speed, seemingly. She extended her arms, hesitated a moment and left the ice. She landed the double axel perfectly, went right into another axel, came out in a spread eagle, into a slow spin, pushed off to do a salchow followed by a toe loop. She picked up more speed and did a double lutz. She under-rotated and wobbled, but she didn't fall.

Thankful I was that she hadn't botched lutz too badly; she might have stayed out there until she got *that* maneuver right. Though a know-nothing observer of the sport, even I realized a double lutz is more difficult than a double axel.

I felt someone beside me.

"She's with you?"

I turned to find a hulk of a man in neatly trimmed dark-brown hair and wearing—despite the season—a long-sleeved sweater, tan

Dockers and brown Oxfords. I judged he was in his middle thirties. He radiated the air of a man used to exercising authority.

I could hardly deny Simone. Why would I care to? She put on a hell of a show. What was more important, no one forced her.

"She must be a competitor," the barrel-chested man deduced.

"Ex," I corrected.

He wanted to look at me, but that required taking his eyes off Simone.

"I bet she's got a ton of medals."

She probably did. Fat lot of good they were since her home was on the wrong side of a line.

No need to go into that.

"Twice an Olympian," I admitted.

A lesser person would demand to know her name and nation. This guy wasn't interested. If he followed the sport, he knew Simone wasn't a major player; those august personages were recognized on sight.

"I believe it," he announced.

This was a chance to advocate. A part of me wanted to keep still, but another part felt obligation toward a woman I desperately wanted to provide an even break.

"She was coaching youth skaters in Kansas City before moving to Lima."

"Really?"

I heard his wheels turning.

Simone skated two more laps in reverse before leaving the ice.

"Is she looking for a job?"

"I have no idea," I confessed. "Ask her?"

That was tantamount to "permission granted."

Simone was upset, but I could take it.

She departed the rink with a satisfied expression to be approached by an enthusiastic fan—or so she thought. Her scowl was directed at me. She said nothing as we returned the skates. She said nothing as I led the way to the parking lot. She remained mute and pouty when I pulled into the parking lot of an independent feed bag.

Once upon a time it was a Pullman car. That's truth. There are places around that looked like railroad cars—and a few resembling airliners. Most, however, are mock-ups. The place in Fort Wayne was as genuine as the food. The menu was simple, work-a-day fare aimed at blue-collar clientele. Nevertheless, the food was prepared by people who realized a favorable reputation with the locals kept eviction notices away.

Even Simone's resentful exhibition melted when she flung a fang into her hamburger. Coming as she did from a country that detested everything American, she might never have experienced a *real* hamburger. Similarly, the fries were homemade on site without traditional baskets or five gallons of sub-par oil. She tasted the difference.

Simone also ordered a chocolate malt. When it arrived, I ordered one for myself to partner my coffee.

She looked across the table with a puzzled expression. Gingerly, she picked up the spoon which came on the saucer supporting the malt's clear glass tower. How quickly she forgot her resentment.

"You won't be sipping that through a straw," I said.

Once upon a time in Logansport, there was a burger joint serving the same kind of malted. It was my dad's favorite treat; we were frequent customers. Then, over the years, that kind of delight became extinct. To discover a resurrection in Wowo justified our outing.

Simone was still not speaking to me. However, her taste buds were in awe.

"If you decide to take a job here, you'll want a place closer to work."

I threw that out just to see what happened.

"I don't know if I want to work at that place," she muttered.

"Ask the waitress if they're hiring."

She refused to speak. For the second time in weeks, she was enjoying herself. She wouldn't tolerate distractions.

She surrendered with her meal half consumed. As she leaned back in the booth, she sighed with a mixture of discomfort and satisfaction. The waitress pounced quickly; Simone's predicament was not atypical.

"Would you like a people bag?" she asked.

The Romanian mightn't be familiar with the concept. Having lived in Kansas City amid all those great steak houses, it's unlikely.

"Yes, we would," I piped up.

After the waitress was beyond earshot, I gestured to my eating partner.

"She'd be insulted if she had to throw that out," I explained.

Not only did Simone get a Styrofoam container for the burger and fry residuals, she got a matching cup for her malted.

"What optimism," I noted. "They don't think your malt will survive long enough to go bad."

Simone's breathing was labored. When her hands disappeared under the table, I was sure she released the top button on her shorts. Circumstantial as the evidence was, it was further supported by the simultaneous reappearance of her hands and a return of normal breathing.

"I'll get a job," she promised. "I will pay my way."

"Simone, I don't want to have to lay down the law, but you don't owe me a thing. You do most of the cooking and cleaning. You even spoiled my fun by being the first to use my new washing machine. I appreciate it, but I don't need your labor; I don't need your money."

She examined me closely. Her hostility was waning.

After one of her deliberately lengthy if thoughtful pauses, she looked away.

"Once, I told my brother I thought—about leaving," she said guardedly, as if the *Securitate* had bugged the catsup bottle. "That was taking a chance. My brother and I used to be like—what you say?—cat and dog."

I sat and waited. Simone was bullied and abused so often that her temper flared at the slightest provocation. Any action on my part to encourage her to finish would meet with resentful silence.

"He whispered that I had no future in Romania. That was all. Do you realize what could happen to him if he admitted that? They have clever ways to make you say what you don't want to say. Just admitting to what he told me could cost him his life. It's the same here. Only, they don't kill you or throw you in prison; they just call you names and hate you because you think differently. I thought, when I came here, I could be free. I was so stupid."

I had no idea what motivated her. I knew even less about how her unsolicited diatribe related to our conversation, so I sat mute.

"I don't want to be your pet, Miles," she began anew. "I am happy that you gave me a place to stay, and I owe you. Finding my own apartment would be an expression of ingratitude. Besides, I'm afraid to be alone. I'm afraid to make important decisions alone—*they* are very careful to make sure you don't get too independent. People would be harder to manage."

There are limits to everything. We finished our meal; a former Pullman car does not offer much seating. Loitering over the remains of a meal made me nervous. There was a high demand for burgers and malts. Had we been in Germany, I'd have pulled out a deck of cards and we'd lounge the day away. In America, people turn petulant over that sort of thing. My nervousness made me either bold or inexcusably foolish.

"I don't blame you for recalling your past," I said, reaching for the check, "but it would be more productive to think about your future."

She pursed her lips, scowled momentarily and slid out of the booth. After leaving a tip, I approached the register to find Simone posted at the door. She was monitoring me. It's off putting. When money exchanged hands, Simone hurried out the door as if fleeing the *Securitate*.

I took my time. Though I provided her with her own set of keys, I recalled seeing her set on the kitchen counter before we set off.

Sure enough, she was leaning up against the side of the car, holding her leftovers, waiting as demurely as a schoolgirl.

"Can you put up with me a while longer?" she asked.

"I could ask the same question."

I tried to unlock the passenger door, but her body covered the mechanism.

"My—panic attacks are not so bad, but I still get them," she confessed. "It's comforting to know there is someone near if—I mean—"

She gave up.

"There are doctors," I began.

"Papa took me to see doctors."

"And?"

"They said they could give medicine, but time is safer and cheaper."

"Simone, if you need medication, I'll gladly contribute."

She shook her head.

"I think—I think—after I tried—after I hurt myself—that—for weeks—they gave me—things. There is no way to know for sure, but there were hundreds of ways they could give me things without telling me. I—I learned—the less I ate and drank the clearer I could think. Most of the time, I walked in a fog—I couldn't see more than a few meters—do you know what it feels like to realize that you aren't in control of your own body? I don't want medication. Please, Miles, no medicine."

"You make that decision for yourself," I insisted. "I promise I won't sneak things into your food or drink. I still think that you should take something for your headaches, but if you can put up with them—It's just—well, I don't like seeing you suffer."

She almost smiled—almost. Instead, she stepped away from the door and allowed me to unlock it.

"You were happy for a few seconds today," I reminded. "It feels good, to see you happy. Promise me, if I can do something to make you happy, you'll tell me."

"I will leave little notes on your pillow," she promised.

She's funnier when she isn't trying.

I was in awe of Simone's ice performance. Figure skating had long been on my list of sports yawns, but, even to my unschooled eye, the skills and precision involved are superhuman. That Simone could put on an impressive display after months of dormancy was nothing short of miraculous.

In deference to my housemate, I refrained from interrogating her about her skating career. Ellen and her family were not so accommodating. On the Saturday night when John was the Sunday-dinner guest, he was grilled ceaselessly. As with Simone, he refused to speak about life in Romania, but he was both ready and willing to talk about his star pupil. Mrs. Good, Ellen and one of her brothers followed both the national championships and the Olympics. Therefore, they knew enough about the sport to ask cogent questions. Later, when Simone was not within earshot, Ellen disclosed a few of the more salient points brought out over dinner.

The Romanian sports bureaucrats were as ignorant of figure skating as I. They didn't know the difference between a toe loop and a touchdown. Therefore, it had to be someone who wasn't yet brain dead who informed them that the delayed axel was a Hamill trademark. No one in the regime would deign to check the veracity of this information. Indeed, they couldn't be bothered to find out what a delayed axel was. Still, they insisted that one or two be included in Simone's free skate.

Albescu's delayed axel looked like a regular axel. As previously stated, Simone was not a jumper. Dorothy Hamill, however, often came down with frost on her eyebrows. Her delayed axel was a thing of stark beauty. Simone could do no better than an epileptic single axel. Still, they practiced it as a part of the routine—especially when one of the government morons was watching.

"Did she do it?" they would ask, because they hadn't a clue.

"Did you not see?" John would ask.

This kept him on the tightrope. He didn't dare lie to an official. If pressed, which he seldom was, he'd tell them that they continued work on the move. In truth, John and Simone both knew the jump was not an enhancement.

When competing outside Romania, John told Simone to leave out the troublesome jump. Simone expressed relief. They had a tacit understanding; if she was ever challenged by the goon squad, she'd make an excuse.

"It didn't feel right," she'd say.

She's a resourceful girl. No matter what excuse she composed, the moron brigade was too ignorant about skating to call her on it. Meanwhile, John would insist that he trained Simone to trust her instincts. This was, decidedly, a very un-communist attitude. Still, if Simone was going to hang, John's "excuse" would ensure that she would not hang alone.

In many ways, Simone is painfully sensible. Having traveled so far to the *Wowo*, it was only natural to have a browse through a shopping arena. Simone remained at my elbow, but she informed me that we could shop in Lima and get the very same goods at comparable prices. It was folly, she insisted, to cross a state line to shop. There was an ice rink in Wowo, but none in Lima. Beyond this, Fort Wayne was as alluring as our soft water.

Sensible and *pragmatic* are the two leading adjectives applying to Simone Albescu. There is one notable exception. Any time we visited a market, Simone purchased a jar of peanut butter. She became addicted in Kansas City and brought the craving to Ohio.

"We don't have peanut butter in Romania," she explained—this and nothing more.

When she walked to the local market, specifically to buy a bag of sugar, she returned with sugar and a jar of peanut butter. There was a cupboard above our sink reserved for peanut butter. Simone had to use the kitchen stool to access that cubbyhole, but she took comfort in maintaining a stash.

Our shopping excursion in Indiana consumed the better part of three hours. I looked for bargains but found nothing I could put to immediate use. I spent some while examining the hardware stores for tools and repair items but couldn't pull the trigger. Simone enjoyed shopping for people. Examining others and their foibles was grand entertainment. She'd freeze up when interacting with strangers, but she enjoyed them from a distance—particularly the children.

When we set off for home that afternoon, we placed all our treasures in the trunk of the car. Our loot consisted of one small jar of peanut butter.

During the outing, Simone dropped her veil and offered me a glimpse into that place where the daemons dwelt. Once strapped in and safely ensconced in our steel carriage, we were again in sanctuary. By tacit agreement we avoided any mention of Simone, her past or her future. Her opening gambit was her wonder over a rainwater fishpond atop a huge castle tower in France.

"Of all the things included in *A Distant Mirror*, why on earth recall something like that?"

Oops! That was a treaty violation.

"You think that's the only thing I remember?" she challenged.

She was sympathetic towards the peasants who, during dry weather, must have schlepped buckets of water up scores of steps to keep the fish alive. Perhaps, they rigged a crude block and tackle. Either way, they'd have to get water from wherever it was to the part of the castle where it was required. I suppose, only a former serf would consider such things. The notion never occurred to me.

After a brief spat over her retentive powers, she peppered me with historical questions. She started with Ft. Amanda and the local environs which I'd researched to who-laid-the-chunk. However, Simone wouldn't be confined to my area of expertise. Soon, she returned to issues discovered in Morrison's text.

"Tell me about the French and Indian War," she demanded.

"Lots of shooting and stabbing and screaming and beating of drums."

She pressed her lips together in annoyance.

"It's in my little book," I reminded.

"I want you to tell it," she insisted. "I like to hear you tell me things."

A revelation!

I began with the reasons for the Seven Years' War and all the political rivalries. My knowledge of the individual battles was minimal since military history leaves me cold. Still, I recounted some of the campaigns from Silesia to Canada. I explored the removal of the Acadians and ended with the treaty line of 1763 and the taxes imposed to pay for the war.

"These," I assured, "made people fighting mad all over again; that's a different story."

That evening, after the peanut butter was properly secured and the supper dishes washed and put away, I felt jaunty. It was approaching eleven when Simone made ready for bed. When she vacated the bathroom, I turned brave. I followed her in my sock feet and watched her turn down her bed. She spun about to switch off the light and was startled to find me there.

"How about a bedtime story?"

She gathered her startled wits and agreed. I urged her to get under the covers and brought a wooden chair to her bedside. It was a beautiful and, perhaps, antique refugee from a dining-room set long since vanished. I bought it at a garage sale intending to use it with my computer. When Simone moved in, I placed it in her room the moment Max pulled out of the driveway.

"Once upon a time," I began.

She listened attentively as I told the story of how the Christmas tree came to America. I never actually fact-checked the legend. Perhaps, I was afraid it mightn't be true. Still, it was historically plausible, so it was plenty good enough for story time.

Simone was satisfied. She thanked me for my time and my story.

I replaced the chair next to the east window and turned out the light.

"*Pa*," her soft voice came through the darkness.

"*Pa, pa*," I returned as I closed the door softly behind me.

This, she assured me, was how her family and relations said good night.

I kept my door partially open—just in case. Still, when I settled into my own bed, visions of sugar plums danced in my head.

CHAPTER THREE

Foolishly, I believed Simone's passion for peanut butter would vanish long before the jars in the cupboard. Unfortunately, she became a slave to her habit. For breakfast, she took peanut butter on two slices of toast. I was never home for lunch, but it was no effort to realize that she devoured at least one peanut butter sandwich with whatever else. After dinner, dessert featured peanut butter—on bread or toast, on apple slices, on—well, some combinations are too horrid to record. On those occasions when we had lunch at home, she made peanut butter sandwiches. For particularly festive days, we'd have peanut butter and jelly.

It was a battle to keep enough bread in the house.

For snacks, Simone took the lid off the jar, shoved a finger in and licked it clean. Were I fastidious, I'd protest this unhygienic practice. Alas, I was resigned; the jars seldom lasted long enough for harmful bacteria to multiply. Further, I doubted that Simone germs were any worse than Miles germs. If anything, they were probably more benign.

As the weeks passed, Simone softened. She smiled more often. These were not polite little tributes. When she assumed a felicitous expression, it was a manifestation of genuine feeling. Whenever I caught her at it, my heart warmed, and my morale got a boost.

Atypically, we were out shopping at the local market. When I pushed the cart down the danger aisle, I issued a brusque announcement.

"We have enough peanut butter."

She wasn't looking at me, but I caught her whimsical expression. My victory, however, was short lived. The following day, while I worked, Simone scurried down and bought a jar. Doubtless, she was haunted by the possibility of a crop failure and vowed to keep our hoard stocked.

"Would you like a story?" I asked nightly.

She, literally, jumped into bed and pulled the covers up. When she looked at me, it was with an anticipatory smile that warmed the house.

Simone accepted the job in Wowo—kind of. She was willing to work with beginners and select intermediate skaters, but—she was adamant about this—she preferred children and total neophytes. Further, she insisted that she NOT offer lessons. She'd assist and provide extra coaching on specific skills. This left her free to work when she pleased. She'd use my car prompting me to lease a used Toyota.

The manager agreed to Simone's terms. He paid her by the hour. He required, however, participation in monthly exhibitions. The instructors routinely showcased their talents to promote lessons and demonstrate staff expertise.

Simone didn't perform a prepared program. She had soured on regimented performances. She eschewed music. She'd open with a double axel, work in spirals, layback spins, a lutz or two, and a double toe loop or salchow. The order was determined by her mood. Though these short, adlib performances lacked an Olympic tour de force, they never failed to fetch enthusiastic applause.

As I left the house one morning, she told me that she *might* go to work. She didn't need my approval, but she got it. As an afterthought,

I suggested that she stop on the way back and get a malt. She flashed a guilty smile which carried me through the rest of the week.

I saw Max, on average, once a week. After Project Gemini terminated Max had assistants to help with networking. My job was customer satisfaction. If I needn't address specific problems, I'd talk to managers and members of the respective staff. It was good PR and a keystone of the company's policy. However, I devoted most of my visits to the trenches. If a worker bee was dissatisfied, the queen or king bee would find out anon; this would result in unnecessary static which, in turn, fell back on me.

I enjoyed being around the lower-level employees. I'm no schmoozer. Ergo, I felt more comfortable and at ease with people not unlike myself. I discovered, to my own best advantage, that worker bees never hesitated to ask for help from a consultant. Most of the underlings went to a supervisor only as a last resort. They feared being labeled inept or stupid. Since I had no power over them, they seldom hesitated to be candid with me.

Most of the problems were mundane and easily fixed. Most often, a user found it impossible to enter certain items because they had, inadvertently, pressed *num lock or caps lock*. Occasionally, I'd encounter a problem beyond my remedy. I'd call Chicago and speak to a tech. I did this in front of customers as a demonstration that we desired instant results. I made it a rule *never* leave anyone with that glib and ever popular "I'll get back to you."

One afternoon I returned home quite pleased. I spent most of the morning in Van Wert. Things were going swimmingly, so I quickly dispatched with the obligatory schmoozing and settled in with the worker bees. One of the employees was smitten by the computer bug, *ergo*, most of the problems were addressed at the lowest level. Still, I enjoyed chatting with the *peasants*. By mid-afternoon, however, it was clear my presence was *persona non-needed*. I arrived home early.

This was a rarity, and I decided to celebrate. I'd invite Simone on a walk or a drive. I'd promised to take her to the Armstrong Museum in Wapak. This might be as good a time as any.

As I stepped into the kitchen, my heart froze.

On the table was a small plate under part of a peanut butter sandwich. Simone did not leave peanut butter sandwiches half-eaten. Further, she cleaned up after herself.

A thousand possibilities flashed through my brain; each one was more terrifying than the one preceding.

"Simone?"

"*Aici*."

My heart resumed beating. Still, something was amiss.

It was four or five steps to the arch, and I set a world and Olympic speed record for traversing that distance. There on the couch, her feet folded under her with an open book on the cushion next to her, lounged Simone. I was blinded momentarily by the whiteness of her teeth. Her smile beamed. In her right hand, she waved a sheet of paper as if it was Olympic gold.

"You—you didn't finish your sandwich," I stammered.

The smile disappeared instantly.

"Oh! I—I must have forgot."

Simone Albescu *forgot* a peanut butter sandwich? It would be easier to believe that a person would sit in a car for eight hours because he *forgot* to start the engine.

"What is it?" I asked urgently.

Simone thought I referred to the paper she waved.

"It's a letter from Ellen."

We'd gotten several of these. Their arrivals never interrupted a peanut butter break. I was flummoxed.

"She's coming home for Christmas and wants to spend a couple days here."

Though I considered Simone eccentric and emotionally retarded, insofar as her ability to *express* emotion, my trust in her was absolute. If she told me what the letter contained, then that was what the letter contained. Nevertheless, and to my discredit, I read the missive before I fully believed.

This was the first of Ellen's epistles addressed specifically to Simone. Hitherto, her letters came to us both.

It was a typical La Goodo letter. There was admirable prose describing her immediate surroundings and select anecdotes. Toward the end, she asked Simone's permission to spend two days in Cridersville. Ellen knew I welcomed her anytime, therefore, my permission was not required.

Why, I wondered, did Simone greet me with that face-splitting smile? She and Ellen were arms-around-the-neck chums, but Christmas was miles away. I could ask the reason for the toothy advent, but that would be supercilious.

At first, Simone said she needed to get the car checked. After a couple days, she decided that the car excuse wasn't plausible; she added a dentist appointment. Had she thought hard enough, she might have invented a student requiring special attention. She stuck to the dentist lie, however. She made certain his office was in Lima and remained vague whenever I asked his name.

Personally, I expected much more from a woman who twisted *Securitate* tails. Still, it was one thing to lie and deceive bullying scum, but it might be more difficult to lie and deceive a friend. Simone was a lousy liar; I took comfort in that.

Simone scurried off for her "appointment" soon after I left to fetch Ellen. I'd never been to the Wowo feeder airport and allotted extra time for navigation errors. Unfortunately, the signs were too good; only a Romanian official could get lost.

After an hour of pacing and fidgeting, the passengers began entering baggage claim. There were several people, in business attire, with carry-ons. They headed for the car rental stalls or were met by associates. One well-togged professional woman marched directly to the exit; presumably, to a waiting limo.

I feared I'd not recognize her, but when Ellen came into the hall, my fears proved feckless. She sported a healthy tan. As I drew near, I noted several freckles she'd cultivated in the southern latitudes.

She waved excitedly and gave me an expression which can best be described as half grimace and half smile. She ran the last few yards, dropped her backpack and threw herself at me. I caught her and struggled to unwrap her arms from around my neck.

"I'm so happy to see you!"

"You look great!"

And *et cetera.*

"Where's Simone?" she asked, disapprovingly.

"Hiding, I expect."

She was confused and looked it. How refreshing to be with someone who didn't mask her feelings!

"It's called *giving us space*," I continued.

Ellen blinked twice during her struggle for comprehension.

"Why, in the world, do we need *space?*"

"Simone seldom shares her thoughts. Three's a crowd? It's only a guess."

It took her a moment to realize I was serious. She may have blushed, but with copper-colored skin, it was difficult to tell. She gave me a coy smile and led me to the baggage carrousel to await her "junk."

She had two bulky bags in addition to her carry-on. We rested twice before reaching the car. She took the opportunity to explain her luggage. She wouldn't return to Costa Rica. The Church was dispatching her to a Native-American mission school in Montana.

"American Indian," I corrected.

"Pardon?"

"I was born in Logansport. That makes me *native* American. Don't use inane palaver, please."

"Tell me how you really feel!"

"Sorry. As Simone likes to say, it is *my time.*"

"Pardon?"

"That's a euphemism for—something."

"Ah! She's well?"

Thankful I am that Ellen never commanded a sailing sloop. Her sudden and drastic changes of course would snap the mast.

"She's better than at first," I replied, "but she's—well, taciturn."

Ellen waited until I finished stuffing the car trunk.

"The minute I heard about Ion, I prayed Simone would find you."

That called for sober reflection.

She waited until I was out of the lot, out of the airport and on the road home before we spoke again.

"You will stay in the Simone Suite while you're here," I told her.

"I never intended that. A motel is fine."

"There are no motels in Cridersville. I suspect Simone figures on you and I having the house tonight. Still, she's put a lot of time and effort into making her room ready for you. She will turn petulant if you don't sleep at our place."

Normally, I don't allow a conversation to lag. Perhaps, it was due to our lengthy separation. It could be due to Simone's arrangements. Despite all our need to catch up, I couldn't get started. Ellen, apparently, was similarly inhibited.

"I'd like to take you to dinner," I began after a couple of miles of highway. "There's a place where I used to wait table. It's up-scale and pricey, but you won't find better food anywhere."

"I don't have anything to wear to a place like that. Save your money."

"I'll take Simone sometime, then."

"Do that," she advised.

She meant it.

Thus, began a new era of silence.

"Did Simone tell you how she got away in Lyon?"

"Simone prefers not to speak about it. How did you know?"

"John told me—that time in Kansas."

"Hmmm."

I was upset. I'd lived with Simone for months, and she steadfastly refused to speak of the old days. Perhaps, it was different with John. They shared a common experience: they'd both escaped. Nevertheless, I was hurt.

"After she made a break for it," Ellen stated, "she looked for a church. Somehow, she knew churches were sanctuaries. She tried a couple, but they were locked. She entered a small chapel. It was filled with candles and people going in and out, but there were no clerics. She found the darkest shadows and hid under a pew or something and shivered for hours before a priest came in. She asked him for help."

I pictured the adventure in my mind. I'd never been to Lyon, but my imagination was not deterred.

"How do you suppose she knew about sanctuaries?"

"Her grandparents probably attended church," I replied. "They may have told her."

"Not exactly the kind of things a person tells a granddaughter."

I stole a glance at her.

"You have a perfect explanation, no doubt."

"Of course, I do," she confirmed.

I nodded. There was no need to inquire.

"Do you know what I've craved for months? Macaroni and cheese!"

I chuckled.

"You're kidding!"

"Honest, Miles. I'd kill for macaroni and cheese."

As we turned south on Shawnee Road, I stopped at a market. We bought two boxes of Ellen's dinner selection—and a small jar of peanut butter.

"That's your present for Simone," I insisted. "She'll love you forever."

"You're kidding!" she protested.

"Trust me."

We were finishing dinner. I was at the sink washing up my portion of the dishes. Macaroni and cheese is one step ahead of dirt on my list of food favorites. I ate what I could without throwing up before willing the remainder to Ellen who acted as if I'd made a great sacrifice. It was her craving, not mine. The moment her back was turned, I'd make toast and top it off with an apple.

It was dark. We saw the headlights and heard the crunch of gravel as Simone drove up. Ellen's attention was divided. She wanted to wolf down the rest of her delicious dinner before being interrupted but made certain her gift was nearby. We wrapped it in the previous Sunday's comic section and left it on the counter next to the fridge. Ellen jumped up, grabbed it and carried it back to the table. The very last of her meal went down just as Simone opened the side door.

The Romanian appeared disappointed to find us innocuously deployed. Conversely, she may have been delighted. One expression is so like the other, there is no measurable difference.

Ellen stood up and awarded Simone a hug. Simone returned the embrace, but there was a decided lack of enthusiasm.

"It's great to see you again! How was the dentist?"

"It was just a check-up."

"And?" I asked.

I thought this would make her squirm. Simone, by habit, does not squirm.

"The teeth are still in my mouth," she replied.

"The best place for them," Ellen responded immediately. "Oh, I brought you something."

"Really?"

There was a glimmer of joy.

She removed the tape with painstaking precision. I'd seen examples of this before. She would resort to nearly anything to keep from tearing wrapping paper. It might be a Romanian thing, but I was too polite to ask.

The smile on her face turned to delight.

"You've been talking to Miles," she deduced.

Smart as a whip.

"Thank you. This is very nice."

She hugged Ellen again. This time, her feelings came with it.

I chased the "girls" out of the kitchen in order to clean up. The first order of business was to get the latest jar of peanut butter in the cupboard. It wasn't easy. Simone must eat faster.

Simone ran, walked, and skated. Daily exercise kept her from looking like the Goodyear blimp. Should she break her leg, I'd have to find a secure stash for all that peanut butter or Simone might never stand again.

The pair enjoyed a lengthy and animated conversation. They talked of their respective jobs and adventures. Simone was curious about Central America; thus, Ellen dominated the exchange.

When, at last, it was time to sleep, Ellen had first shot at the bathroom. After flying for twenty some hours, she opted for a bath.

"Running water" in my abode is a euphemism. Ellen would enjoy a lengthy wait before obtaining an appreciable amount for bathing. This gave Simone and me ample time to prepare the couch. It was a great opportunity to scold her for an imaginary appointment with an imaginary dentist, but I gave it a pass.

Simone was an adult. She'd endured hundreds of times more crap than I knew existed. Chronologically, I was eight years older, but she was the wise old sage. Perhaps, one day, she'd share. At that moment, it wasn't right to confront her.

She changed into her pajamas. I heard her bare feet on the kitchen linoleum as she came up behind me. I was halfway through my apple.

"May I join you?"

I don't speak very well with a mouth full of half-masticated fruit. I took a step back and gestured toward the fruit bowl. She picked up a banana only to think better of it. She exchanged it for an apple and crunched out an impressive bite.

"Didn't you eat anything?" I asked.

"If you took Ellen out for a nice dinner, I could have fixed myself something," she pouted.

Ellen insisted on macaroni and cheese. Simone believed it but only after some fancy explaining. She scolded me for preparing a cheap homecoming meal.

"I love Ellen," I confessed, "but it's you I want."

I was tired of walking on eggshells. It was time to chop wood.

Predictably, Simone froze and glared a hole through me—two holes.

"You don't love me," she accused.

"Not true," I objected. "I've loved you for years. I think I'm near the point where I am *in* love with you. I say *might* because—let's face it, you're difficult."

She chewed slowly and glared mightily.

"Suppose I'm not in love with you?"

"Tell me to kiss off. That won't change anything. You're welcome here as long as you can stand me."

She took another bite and munched, but her x-ray vision made me sweat.

"*Kiss off?*"

I stood in stunned silence. Was she telling or asking?

"You've heard that before," I assured. "*Kiss off* means—what? Ah—*terminat*, right? *Finished, over, forget it, go away, eat hatchi.*"

"*Eat hatchi?*"

"*Terminat.* Understand?"

"*Eat hatchi,*" she repeated.

My heart sank. Simone assumed I had a spare in the bathroom. I didn't. Ellen was serious about her work and excited about an opportunity to teach. I, however, refused to follow her around from one wide spot in the road to another for the rest of our lives. I, certainly, did not want Ellen following me around from one computer to another.

I'm nowhere near as stoic as Simone. Whatever I feel ends up on my face regardless of intentions. That's why I can't lie—no matter how hard I try. Yes, I lied my head off in Chicago with the Romanian Tweedle-dum and Tweedle-dee, but I was too pissed to care. I wasn't deceiving them; I was distracting them.

We stood there and finished our apples.

"Eat hatchi," she said again.

"I heard you!" I snapped.

Her eyes, which stabbed me so brutally, were suddenly wide with horror.

"Miles, no! I was repeating to remember! Oh, Miles, no, I do not want you to think that I want you to take a *kiss off*—whatever. I was talking to myself."

Relief, I knew, reflected in my face. For this I was awarded a smile. It wasn't much compared with other people's smiles. For Simone, however, it was effusive.

I didn't know where I stood. I was still flying. She hadn't shot me down—yet. Suddenly, however, I was the one tossing and turning in bed. I feared hearing those two fatal words: *Eat hatchi*!

CHAPTER FOUR

Twice, I hinted my feelings for Simone. In truth, my *hinting* was a subtle as a hammer blow to the foot. Simone is intelligent. She reads the most esoteric history and fiction and understands everything save English slang and colloquialisms. After *War and Peace*, she started in volume one of Gibbon's *Decline*. Even I struggled with that, but Simone turned the pages with enviable alacrity. Periodically, I'd ask for a synopsis. She not only detailed her discoveries but included her biased commentary. She does not approve of murder, slavery or political coercion.

Simone didn't require a large, painted picture. My two allusions of my feelings were clear.

It was Simone's move.

For weeks, I kept an aesthetic distance. My position was fragile. Should I make a false move or drop an unguarded comment, my suit might shatter. Additionally, I was ultra-sensitive to anything which fed my (alas) *hope*.

Simone let me starve.

Somehow, despite her formidable façade, I sensed intense rumination. This was no linear equation. Behind her she had friends, family, a culture and a myriad of experiences I neither understand nor appreciated. Presently, she had a job providing her with (in her words) "peanut-butter money."

What had she brought to America? She could speak basic German, Hungarian and French. She could grunt her way through elementary conversations in English. She skated well. She read voraciously.

That was the sum of Simone Albescu.

With her intelligence and reading comprehension, she could be a lawyer, teacher, fashion designer or any number of high-earning professions. Alas, she was starting anew at twenty-one without, what Americans would consider, a proper education.

Ion Lupei, a.k.a. John Wolf, took her in. The sum of them both: skating.

Reluctantly, she strapped on her equipment and shared her expertise with younger people. She enjoyed their company and their delight in an activity Simone had come to resent. Eventually, she recovered a portion of the skating joy she'd lost.

There was one quality which resided deep within that maddening stoic edifice: Simone had a will and determination far above mere mortals. I saw it on her face when she bobbled that first attempt at that double axel. She'd no intention of showing off or delighting the peons; they were invisible. Nor was she the least interested in sharpening or even maintaining her skills. She just refused to accept defeat.

In Lyon, she refused to be cowed or exploited further. Without any preparation and devoid of a plan, she walked away from her jailers.

Simone had a contingency plan. I don't know how she intended to see it through, but I know as surely as I know my own name: Simone Albescu would return to Romania in a box.

After placing my heart at her feet, I waited. I admit to *hoping* (that damned word) for a spontaneous display like that of Lyon. More likely—and more frustratingly—Simone would reach a decision only after prolonged self-examination. There were thousands of reasons, all of them sound, concerning my unsuitability. As I saw it, I had only two cards to play. I could provide her with a safe environment, and I could daily assure her that I cared for her.

Max came to appreciate Simone's wit and intelligence, but he insisted I was a chump. It was the first point of discussion whenever our paths crossed.

Once, every great while, I'd catch Simone looking at me. I never bothered to smile. I'm as charming as a pile of dog dew. Should I smile, it would come off as a self-defeating leer. Instead, I'd look away and let her stare.

She waited long enough, but she Anglicized her name as Ion had. Everyone called her a cow—Al-bes-COW. One neighbor created a mnemonic, Al's-best-cow. That prompted Simone to introduce the English translation, *White*. There were, however, two links remaining. She *insisted* on the German pronunciation (zee-MONE-ah) which even complete dolts managed—after minor, if emphatic (verbal) bruising. Also, she dogmatically continued to introduce herself in accordance with Romanian custom: "White, Simone."

People thought nothing of this. Many assumed she'd served in the armed forces. Alternatively, they labeled her eccentric.

I, however, formed a different perspective.

There was a subversive side to Simone White. Owing to her upbringing and environment, this is not surprising. Being both naïve and prone to trust others without evidence of their trustworthiness, I fell right into the tiger pit. Fortunately, I had an ally.

Through her job, Simone had an Indiana address. She could, and did, communicate across a thousand miles without my ever suspecting.

In a practical demonstration of irony, I finished shoveling snow off the front walk. No one, save the mail carrier, used it. Still, that single individual was enough to suffer injury and leave me in a fine kettle of litigation.

Simone, sober as a judge, had her nose in one of her library books.

I removed my shoes, hung up my coat on the hall tree next the front door we never used, and escorted the snow shovel to its place at the top of the cellar steps. As it was time to think about supper, I made a move toward the fridge when I experienced a head-slapping moment. After shoveling the walk, I neglected to bring in the mail.

Back through the arch and into the living room.

Simone White didn't look up.

She'd adopted a new habit: whenever she returned from work, she'd rinse herself off (I must install a shower) and climb into the pajamas I got her for Christmas. In that and a pair of woolen socks, she'd curl up on the couch. With a blanket over her shoulders, she'd wade through the books she kept on the floor near the couch.

On those days when she didn't work, she'd read fully clothed. Thus, I never need ask if she'd been in Wowo.

I did, however, wonder what this gripping compulsion was of changing into her pajamas early in the day. Perhaps, it was her way of telling me that she appreciated her Christmas gift. When she put on her old, worn *jim-jams*, it was her subtle way of telling me to do the laundry.

I opened the door quickly to minimize the escape of warm air. Lifting the lid on the mailbox and seizing its contents was quick, easy and simple. However, without my shoes, it would take time to warm my toes.

I lusted for an all-junk-mail day. I took delight in dumping unopened mail; it meant there were no bills. Other than Christmas cards, there was seldom anything personal.

Not, that is, until the day currently recounted.

The return address was one word: *NoGood* and post marked Cedar Falls. There was no mistaking this for junk. My name and address were hand printed.

Curious about what Noah wanted, I adjourned to the kitchen. I placed the junk mail in the out box before settling down at the table. When I opened the long envelope, I discovered a sealed, short envelope.

El wanted me to pass this on. She gets weirder every day.
School is exhilarating. Otherwise, nothing happening.

N.G.

I was nervous. Apparently, Ellen intended the message for my eyes only. What needed to be kept a secret from my housemate?

Instinctively, I listened for footfalls. Assured Simone remained on her perch, I quietly tore open the envelope. Inside was a single lilac-colored sheet from a memo pad.

You big Lugen! That woman is waiting on you.
Don't make me come out there!!!

The penny dropped.

Scarfed up by the State as a young girl, Simone was placed in a special school. She learned sums, patriotic songs, reading and writing. Doubtless, her innate intelligence earned her many gold stars (*Red* stars in her case). Concurrently, she trained between six and ten hours a day. There were no boys, no dating, no parties (other than *the* Party) and no dances. She got time off only if she were injured (or recovering from a botched suicide). Even then, she was closely supervised (guarded).

Communicating with Ellen, Simone, apparently, summarized our courtship thus far.

F1!

For all the reading Simone did, she must have learned something! Regardless, she was stymied. Socially retarded and emotionally repressed, she failed to respond to my overtures because—to be perfectly blunt—she didn't know how. She made it clear weeks before that she'd not rejected me. Following that, she was lost.

I felt like the world's greatest fool! The narrative to this point will vouch for the fact that I must be among the finalists.

I took a breath and escorted the clandestine missive to the sink. I soaked it, Ellen's envelope and Noah's. After kneading the paper into mush, I checked to make certain the ink was sufficiently smeared and indecipherable. I wadded up the mess and squeezed the water out until it stopped dripping. Only then did I toss it in the trash.

Every few seconds, I glanced over my shoulder to ensure my covert activity remained covert. Never, to my knowledge, had Simone inspected the garbage. Knowing my luck, this day would constitute the exception. By the time I finished my operation, I worked out a plausible explanation for the soggy paper ball—just in case.

One problem down, but there remained another, just as delicate and, possibly, dangerous.

I took another breath. There'd be time to plot strategy later. This was a task which must be handled with tact and delicacy. With luck, I'd acquire those qualities between the kitchen and the living-room arch. I was shaking for want of confidence.

I moved to the arch and leaned against it. I stuck my thumbs in my pants pockets to steady my hands and keep them from trembling.

"Working Friday?" I asked, trying to sound casual.

She was riveted. I allowed her to finish a paragraph.

"I hadn't planned on it," she replied.

She looked at me. Try as I might, I detected no signs of suspicion.

"Don't start dinner," I instructed. "When I come home, I'll get cleaned up and take you out."

Instantly, she looked suspicious.

"Where?"

There were times we went over to the Dixie Highway to eat when we were too lazy to rattle a pot. Fine for the occasional meal, but such outings hardly rated premeditation.

"We'll go to Lima," I shrugged. "There's a place I know. We might dress up a little."

Her suspicion disappeared. What took its place, I daren't guess. It might be anticipation; it might be curiosity.

"Do I have to put on a face?"

What?

There were days when she wanted to look nice. She kept timid eye shadow and equally timid rouge on her dresser. To my knowledge, that was her entire inventory. How one can *put on a face* with such a dearth of material?

Stumped for an answer, I held up my index finger—quickly, in case it trembled—and moved toward the phone. I dialed the number I knew well. I asked for a seven o'clock table for two. The lady took my name and—that was that.

"Yeah," I said, replacing the phone, "put on a face."

The following night, or the early hours of the morning, I heard a commotion. It was enough to wake me from one of my infrequent, weird but enjoyable dreams. I listened for a moment. If I heard thrashing, I'd spring into action. We'd managed several weeks without a panic attack and were overdue.

I heard rustling from the room at the end of the hall. Refusing to get up for anything less than troubling noises, I lay staring into the darkness with a heart rate higher than a cat's back. There was a *thunk*.

It was her feet hitting the bare wooden floor.

She was out of bed.

I heard the creaking of the floorboards followed by the opening of her door

I swallowed hard.

Perhaps, it was her time. She no longer reported as if I kept records. On the contrary, she became overly tactful. The thumping of bare feet on the floor was *not* tactful.

She was in a hurry. Instead of turning into the bathroom, she continued straight on. The moment her heavy feet ceased stomping, the door swung open.

"Miles!" she whispered frantically.

"What's wrong?" I whispered back.

She sobbed.

"Are you okay?" she demanded.

I threw back the covers and got my legs over the edge of the bed, ready to move at a moment's notice.

"Are you okay?" I asked in return.

She said nothing, but her breathing came in gulps and gasps.

"Sorry I woke you," she whispered, finally.

Without any explanation, she pulled the door back to its slightly open configuration. I heard nothing more until her door clicked shut. A moment later, I heard the muffled creaking of her bed.

Silence.

After a while I lay back and covered myself, but it took time for my near panic to subside.

I made no mention of the midnight ruckus. Simone, likewise, kept silent.

Regardless, neither of us would forget this disruption for a long, long while.

CHAPTER FIVE

Expecting Simone to wait so long for her evening meal was problematic. She often had a late breakfast and skipped lunch to begin dinner early.

When I arrived home from work, on the afternoon of our "date," I discovered one stray strand of peanut butter on the kitchen table. This I removed with a napkin, vowing to make no mention.

A book lay open on the couch, spine up. The reader, apparently, was so distracted by dust on the coffee table that she had a rag in one hand and a spray can of polish in the other. After dispatching the table, she graduated to the windowsills.

"Let me get dressed and we'll leave," I suggested.

She glanced at her watch. It was a cheap toy intended only for a short stint on her wrist. Ion bought it for her; therefore, it was sacred. She'd go to great lengths and greater expense to keep the thing running. I suspect it would remain on her wrist long after it ceased functioning.

"It's just after five," she observed.

"I thought we could have a drink before dinner."

"Oh."

I'd wash up a bit before changing and leave Simone alone to determine her plan of attack. As was her wont, she would not leave a task half finished. I, on the other hand, do not care to spend much time either at housework or dressing.

I hung up my shirt and dug wallet and change out of my pants pocket. I threw the pants across my computer chair. I'd wear them again in the morning. Next, I got out my dress slacks and removed the plastic from their most recent sojourn at the cleaners. My favorite yellow shirt, my favorite tie, my dress shoes and my only blazer rounded out the evening's ensemble.

While waiting on Simone, I sat on the couch and examined the book she left open. It was a Dorothy L. Sayers mystery. I didn't own it. It wasn't a library book. Someone lent it her.

None of my business—don't even ask.

She reappeared in a nice, new pair of black jeans and a solid blue shirt. Though she had, indeed, put on a face, it was as casual and unassuming as the shoes she wore.

She took one look at me and let go with a childish "Oh!"

This was awkward. She wasn't accustomed to dressing for dinner. As ever, this was entirely my fault. Being one of only two people who washed our clothes, I had intimate knowledge of her wardrobe: three (now four) pair of jeans, two pair of slacks, three shirts, two blouses and two long-sleeved knit sweaters. I didn't run shoes through the machine, but I was certain she had only two pair.

The expression on her face was unmistakable. She blamed herself for ruining our dinner before the fact. It was so like Simone to believe that she was the source of all domestic misfortune. Even in her darkest mood, she never considered the obtuse dunderhead who lived with her was at fault.

"That's fine," I assured.

Simone knew better. She could wear that stoic face all night long, but her subdued *oh* gave her away. Why hadn't I suggested that she buy something formal? It was, of course, because I'm a big

Lugen—whatever the hell that is. The fact that we never went any-where other than casual venues didn't matter.

"Didn't I see you in a hat a couple weeks ago? Go get it."

She is a trusting fool. If I told her to grab a live electrical wire, she'd obey without question. To my credit, I'd never betray the trust she'd assigned to me.

She'd been given or awarded a black fedora by someone in Wowo. When she brought it home, we enjoyed a merry laugh—a relative term when applied to Simone. Thereupon, it was summarily banished.

While she searched, I removed my tie.

"You should have told me we were going to one of *those* places."

She wasn't scolding. She wasn't whining. She merely stated fact.

"You've been in America long enough to know we're pretty informal," I reminded. "In England, they might keep you out of a snooty club for improper attire, but we don't do that here."

I took the fedora from her hands and placed it on her head as if it were a jeweled tiara. I turned up her collar and threw the tie around her neck. I buttoned the top button.

"Turn around," I advised. "I have to pretend that this is my neck."

Again, there was no questioning in word or deed. She turned and allowed me to tie a snappy half-Windsor. I spun her about.

"That's too much," I admitted.

I loosened the knot slightly and undid the top button.

"That's good," I announced.

Any other woman on the planet would ask if I was sure. Simone is not any other woman. If I said she looked good, she believed. For my part, I counted on the American penchant for eccentricity. As a former waiter at the establishment, I can testify to the wide range of togs in the dining room. Most people dressed up, but no one was turned away for showing up in a t-shirt and shorts.

I made a point of helping Simone with her coat. She took care of a woolen scarf on her own.

We took her car. I preferred to exercise both vehicles during cold weather. We arrived in better time than expected. I helped her off with her coat and, with her scarf, hung it up next to mine. The reception-ist's podium was located across from the coat rack, so our wraps were under surveillance. I left my name, and we went into the lounge.

Unlike the popular watering holes about town, this one was well lit. The recessed lighting, however, feigned dimness for the romanti-cally inclined. There was no blaring television or cacophonic music blasting at us. Instead, there was a recorded instrumental in the back-ground, one step ahead of elevator music. The same music was piped into the dining room. It was intended to establish a mood: subdued.

The cocktail waitress was unknown to me. She wore a gaily colored two-piece print—thing. It looked like a set of pajamas. Nevertheless, her blond hair was meticulously brushed and lacquered. Additionally, she had a set of curves that may be illegal in some states.

Simone ordered a red wine. Since I was driving and refused to take chances, I ordered a Shirley Temple in memory (and honor) of Ellen.

Before Simone lifted her glass, I proposed a toast.

"Here's lookin' at you, kid," I said.

Bogie, forgive me.

"Pardon?"

She'd never smile, so I did.

"We are celebrating our tenth anniversary," I reminded.

Mt. Rushmore simply stared.

"It was ten years ago, almost to the day, that we met in Innsbruck."

Dumb Kopf! That was exactly the wrong thing to say.

Simone made studied attempts to blot out everything prior to her American life. She considered her arrival at Ion's home as her date of birth—the beginning of life. My thoughtless comment, probably, scotched the entire evening.

Imagine, then, my amazed delight when I saw the corners of Simone's mouth curve upward. We clinked glasses and sipped our drinks.

Simone looked at the menu and set it down.

"Miles, we can't eat here."

"*Dimpotriva,*" I whispered.

She was dubious, but she reverted to her trust in me.

Gingerly, she picked up the menu and looked at it, keeping her head turned slightly aside.

"If you order crackers and milk, I shall be cross," I warned.

That was not on the menu, but I suspect she looked for it.

"I don't know what most of this is," she complained. "Why don't you order?"

Everything, it seemed, was my responsibility. She set the menu down and renewed her sip assault on her red wine.

"Miles," my Marine friend and former colleague hailed. "Long time; no see,"

"Ditto. James, meet Simone."

Automatically, her hand was extended. This flummoxed my friend for a moment, but he shook her proffered hand.

"White," she said.

"Mitchell," he replied in kind.

James had no way of knowing its rarity, but Simone's smile was so bright, it temporarily blinded me.

"This isn't my table," he apologized, "Maggie will be with you in a minute. I just wanted to say hello. Don't be a stranger."

"You still in the same digs?"

"Oh, yeah."

"I'll call you. Let's have a brew or two some night."

He turned to my companion.

"I hope you come along," he said.

Twice!

Twice! Not just in the same evening, but within a matter of seconds; Simone flashed a smile that would have animated artificial flowers.

"Enjoy your meal," he said. "Nice to meet you, Ms. White."

"Nice to meet you, Mr. Mitchell."

"I'm jealous," I hissed. "You never smile like that at me."

Thrice!

Never had I so profoundly enjoyed being proved a liar.

I ordered the grill platter for two with mild trepidation. There were, in addition to beef and pork, two varieties of fish. In Ohio, one harbors concerns for the freshness of fish. However, Simone's trusting nature rubbed off. I knew the establishment, its owners and the kitchen staff.

We were not disappointed.

Simone sampled everything, but she was particularly excited about the vegetables. When I witnessed her enjoyment, I willed all the vegies to her and was rewarded with another smile.

Ellen, thou art great! Had I the intellect of a sand flea, I'd have figured this out long before.

Maggie was not some aging old crone as her name implied. She was slightly plump, but she was an absolute striker! I mention this addendum because, during our dinner, I never noticed. Simone's smiles were so overpowering, I was blinded. It wasn't until we were on our way out that I happened to look back. Only then did I realize what I'd missed.

To say truth, however, I hadn't missed a thing. *Dimpotriva*, Simone's smiles fueled me through the entire week following. For a few minutes, I experienced the real person inside that, hitherto, impenetrable armor.

After a great meal, we were heady. We came down the Dixie Highway and stopped for coffee at one of the low-end cafes. We took our stout cups to a booth, slid out of our coats and sipped reflectively on our dessert.

It was here that I briefed Simone on the established protocol. It was customary for the male to see his date to the door and kiss her goodnight. Since we shared the same door, I suggested that I see her home after which I'd return the car to the garage and secure it. Simone listened in silence. She nodded occasionally.

This conference was a result of deep apprehension. Eager was I to avoid bruising my delicate ward. This explains my oafishness. I didn't dare make any sudden or unpredictable moves. Simone maintained such a formidable exterior that it was easy to forget how delicate she was. My strategy, at the very least, afforded her the opportunity to register objections before an issue graduated to a crisis.

She paid attention, as she always did, but appeared far more interested in observing passing traffic. As a result, I was as nervous as a deer on opening day. There was so much more at stake than bruised egos. If she rejected my advances, my house of cards would fall.

I drove extra slowly. Nevertheless, we turned into the driveway far too soon. I jumped out quickly in hopes of opening her door Andy Hardy fashion, but Simone was too independent for chauvinistic if innocuous customs. The best I could do was close the car door, take her arm and lead her up the steps to the side entrance.

The first time I kissed a girl, she was—indeed—a girl. Susie Peterson was the prettiest, most curvaceous and seductive seventh grader in the whole of central Indiana. We hated each other, of course, but there was one evening of the sports jamboree—

I was entered in the chin-up event because I excelled in that skill. I was a heavy favorite to win. However, no one bothered to inform me that I had to grip the bar palms out rather than palms in. I'd never delivered chin-ups in such an unorthodox fashion, but what was I to do? Thinking thoughts I daren't express aloud, I rubbed the chalk on my palms and stepped up to the bar.

Susie participated in both the basketball free-throw and the up-and-back sprint on the gym floor. She was rested when she sat in the bleachers next to the chin-up station. As I jumped and grabbed the bar, I pulled for all I was worth. It was a struggle. Using my preferred method, I could whip off forty with ease. After my first two at the jamboree, I realized that I'd be lucky to manage twenty.

Tumbling mats were on the court. Ropes dangled from the rafters. There were, at least, four other activities going on as I struggled on the bar. Panic set in when I saw Susie watching me. This was no accident. She had to twist her body and bring her head around to watch my progress.

I gritted my teeth and struggled. I blew out a wet bugger which came to rest on my upper lip. It wasn't enough that this happened during a competition I could not win! No! I had to endure Susie witnessing my humiliation. Blowing snot was an additional, unendurable aspect to the most embarrassing moment of my life.

I dropped after fifteen chin-ups, wiped my nose and mouth on the sleeve of my t-shirt, and raced for the locker room. After a few minutes of hiding in the corner, I got dressed and did my best to slink out of school unobserved.

Susie happened to be passing as I exited through a side door on the far end of the school—the dark side. I followed her toward the street. Just as we got beyond the range of the exit light, she stopped. When I drew even with her, I stopped. We looked at each other for a few, silent moments. I realized my embarrassment could not possibly get any worse.

That first kiss was a heart-stopping, boot-quaking, mindnumbing experience. It was more explosive because Susie co-operated. There was a moment during which I thought I'd faint.

I didn't faint. Instead, we went our separate ways in silence. The following week we reverted to hating each other. Nevertheless, that first kiss had me walking on air for days.

Simone's kiss was not as dramatic, but it was nice—very, very nice. Despite the bundle I plopped down for dinner, I'd have parted with twice the amount, forgone the meal and been superlatively satisfied with that kiss.

"*Pa*," I whispered.

"*Pa*," she replied. "*Mersi.*"

She dug the keys out of her coat pocket and let herself in while I put the car away.

She was walking out of the kitchen with her index finger in her mouth. Were I capable of cogitation, I'd have offered her a slice of pie at the roadside drive-in in addition to the coffee. She enjoyed the vegetables no end and sampled all the meat and fish, but she *needed* that little extra rush.

After tossing the keys onto the counter, I hung up my coat and pulled off my blazer. It was still early. I opted to lounge in my shirt and slacks. Exchanging shoes for slippers ensured comfort.

The door was wide, but Simone knocked respectfully on the frame before entering.

"*Multumese*," she said, quietly, handing me my tie.

"You're welcome," I replied.

She watched as I draped the tie over a hanger with its four companions. There followed one of those extremely awkward moments when neither of us know what to say or do. After an interminable delay, Simone turned to leave. Barely had she taken a step before she spun about. She took hold of my sleeve with two fingers below my elbow and tugged, ever so gently.

"*Te rog*," she whispered.

She pulled herself to me, turned her face upward and found my lips with her own. Because this action was not premeditated, it was more enjoyable than our lip-lock outside.

"You don't have to ask permission," I assured.

To underscore my point, I leaned forward and kissed her back. She hesitated a moment longer before leaving me standing there with my teeth in my mouth. After coffee, I required the bathroom. While there, I brushed and rinsed—just in case.

I found Simone on the couch with a volume of *Decline and Fall* in her lap. I sat next to her, put my arm around her and drew her near. She shifted her posture slightly and nuzzled against me, but she did not abandon her reading.

We sat silent for several minutes enjoying each other's warmth. For the first time in months, I didn't think what was proper or appropriate. In fact, I wasn't thinking. I enjoyed sitting with my arm around Simone.

Saturday was creeping up one tick of the second hand at a time. I was content to remain on that couch with Simone for the entire weekend. It was a pleasure and a privilege to watch her read.

Finally, she marked her place, closed the book and leaned further into me.

"Do you know Edward Gibbon's favorite word?" she asked, speaking into my shirt.

"I wasn't aware that he had one," I replied.

"That's because you probably didn't have to look it up," she stated slowly, effortlessly.

This was most *un*-interesting. The fact that Simone spoke made it vital.

"*Te rog*," I prompted after a lull, "what is Edward Gibbon's favorite word?"

"*Felicity*," she reported.

Stop the presses!

Why in the world would Simone feel it necessary to report a perfectly innocuous and—for me—highly pedestrian observation? I cared only for the sensation of her resting against me.

"He's writing about—about a hockey game gone horribly wrong," she reminded. "Yet, he uses the word *felicity* often."

I was obliged to contribute. I forced myself.

"For people like you and me, life was probably secure—like now. I feel felicitous sitting here with you. The world is going to hell in a basket, but I feel satisfied here—with you."

"Me, too," she muttered.

"You took me by surprise in Innsbruck," I confessed. "It made a huge impression on me. I followed your every move after that— well—you know what I mean. Then, when I saw you again—in person—in Chicago…Gibbon might say *vicissitude*. It was as if we were destined to be together."

She didn't move, but her voice betrayed feeling.

"Miles! No! *Vicissitude* implies misfortune."

"Neither of us was dancing the highland jig that night," I reminded. "Still, you have a keen perception of English nuances; I bow to your superior knowledge."

"Well, we are here now—together," she affirmed. "I call that *felicitous*."

There was nothing to add or to amend. I let silence speak for me.

I must impose an addendum.

The day before Simone's arrival in Ohio, I placed her hairbrush in the medicine chest. It was the one I removed from her room in Chicago. I'd examine the strands of hair adhering to the bristles from time to time.

When she took over the guest room from Max, she placed her hairbrush and her sparse makeup items atop her bureau. She brushed her hair in the morning and again before going to bed. This she did without a mirror. Other than the twice daily ritual, she didn't attend her hair save for the occasional trim.

On the night of our dinner and no dancing, she felt brave enough to ask me a question.

"Miles," she called.

I padded softly from the couch to the bathroom.

The door was half open. I pushed it wider to find her putting away her toothbrush. Rather than close the cabinet, she reached for the hairbrush.

"This isn't yours," she deduced.

She could tell from the strands of hair that it didn't belong to either Max or Ellen, yet it had been in the medicine cabinet from the first day. Perhaps, the exchange of kisses pricked her curiosity. Did she, suddenly, suspect me of having a paramour?

"That's yours," I informed.

She studied it anew.

"I took that from your room the morning you left Chicago."

She stood silent, but tears filled her eyes.

"I'll throw it out!" I announced quickly.

Idiot! She didn't want souvenirs of that horrible night. What was I thinking?

She shook her head violently.

"Don't you dare!" she warned.

It was the first time I heard her voice break. This time, crying was not limited to her eyes.

"I bought it in Chicago," she choked. "Ion—John—he was with me. I lost or forgot mine. After Ion—left—I didn't dare return home with anything American."

This was a precious memory. Now, John was gone, and she grieved over the loss. She'd lost him twice.

She came to me, leaned against my chest and had a good cry. I held her and soothed her with my silent embrace.

When she finished, she sniffed, returned the brush to its shelf and closed the door. She blew her nose, washed and dried her hands and looked into my eyes. Hers were puffy. Mine, I suspect, were a bit red. I'd shared in her moment of grief.

"Thank you," she said softly. "Thank you for keeping it."

She gave me a soft little kiss on the side of my face and went to her room.

The brush, by the way, was *not* American. Simone was smart enough to make out the letters embossed upon the plastic handle. She'd lied. Her reason for leaving the brush had nothing to do with its origin. The fact that she wouldn't say truth was warning enough; I'd make no inquiries.

PART THE FOURTH

CHAPTER ONE

Chance was not finished with Miles Nelson. The end of Ellen Good's eighteen-month stint at a Montana Reservation added more laurels to those garnered in Costa Rica. She was making a name for herself in the higher echelons of the church.

Suddenly, a ministry fell vacant in Keatsville, Indiana. The resident cleric was evicted by the elders for less than honorable conduct. The actual transgression, one which would prove perfectly innocuous elsewhere, had so offended the local gentry that they insisted the regional authorities transfer, transport or remove the offending clergyman and his family *toot sweet*.

There was considerable consternation at the regional administrative office. They knew how arbitrary tradition-laden congregations are in Breadbasket communities. Keatsville, not atypically, is an ultra-conservative town which closes business doors on Washington and Lincoln's birthdays. If the State and Federal governments had a problem with such conduct, they knew where to deploy the troops! Keatsville citizens aren't easily placated. The locals wanted a replacement pastor, or it would raise a stink in inverse proportion to the population of under two-thousand souls.

The administrators didn't want a stink. Though they promised a replacement at the first possible moment, they must deal with a cumbersome and slow-moving committee process.

Someone brought out Ellen's vita and tossed it into the mix. She was awaiting reassignment and was, in fact, headed home to Waverly for two weeks. True, she was female which might create problems with the stiff-necked folk of Keatsville. Further, she wasn't ordained. Regardless, she'd earned a chance. If she held the fort until the committee could select a proper replacement, it would be another feather in Ellen's well-plumed cap.

The only Good daughter was half a day and one night with her family before ordered on the road. She arrived in Keatsville on a Wednesday morning. Instead of scheduled Bible study, the church wives organized a potluck, get-acquainted dinner for the new (almost) reverend. There remained considerable reticence among church members about a youngish, single female taking over the pulpit, but that could not override tradition-driven hospitality.

There are no motels in Keatsville. Therefore, Ellen was driven directly to the Parsonage, a three-bedroom furnished house cleaned to a fare-thee-well by church members. There being no other lodgings available, the reverend (*pro-tem*) was ensconced in the official trappings of office prior to the exchange of "howdy-dos."

Her temporary home sat across from the school (K-12). There, she was presented with bed clothes, towels, and cooking utensils to get her started. Almost immediately, she was whisked back to the church basement as guest of honor.

By way of introduction, she provided a short biography and a precis of her professional history. This, in addition to the obligatory schmoozing, gained for her extremely high marks among the ladies and no few of the daughters. Most of the men, foolishly, announced they'd never attend services so long as a woman presided. Ellen so impressed church wives that their recalcitrant husbands were soon to experience the lowering of the proverbial boom.

It was well after ten in the evening when Ellen was, finally, left alone in the Parsonage. Fatigued though she was, she took the opportunity to call.

"Your mother called yesterday," I announced. "We'll be there Sunday."

Thursday morning Ellen began with routine shopping. In addition to victuals, she needed soap, a broom and mop, and sundry other items seldom thought about until an analytical mind set to work. Even as her groceries were rung up (by hand), Ellen was ambushed by a church wife. Without thinking, Ellen disclosed her plans for the day.

"I was told I'll have to drive to Decatur for some things," she added, tactlessly.

"You just go back to the Parsonage and relax, dear," she was advised.

Ellen is pro-active by character and upbringing. Nevertheless, she couldn't disobey a direct order from an employer. As an AlmostA-Reverend, her authority to be her own agent was limited. Though she returned to the Parsonage as instructed, she wallowed in anxiety and trepidation.

One by one, the women came by to loan certain necessities. True to her instincts for order, she kept a written record of every item and to whom it belonged. In less than three hours, Ellen found herself with a considerable collection—

- Vacuum cleaner
- Bed clothes
- Flatware
- Cups and saucers
- Glasses
- Plates
- Carpet rake
- Shower curtain
- Two fans (for the warm weather)
- Radio
- Portable black and white TV

- Shovel (?)
- Bicycle
- Waste baskets × 3
- Coasters
- Iron and Ironing board
- Laundry powder
- Tennis racket and balls
- Coffee maker
- Clothespins
- Laundry basket
- Hamper
- Microwave
- And, etc.

So fast and furious were the women descending that Ellen had no time to stow the loot. Of course, each woman loitered for a get-acquainted chat. Thus, Ellen ended her day with a living room resembling a second-hand shop. There was no time to sort things out because she was invited to dinner by one of the elders.

The next night, it was the deacon and his wife.

The next night, it was another elder and his wife.

On Sunday morning, she woke early and got to church quickly. She locked herself in the pastor's study and reviewed the service which she hurriedly planned amid a blizzard of social obligations. She was confident she could handle the big stuff, but she was sore afraid that she would bungle the details. She noticed the secretary made two glaring typos in the church announcements. She tossed and turned the previous night wondering if it was worse to point these out and—possibly—embarrass the volunteer or ignore them and be thought an inattentive dolt. In the end, since hers was a temporary assignment, Ellen decided to make no mention. She would, however, have a private word with the secretary the following week.

Simone arrived in a dress. It was the only one she owned. In truth, it was a recent purchase specifically in honor of Ellen's debut.

Additionally, there were (now) two skirts in Cridersville, but they had yet to venture beyond the closet.

She was inside a church years before and under circumstances she'd rather forget. As a result, she held my arm tightly. She nearly panicked when she saw a crowd already inside the doors and a legion arriving behind us.

There was a slanted floor with long pews divided by a red carpet leading from the interior doors to the altar. There was room for, perhaps, two hundred and fifty worshipers with room for two dozen or more in an interior balcony which, apparently, had fallen into disuse.

Simone, reverting to old habits born of paranoia, wanted to sit on the aisle and have a clear path to the door should the need arise. She squeezed my arm as if attempting to arrest circulation.

She was in full stoic mode. Nothing would alter that bland expression. When a young girl in a white robe marched slowly to the altar to light the candles, Simone watched every move with suspicion. When the organ burst forth and the congregation stood to sing the processional, Simone didn't even glance at the open book in my hand. She remained on the alert, ready to yank me out of the pew and initiate flight.

Finally, Ellen in a white robe came down the aisle with hymnbook in hand and singing for all she was worth. All the men turned to get their first look at the woman about whom they had heard so much. Simone relaxed her grip on the arm. Fear was manageable so long as Ellen was nearby.

I shall leave this anomaly for the professionals to explain. At that moment, I was relieved by the renewed circulation of blood to my hand and lower arm.

If there were any glitches during the service, they eluded me. Ellen could be mistaken for a minister of many years' experience. Her sermon was safe. Without the opportunity to gauge the communal pulse, she took as her theme the shower of God's grace. Her speech was crammed with three historical anecdotes. One of them dealt with a young woman fleeing Eastern Europe against incredible odds.

Simone took my hand and squeezed hard.

"She's talking about me," she whispered superfluously.

Only when Simone's anonymity was assured did she release her death grip.

After the service, Ellen stood at the exterior door and spoke with members of the congregation as they filed out. She gave Simone and me heartfelt hugs and thanked us for seeing her through her inaugural service. She invited us to come and visit, but she must attend a luncheon scheduled with members of the laity. Later that evening, she was back on the banquet circuit. Regretfully, we couldn't tarry.

"You can trust Miles in all things," Ellen assured Simone.

"I know this," the Romanian reported with a gaiety hitherto unknown to an audience of one.

In Keatsville nearly everyone attended church. Some were more fastidious than others, but there were few Sundays when the spiritual houses were ill attended.

The Catholic church headed membership rolls, followed by Ellen's. The Baptists and Congregationalists lagged, slightly. The Assembly of God had fewer than two dozen members. However, what this congregation lacked in size they made up in fervor. In many ways, Keatsville was the typical Midwestern farm community: hard working people who squabbled and gossiped but were ever ready to lend a hand to neighbors in need. Communal hatred existed only for the nameless and faceless externals beyond their rural enclave.

The 1875 vintage courthouse dominated the town square. The streets surrounding this Victorian-style monument were paved. The only other paved streets ran past the Catholic Church on the Northeastern end of the square and Ellen's edifice on the Southeastern end. There was a post office, two small markets, a hardware store, drug store, two lawyer offices, two doctor's offices, a pharmacy, a tiny apartment complex, a variety store, a two-lane bowling alley, a hole-in-the-wall tavern, a café, a flower shop, a mom-and-pop fast food drive-in, and a bank. Most of these establishments fronted the town square.

The former Elks Lodge was converted into a roller-skating rink in the 1950s. An abandoned radio station (with its transmission tower still standing) stood forlorn and surrounded by farm acreage. A combination service station and convenience store resided near the town's only traffic signal, a flashing yellow light, at the highway intersection. A doughnut shop, formerly a rural service station, sat on a ridge two miles north of town on the highway to Decatur. Shadetree mechanics utilized vacated garages. A farm co-op resided south of town. There were two barber shops. The DMV was represented by an elderly grouch spending most of his time napping behind a counter in the back of one of the barber shops. The sheriff's office and jail were in the courthouse basement. There was one patrol car and one deputy. The town hall was perched on a nearby hilltop.

The fire station consisted of a single pumper (c. 1945) and an ambulance only slightly newer which made many midnight journeys to the county hospital thirty miles distant.

The school is a small squat building with a paved bus loop in front. The original building had been added to so often that it was an architect's worst nightmare. The elementary school was an office, a multi-purpose room and six small classrooms. The high school was seven rooms, a main office and conference room, library, cafeteria and gym. The football field was a depression east of the gym and surrounded by a corn field abutting the main highway, a pathetic secondary road providing access to an intersecting road—both in need of repair.

In short, few people ever traveled to Keatsville. It was either a destination or an aid station for the lost and hopeless.

Ellen, initially, felt hopelessly lost. She needed a few minutes every day to plan Sunday service and attend the secular concerns of a building requiring utilities and other services. Moreover, she needed time to kick off her shoes and relax. She'd scarcely time to breathe.

In addition to being wined and dined by all and sundry, church members needed tending, there were hospital visitations, and guest appearances in and around town. This was an essential part of the welcome-wagon routine. Ellen rose early and retired late.

"I feel like I'm running a marathon at a dead sprint," she confided to us one evening by phone.

Her first outreach was a young sophomore girl. Her father died of cancer and she was orphaned in a car crash in which she was a passenger. She was taken in by a widower uncle, but her emotional state was questionable. Her grades dropped; her concentration evaporated; she stopped eating. Local doctors agreed that she was, physically, recovered. She met with quasi-shrinks through county social services. They made (so they claimed) some progress, but everyone was alarmed by her severe weight loss.

One morning during gym class, a classmate passed her a basketball. It knocked her over.

General Quarters!

Ellen, living across the street, responded.

She met with young Diane later that day. Not unexpectedly, the two hit it off. From that day forward, Diane was granted permission to leave campus for lunch. She walked across the street to sit at Ellen's table and eat a modest but nourishing lunch.

There was no preaching, no scolding, no cajoling, no Bible thumping. Ellen would sit opposite the young girl and talk on any subject that sprang forth. Diane became so engaged in the dialogue that she ate, absent mindedly, her soup and sandwich and drained a glass of milk. Minutes later, she was back in school.

The difference between the malnourished Diane and the post-lunch Diane was instantaneous and drastic. Though the girl had a long road ahead, her recovery appeared underway.

Ellen cherished her few, uninterrupted, daily minutes with Diane. It was a relief from the duties, social and professional, of office. The people of Keatsville and the surrounding farms were generous and caring. Nevertheless, too much love is as harmful as too little. In sheer desperation, she dreamed up an outside-the-box strategy.

She picked up her phone.

"Father Zukowski, would you allow a poor sinner to serve you dinner Thursday evening?"

There was a pause.

"I—think it might be possible," he murmured warily. "It would be nice to know who is poisoning the wine."

Ellen laughed. She'd been as taut as a wet hat band. Suddenly, she felt she'd discovered a kindred spirit.

"My name is Ellen Good—"

He cut her off with a cherry voice.

"Not *the* Ellen Good! The Costa Rican missionary and reservation schoolmarm and Iowa farm daughter who has the audacity to nurture heathenism in our midst!"

She laughed again.

"Guilty."

"At the Parsonage? Do you think it wise?"

"I'm only here for five more weeks. To fire me would be—redundant."

"How can I decline an invitation from a courageous daughter?"

"Seven o'clock?"

"Fine."

"BYOB—bring your own Bible."

This time, it was Father Zukowski who laughed.

She felt better. If invited out on Thursday, she'd an excellent excuse to decline.

She'd never met Father Zukowski, but his name was on everyone's lips. Even if they spent the evening in guarded silence, Ellen would enjoy *not* being an exhibit. If she dropped her salad fork, it wouldn't circulate until a report appeared in the local bugle.

She prepared a simple menu: spaghetti with store-bought sauce "jazzed up" with a few spices, garlic bread doctored in the kitchen from two store-bought mini-loafs, a green salad with a home-made vinaigrette and vanilla pudding and coffee for afters.

Father Zukowski is thin and not much older than Ellen. This farm lad was muscular. He was the Pennsylvania high-school state champion wrestler in his weight class both his junior and senior years.

He wore dark slacks and a casual yellow shirt. Save for his collar, there was no way his demeanor would indicate he was a Catholic prelate. He was polite and amiable. It was a perfectly innocuous meeting of a farmer's son and a farmer's daughter.

Would he like a glass of red before dinner?

He would.

They sat in the newly cleared and cleaned living room. They chatted and sipped until the water came to a boil. As Ellen busied herself with monitoring the noodles, Father Zukowski stirred the bubbling sauce as needed.

Upon Ellen's invitation, Father Zukowski crossed himself and returned thanks. From that point forward, the pair exchanged biographical anecdotes and information.

"My father came to America in his early thirties," Zukowski related. "He married a second-generation Austrian and raised a family on farm outside of Philly. He wanted me to be American through and through, so he insisted that I be named Bob. He said I could spell it backwards; something one cannot do with *Robert*. He felt it reeked of America. It was a battle when I wanted to take Latin in school. Dad didn't want me to speak anything other than *Merican*."

"So, you got *the call* in high school?" Ellen asked.

"Oh, no," Zukowski replied. "I didn't get the call until I graduated from college."

"The same with me," Ellen reported, excitedly. "I went to Northern Iowa. It was less than an hour from home."

"Slippery Rock," Zukowski announced, rolling his spaghetti.

"That's more than an hour away from Philly."

"As much as I love my mother and father, I didn't cherish reporting in every night—or even every week. I wanted to enjoy a beer or two and not have to face a Breathalyzer when I got home."

Ellen giggled.

"I have a weakness for vodka martinis," Ellen confessed.

Zukowski leaned back in mock horror.

"I hope this place isn't bugged! Don't let anybody around here know that!"

"I got the word the day I arrived," Ellen assured. "I've gone without a martini for many, many months. I'm confident I can last five more weeks."

"You like it here?"

She didn't hesitate.

"It's more provincial than I like, I admit. Still, the people are friendly—maybe, too friendly at times. I invited you here because I wanted to take a break from these endless evening fetes. They wear me out!"

"I know, I know. I went through the same thing when I first arrived. Once you get settled in, it tapers off to once or twice a week. Fortunately, all these farm wives are first-class cooks."

Ellen patted her stomach noisily.

"Don't I know! I must have gained twenty pounds this week. Coming from farm communities, we know it's a sin to refuse the hostess's cooking."

"Amen."

There was a short pause.

"At the risk of sounding importunate," Ellen began cautiously, "what bishop did you piss off to get sent to this place?"

He laughed again. He had a soft, pleasing laugh; it was devoid of grand production. It was the laugh of a man who enjoyed humor but who knew its dangers when mixed with his profession.

"It was a rescue mission not so unlike yours," he replied. "I found it interesting, and I was satisfied with my accomplishments—not overly satisfied. I've known failure. That's never easy to take. Still, the place grows on you. These people are family. We have our differences and, at times, exchange blows. Still, there it is."

"I haven't really experienced failure—yet," Ellen reported with concern. "There've been many disappointments, but I'm waiting for that first big kaboom. I'm not sure I can handle failure."

"I can't take your confession," he responded lightly.

Ellen smiled.

"I'll say ten Our Fathers anyway," she promised.

Confronted with an unexpected moment of seriousness, Bob felt obligated to carry on.

"We both work for the same Boss," he reported. "He's pretty understanding."

She smiled again. Father Bob's diction was comfortably down home. "*Boss?*"

He shrugged his shoulders.

"I read about a headstone out West—a frontier town where the graves have wooden markers. This may be apocryphal, of course, but it's stayed with me. As I recall, it said *Here lies So-and-so; He did his damnedest.* That covers a lot, doesn't it? If I can look back on my service and honestly say I've done my damnedest, I won't fear meeting the Boss. Failure, to my way of thinking, is no sin. Not trying—that, in my estimation, is the *eighth* deadly sin."

Ellen took great comfort in these unsolicited words. Indeed, she took great comfort in Father Bob's visit. He may be of a different persuasion, but he'd experienced the hot seat longer and was eager to help her manage her brief appointment.

CHAPTER TWO

Ellen rolled out of bed at five in the morning determined to go to war with forced feedings. In a sweat-shirt, shorts and running shoes, she jogged over to the school, down the hill and onto the track. One of the elementary teachers and a woman of middle age were walking power laps, water bottles clutched firmly in their fists. The only runner was Father Bob in a t-shirt and shorts. Ellen waited for him to come around and fell in step beside him.

They ran five laps before Father Bob peeled off.

"I want to do three more laps," Ellen said, pulling up.

"Meet me at Crazy Bob's at seven."

"Crazy Bob?"

Father Bob wiped his forehead on his t-shirt.

"He owns the café. I go there every morning to bless the coffee."

"You're kidding!"

"That's what Crazy Bob calls it. He gets restless if I don't come 'round first thing."

Ellen suspected her leg was being pulled. Nevertheless, after her laps, she took a nice shower and settled in with the notes for her Sunday sermon. Shortly before seven, she walked briskly to the town square and ambled into the café.

Father Bob sat at the end of the counter. Ellen sat beside him and ordered a coffee. It came in a large, brown, earthenware mug.

Father Bob informed her that Keatsville produced four staples: wheat, soybeans, cockleburs and Bobs. He was Father Bob; the café owner was Crazy Bob (for trying to make a go of a breakfast/lunch hash house with no appreciable, transient clientele). Additionally, there was Farmer Bob, Dr. Bob (the pharmacist), Cowboy Bob (who owned horses), Tinker Bob (a mechanic), Trader Bob (manager of a food-chain outlet), Senator Bob (a lawyer who once served as a state representative), Old Bob and Big Bob and Tiny Bob. In addition, there were a dozen or more school kids, Little Bobs. This included a cute ten-year-old Catholic girl christened Roberta who, also, answered to Little Bob.

"If you ever come up behind a group of kids, just yell *Little Bob*! It's funny to see eight or ten heads whip around."

Ellen found that a harmless form of amusement.

"Is this coffee properly blessed?" she had to ask.

"Crazy Bob thinks my presence is blessing enough. I invited you, let me get yours."

"Thank-you. My father insists that indigestion is the result of un-blessed food."

Father Bob laughed.

"I should like to meet your father," he said sincerely.

"He's coming for service this Sunday," she informed. "He was disappointed to miss my debut, but the time was too short to arrange a trip out here. My mom and little brother are coming, too. If you are free in the afternoon, I'll be proud to introduce you."

"I will make that happen," he promised.

"Well, I have to run."

"Me too. So many indulgences; so little time."

Ellen laughed.

"I'll be nailing something to your church door later," she warned.

Father Bob rolled his eyes.

"Here we go again!"

The fifth week of Ellen's reign featured communion. Ellen was not officially sanctioned, *ergo*, one of the regional supernumeraries was dispatched to take over. Ellen was busy on the phone for several minutes taking notes and planning. The communion service was a week and a half away, but she did not want to be left stranded by some bureaucratic *oops*.

Once free, she made soup and sandwiches.

Diane arrived with a cheerful countenance. She'd regained some color, but it might have been an illusion brought about by her infectious smile.

It was only her fourth luncheon with Ellen, but Diane was comfortable at the table. She summarized the events since their previous meal. Despite her nearly continuous narration, Diane ingested the contents of her bowl and every crumb of her tuna sandwich. Ellen offered her an apple. Diane pondered for a moment. She was stuffed, but the apple looked luscious.

"I'll split it with you," she announced.

Ellen reached for a knife. It was hard to tell who was the happier—the young orphan who was, at long last, regaining her appetite, or the witness to this welcome transformation.

Diane was escorted back to the main school entrance. Upon her return, Ellen heard the phone and rushed to answer.

"Ellen Good here," she answered.

"Simone."

What a great day!

"Thanks for coming last week. I'm so sorry we didn't have time to visit."

Prolonged silence.

"Simone?"

"I'm—I—uh—"

Ellen's smile faded.

"Simone, are you okay? Where are you?"

"I'm okay—well—yeah. I'm at home. It's—well, I need to talk."

"I'm sorry, Simone, but I'm tied down for the rest of the day. Could you come by—maybe, tomorrow?"

"Ah-um—I—well, we will come Sunday."

"Great!"

"Well—I'm so—confused—"

Ellen gripped the receiver tightly.

"What is it?"

"I'm—going—to have—a baby."

"Congratulations! I'm so happy for you!"

Silence.

"What's wrong. Simone? Tell me."

"It's all wrong," the Romanian replied. "I—I am happy about the baby, but I'm so miserable."

"Why? What does Miles think?"

"Ah—well—I haven't—told him—yet."

"Simone, you have to tell him right away. Why would you tell me before you tell Miles?"

There were a series of scenarios racing through Ellen's brain. None was favorably propitious.

"If that man doesn't want to marry you—"

"He does," Simone insisted. "He's told me several times, but—but—but it is—possible—that I am the only living Albescu. I—I want my baby to have the family name. I'm so afraid that Miles—that he won't like that."

"There are ways, Simone," Ellen promised. "We will be sure to talk on Sunday."

"This isn't the plan," Simone bellowed. "Miles is learning Romanian. He wants to ask my father's permission to marry me. He talks about it often."

"Simone, listen to me: we can talk this through on Sunday. I promise we can make this right. Let's wait until Sunday. Can you do that?"

"Ah—there's just one thing—ah—that I think about."

"What's that?"

"Ah-um—when Miles and I get married—ah—we—that is I, and I'm sure Miles feels the same—that is—we want you to marry us."

Ellen gulped. This could be a problem.

"I'd be honored, Simone. See you Sunday."

"Sure."

"Good girl. Now, tell Miles. Tell him today. Promise."

"I promise."

CHAPTER THREE

Eight days following our first *date*, Simone moved into my bed. At first, *I* experienced restless nights. Every time Simone moved, I was awake and alert. The middle-of-the-night panic attacks, however, never materialized, and soon enough I was sleeping the night through. There was one morning, however, when I attempted to sneak out without disturbing her. Just as I exited the house, I heard an hysterical scream.

Racing back, I discovered a hyperventilating woman propped on an elbow. When she woke and found herself alone, she was instantly transported back to that horrible Shawnee Mission morning when she realized that Ion, the only person she trusted, had left her— again. The moment she screamed, she realized where she was, but the adrenalin rush was so powerful it took time and reassurances to quell her racing heart.

After that performance, I woke her whenever I got out of bed. Most days she'd spring up and pitch in with breakfast. There were other mornings when she'd grunt, turn over, and go back to sleep.

Simone continued to work with young skaters, but her heart was no longer in it. John was not there to be proud of her. Of course,

I was proud of her, but I was an outsider; it wasn't the same. Without John, there was little joy.

"I don't care if I never see ice again," she sighed one evening during her reading.

I gave her a reassuring neck message but said nothing.

She never bought new skates. The arena kept a pair for her exclusive use as a "perk." Save for her periodic performances, Simone never skated except to get from one skater to another or to glide around while observing students.

Through me, she came to know James. When he got a new girlfriend, we'd double date. Sometimes, James came by the house for a coffee and a chat. Other times, we'd drop in on him in Lima and enjoy a game of Scrabble or watch a movie. As time went on, Simone expressed interest in working at the fancy eatery. James said it was possible, but the turn-over rate was low.

"Except for Miles here," he pointed out, "there aren't many people willing to toss off those tips. Maybe, you could get work bussing tables. That doesn't pay much, but you'd be on the short list if the boss needs a waitress."

I thought the notion absurd. Simone was too talented to be scrapping and stacking plates. She, however, argued that it was her duty to secure steady work.

"I'm tired of being cared for," she barked. "I want to help out instead of being carried."

It was fruitless to argue with Simone once she built up steam. Instead, I bided my time and offered rebuttals during rare pacific interludes.

"*Lubita*, I don't care if you never work another day in your life."

"But I do! I love you, Miles, but I need to respect myself. I want to help."

"You do," I objected. "You help by being here and putting up with my crap."

She gave me a hug of appreciation.

"You are too good," she whispered.

Then, she released me and went back to the reading couch.

"Now, I must work on self-respect."

I sighed. As always, Simone had the last word.

I was not her keeper. If she wanted a *real* job, I'd be supportive.

Twice, Simone and I spent evenings with Max and his intended. The girls got on quite well. Simone laughed at nearly every jest Brenda invented. This was not in the service of politeness; the Romanian's appreciation of sharp wit was genuine. However, I found it irritating.

"You can be funny," I reminded in private.

Simone's humor was drier and deeper. Brenda was more of the stand-up variety. It was my desire to witness both women in full stride. Max and I would injure ourselves laughing.

"I can't be funny when I'm relaxed," Simone confessed. "I only say funny things when I'm afraid or anxious."

That made no sense to me, but I was not foolish enough to doubt her word. Simone's love and friendship meant more to me than any other thing. That she reciprocated my feelings was miraculous. I'd chance nothing which might rock the love boat.

Simone was certain a baby was coming. She didn't make a big production. Certainties had failed her before. Just as with me, she rejected anything that might threaten our alliance. She'd relied upon John as a mentor, father confessor and greatest of all friends. With me, it was love between equals; our relationship was based on mutual support. I could teach her many things, but in matters of frugality and practicality she was the master.

In her experience, sex was cruel and sadistic. Yielding to me was expected of an obedient, subservient leech. Surprisingly, she realized that I wanted her for herself and not to punish her or collect payment for services rendered. Eventually, it became stimulating and enjoyable.

"It's always better when both people participate," I whispered after our first encounter.

Simone said nothing.

It was a startling revelation for her to realize that she did not have to wait for me before becoming amorous or seductive. If she made it known through her actions that she was eager to go to bed, I seldom begged off. There were a few times when one or the other was simply not up for it. That was another startling revelation: if Simone didn't feel playful, I'd not force the issue.

In time, she felt comfortable and safe. Save for her own father and John, Simone had never harbored such unconditional feelings for a man.

Whenever we frolicked, however, a baby was always lurking in our thoughts. Afraid of motherhood and a myriad of external concerns, she didn't want a child. Nevertheless, there was a part of her which secretly hoped that *this time* it would happen.

I performed a series of small tasks and rituals to ingratiate myself. Simone was delighted that I treated her as the most important part of my life. Well, she is.

I spoke only in Romanian for thirty minutes each evening. In the early days, I was limited to a dozen or so words. I'd jot down phrases or words I wanted to use but couldn't; later, when time expired, I'd consult with her. This was how Ion had worked with her. Now, she worked with me. Little by little my grammar and vocabulary progressed until I spoke in complete, albeit short, sentences. Eventually, we engaged in rudimentary conversations. Whenever Simone said something I didn't understand, I need only give her a questioning look. She'd proceed to explain with gestures and elementary vocabulary until I grasped her meaning.

During the daily language half-hour, Simone through laziness or frustration would slip into English. Whenever she did, I spoke sharply.

During her abbreviated life with John, Simone learned English from him and a series of night courses. Since he refused to speak anything except English, it was Simone who was often cross with him. She persevered. Her constant reading was a wonderful tool, but I was never remiss in applying on-the-spot corrections. At first, I feared she would not wish to be corrected in the presence of others, but Simone scolded me.

"If you do not correct me, I will sound foolish or stupid," she explained. "If you correct me, people know I want to learn."

It was a tedious process, but we persevered together.

Simone loved the Romanian language. It had the musicality of French and the boldness of Italian; it delighted her ear. Even as her English improved, she retained certain native sounds and imposed them upon her adopted tongue for no other reason than it pleased her.

I found the mixture of Romanian pronunciation and English vocabulary cute.

Simone's favorite music is Enesco's *Romanian Rhapsody*, (the first one, particularly). It was among her earliest memories and it invoked pastoral images of gaily attired peasants dancing and romancing amid harvested wheat with purple mountains dominating a distant horizon. This was the Romania of the imagination—pure fantasy, devoid of bleak reality. She never saw such scenes in real life, but her dreams could neither be taken away nor prohibited.

She thought of her father who, unlike Simone's mother, never pushed her away. His lap constituted a welcome refuge. When he was reading, talking to his wife, or trading observations with a neighbor his mighty arm around her kept fear and want at bay. He never made demands. If Simone was recalcitrant, it was mater who scolded, cajoled, or swatted her bottom.

When Simone left for boarding school, she and her father both cried.

Simone's mother was a lithe yet muscular Romanian woman who aged quickly under the demands of life. She was never idle. There were clothes to make, laundry and mending to do; meals to prepare, errands to run, beds to make, floors to sweep and mop, water to fetch, and dozens more daily demands. She showed her love in subtle ways that Simone recognized only as an adult.

Her younger brother was a pest. Simone competed for attention, and she hated him whenever he occupied Father's lap. Lucian, however, looked up to Simone and followed her example in anything gaining parental approval. Only after she left home did she long for his company. Though younger, impish and more felicitous than any Romanian had reason to be, he was her confidant. Never, even when angry with her, did he betray her trust. Similarly, Simone kept her brother's secrets—even from me.

She hinted about leaving to Lucian only. Many of her worst nightmares were induced by thoughts of her brother. When she defected, he'd suffer worst of all in the hands of the *Securitate*.

Simone was fortunate enough to attend Lucian's wedding. Unfortunately, her rigorous training schedule allowed only a few short hours. She met her sister-in-law but had no chance to know her. What Simone learned of Silvia Albescu came in those few terse letters not confiscated or highly censored.

It caused great heartache when memories of her family faded. She was eight-years old when she was taken away. Her subsequent visits were short, few and far between. In a very real sense, Simone Albescu was a creation of the State. The little girl who treasured the safety of her father's protective embrace died the day she was spirited away.

The Party proved a miserable surrogate parent. Her job in the State apparatus was to learn what she was ordered to learn and do what she was ordered to do. If she stumbled or failed, the punishments were severe and creative. Her keepers quickly discovered that corporal punishment made her defiant and uncooperative. Any mention, however, that her masters might be forced to speak with her father made her instantly malleable.

Over the length of her sentence, Simone went through seven coaches. She listened; she followed instructions; she put up with discipline whenever she failed to please. She seldom spoke. She might have kept total silence, but her keepers employed the strategy of direct questions. The punishments for not answering authority were memorable.

When Ion took over, she obeyed him. Somehow, she sensed that Ion was different. When he stood rink side and watched others go through exercises, skills and routines, his protégée was required to be with him. He would point out the strengths and weaknesses of the other performers and made Simone more aware of her art. If, however, they were by themselves, he'd point and gesture, but he'd speak of things far removed from figure skating.

Ion would tell jokes, describe his hometown, and explain foods and objects few Romanians experienced. It didn't bother him that the lump beside him never asked questions, made comments, or spoke. Gradually, however, Simone viewed him less as a task master and leg swatter and more of a substitute father. She responded better and more quickly than with previous instructors.

Simone no longer skated to placate the authorities; she skated to please Ion.

After confiding in her, Ion's life was in her hands. Should she, for any reason, tell the *Securitate* what Ion said in private, he'd be severely disciplined and, likely, imprisoned—or worse!

She never took advantage of her hold over him. Instead, she made comments which would not meet with the approval of the authorities. Soon, they each had enough evidence to get the other in serious trouble. Rather than become paranoid, the realization that they could inform on each other made them *free*. There was nothing they could not talk about—provided they were not overheard.

Ion was the first person outside her family Simone viewed as a friend. Within a few weeks, they trusted each other implicitly. Moreover, they relied on one another.

When he left in Chicago, Simone understood. She, silently, wished him luck and good fortune before reverting to the sphinx, requiring coercion to smile for the crowd.

She joined Ion in Kansas City and they took up where they left off. Now, however, Simone was free. She didn't want to skate; John refused to force her. They lived in peace and harmony as father and daughter.

Then, when the sky was darkest, I took her in. I was not John. No one can take his place. No one had shared the years of slavery with her. Yet, in my own quiet way, I became a pillar of strength. She worked at pleasing me in recompense for food, lodging and safety.

After a career as a silent, morose automaton, Simone Albescu's greatest fear was being alone. When violent dreams drove her to frantic thrashing, she'd wake to find me tending her. I'd bring her water or juice. I unraveled her bed clothes and made them functional once more. Sometimes, I'd sit silently beside her and stroke her hair until terror receded. If she wanted to talk, I listened. If she wanted conversation, I'd join in. If she remained mute, I respected her silence.

Gradually, she fell in love. I hope it was love and not some tawdry expression of gratitude. It appeared genuine, but Simone's waters run deep.

What to do? She knew nothing but filial devotion—and damned little of that.

She didn't dare be overt. She mustn't appear too eager. She refused to play the vamp; even if she did, she wouldn't know how. What she found in novels was exactly what she did *not see* in life; she couldn't imitate mass culture for fear of being laughed at or mocked.

The one person in whom she could confide was dead.

There was, however, one other she trusted.

She began feeling queer.

Simone, far more perceptive than her stoic façade indicates, had a solid idea as to the cause of her malady. She bought a book, which she kept in her dresser drawer—safe because I respected her privacy. She read magazine articles.

Simone knew.

She was frightened. As thankful as she was to be out of *that damned country*, she took a perverse pride in her nationality. She thirsted for American citizenship, but she felt, somehow, it constituted a betrayal. She wanted her baby to be American, but she must honor her father. If her family was dead, as was rumored, she'd not allow her family's name to be erased. The child *must* be an Albescu in defiance of the monsters who, twice, drove her to the brink of destruction.

How would I react? I'd every right to expect our child inherit my name. She squirmed and suffered, fearing I'd lay down the law.

Maybe—just maybe, she thought, I didn't want the baby. It isn't something we discussed. For all Simone knew, I might refuse to marry a pregnant woman.

I once gave her a nice little band. There was no production, but I made clear my desire to marry her. She slipped the ring on the appropriate finger and admired it several times a day. Would the baby deepen my commitment or cancel it?

Simone thought she knew the answers, but a lack of certitude haunted her.

Whenever I went on an overnight, Simone insisted on coming. She could not eat or sleep on my expense account, but I, unhesitatingly, parted with the difference. I enjoyed her company as much as she needed mine. Occasionally, I'd pull over and ask her to drive. This made her doubly thankful to be along; she didn't want me driving while fatigued.

We drove to Marion with a stowaway. She wanted to tell me, but a vision appeared of her standing alone by the side of the road as I drove away.

He would never abandon me!

Still—

Maybe, it would be best to tell him when the car is not in motion.

Somehow, she could not.

The following day, we drove to Toledo. We stayed over for a service call at two area venues. We talked of many things and enjoyed a few laughs. Simone came very near telling me then, but she wasn't certain. Why create a fuss over a possible false alarm?

When I drove away for a day in Findlay, Simone remained behind. She didn't explain; I didn't ask.

She consulted with a woman doctor who treated her for reoccurring headaches and, once, for a staph infection.

"What can I do for you today?" the graying doctor asked after dispensing with the opening banter.

"You can tell me if I'm carrying a baby."

The word *pregnant* was problematical. There were certain words Simone confused with similar but different words. Out of fear of bungling in front of a near stranger, she opted for a less oblique approach.

In a matter of minutes, Simone's do-it-yourself diagnosis was confirmed. She left the office with literature and the clear realization that important issues must be addressed.

Simone Albescu, a.k.a. Simone White, desperately wanted to trust me. She had a great deal of faith, but she came from a culture where trust was dangerous and, often, deadly. She couldn't commit herself—yet. Perhaps, she never could. Nevertheless, she must tell me about the baby and *believe* that I'd react amicably. As the events of the previous few days testified, Simone realized she couldn't trust herself.

There was, however, one person in whom she had confidence. Frequent exchanges of missives provided comfort and release. Perhaps, the physical distance separating them cemented their ethereal bond.

Sitting with me in a church aisle seat, Simone looked nervously about. Several times, she glanced over her shoulder as if expecting a *Securitate* raid. This paranoia was well-understood; she'd acquired it through experience. However, there was something more urgent. Simone imagined the (not yet verified) baby growing within. She imagined everyone watching her bulging before their eyes. She was sure I'd notice. I would, she thought, have every right to be cross.

Ellen, adorned in white and carrying a dark-blue hymnal, walked within inches of Simone. Instantly, a wave of relief caressed her, and fears vanished. She experienced a rush of camaraderie. She'd experienced the feeling only twice before: once with Ion and, a few months later, Lucian.

It was time, she told herself, *to be bold and take the supreme risk.*

The moment she concluded her walk home after the doctor's examination, she went to the telephone stand. She reached on the lower shelf for the phone book. There on the cover, in large, blue-inked characters, was Ellen's number. She knew to whom they belonged because she witnessed my recording of them the evening of Ellen's initial call.

Her hand trembled, but there was no temptation to abort her mission. There are certain times, she told herself, when a person must be brave. It was not, however, easy. In fact, dialing the number on an ancient relic was far more nerve-wracking than outrunning the *Securitate* in the darkness of Lyon.

"Ellen Good here."

Simone took a long, deep breath. She swallowed hard.

"Simone," she whispered.

The first, brave step was taken.

PART THE FIFTH

CHAPTER ONE

The moment I pulled into the driveway, I felt something was bent. Simone agreed to come with me to Findlay only to beg off at the last minute. She noticed my expression of disappointment and mirrored it. She didn't like disappointing me. I reminded her, on several occasions, that her life was her own. Respect for my feelings was not intended to override her personal wants and desires.

I hadn't asked why she changed her mind. Firstly, it was none of my damned business. Secondly, if she wanted me to know, she'd tell me.

After putting the car away, I entered the side door and found her in the kitchen. She sat at my place on the far end of the table. There was an open jar of peanut butter in front of her with gouge marks where her fingers had visited. Her hands were under the table and in her lap. She looked at me askance with whipped-puppy eyes.

"What did you break?" I asked.

I didn't really care. My tone of voice was intended to make it clear. This, however, did not modify her guilt-ridden expression.

"Could you sit—there for a minute?"

She brought up her right hand and gestured toward the place opposite. Rather than rejoin her other hand, she planted her elbow on the table, tugged nervously at her hair before playing at her ear with finger and thumb.

Her serious visage frightened me. It resembled her stoic countenance that, I feared, presaged another emotional shut-down. After seventeen months of effort bringing her out of her shell, I wasn't sure I had the resources to start anew.

She held all the cards. I pulled out the chair habitually occupied by her during meals. I planted myself and placed both arms on the tabletop. I looked directly at her. She averted her eyes.

"Don't be angry with me," she pleaded in a mousey voice that made me cringe.

"That would take a lot of doing," I reminded.

"I—I called Ellen today."

I took a breath.

"Is she okay?"

"Oh, yes," she replied instantly. "It's just—well, I kind of needed to talk with—somebody—and—uh-um—"

Two and two is such easy math.

"You're pregnant!"

Her eyes snapped. She desperately studied my expression. When she realized I was pleased, she sighed with relief and—barely detectable to a casual observer—initiated a smile.

"You thought I'd be angry?" I asked incredulously.

"Miles," she began as a supplicant, "I—well—Ellen thinks there is something we can do—maybe, I'm being—foolish—or silly. It's probably selfish—"

"Are you fishing for a proposal?" I demanded with a light heart. "Simone, I will marry you this minute. All you have to do is say *yes*."

She balked. She brought up her under-the-table hand to join its partner. She wove her fingers together and raised them to her chin. She rested her face on them for a moment then dropped her hands to stroke her thighs nervously with her palms.

"Ellen promised that we can talk Sunday after church."

Ah! If Ellen said we would have a meeting, Simone was bound to think everything would be hunky-dory. Well, the odds were greatly in her favor.

"Simone, please, tell me what's bothering you. I thought you'd be over the moon; I know I am! What, exactly, is the problem? Obviously, there's a problem. Why should there be a problem?"

She continued to wipe the sweat off her hands by rubbing her jeans. Finally, she made a command decision. She laid her hands flat on the table, leaned forward and looked me directly in the eyes.

"*Te lubesc,*" she said.

"Glad to hear it," I replied, "I love you, too. That's settled. Now, what, exactly, is the problem?"

"I want baby to have my family's name," she announced.

"That's it? That is your big worry? Simone, why would you ever think I'd possibly object to that?"

She was genuinely amazed. I saw it on her face. For once, there was no mystery about her emotional state. She smiled briefly before assuming that damned expression of torment.

"It's just that—well, it—"

"I know the reason, Simone," I assured. "I think it admirable. This isn't a matter of asking for my approval. I agree—absolutely. It's your baby."

"Yours, too," she insisted.

I snorted.

"I did the easy part, *Lubita,*" I reported. "You're the one who must skate."

CHAPTER TWO

Sunday dawned clear and crisp. The spring we longed for was on the way. We needed heavy jackets when venturing forth into the brisk morning air, but the clear skies promised us a temperate spring afternoon.

Since we opted to take Simone's car, she climbed behind the wheel.

"We have plenty of time," I reminded.

Simone, as was her wont, grunted. She disliked being informed of the obvious. Nevertheless, my peace of mind was much more important than her attitude.

After backing out, she turned north. I said nothing though I noted that her route, miles longer, was along wider and better maintained roads. No fool she. I admired her caution but knew better than to complement her judgment.

We parked on the west side of the square in front of the tiny whitewashed building housing the local branch of a Midwestern grocery chain. The temperature was reasonable, so we left our coats in the back seat. Thinking better of it, I grabbed Simone's jacket and draped it over her shoulders. She made no comment.

"Let's go this way," I suggested.

She smiled at me. That is correct; she smiled approvingly. Though she'd been habitually smiling for some months, any demonstration of felicity remained a novelty. I'll never take it for granted.

We walked the long way around the square. Sunday morning traffic is a rarity.

Despite our careful drive and our leisurely walk, we were early. Mass began at nine. It was just few minutes after ten; we could expect a significant increase in both traffic and pedestrians. What caught our eyes, however, was unexpected.

Coming up the street from the south were three people enjoying an unhurried stroll. Even from a distance and despite the lapse of time, I recognized the party immediately.

"Ellen's parents and her youngest brother," I told Simone. "They probably parked in front of Ellen's house."

I could think of no other explanation. It was quite a stretch of the legs from the Parsonage for mature people. The down-hill portions would be taxing but walking up hill would separate the sheep from the goats. Alas, Mr. and Mrs. Good were spry enough to handle the task.

I waved. Noah returned my wave instantly and informed mater and pater. Their wave came moments later.

We stood on the corner with the church at our backs and the steps and main doors slightly to our right. The distance between our parties decreased rapidly, but Simone stood at my side without the slightest impatience. Usually she fidgeted when unoccupied.

Two minutes later, introductions were made, and hands clasped by all in turn. The scene required only a man in a zebra shirt and a coin.

"You're married," Noah observed. "Congratulations!"

"Not quite," Simone responded before I had a chance. "This is the Romanian engagement finger."

Noah was not embarrassed. He wasn't the type.

"Premature congratulations."

"Thanks!"

Simone and I shared a laugh over our, in-unison, reply.

I expected Simone to be filled with trepidation. Somehow, she decided to leave her disquiet in Ellen's hands. There was an inexplicable bond between them which I envied but never understand. I recalled that pathetic scene in a Kansas City dive, and the words of comfort I gave. Between me and a stiff belt, Ellen was placated. At the time, I thought myself a clever fraud. Suddenly, I wondered if I'd been swindled. Had I the *power*—what other word can I employ?—Ellen exercised over Simone, I'd rule the world.

We decided it was not a violation of law to let ourselves in the church before the appointed meeter-greeters assumed station. Indeed, they were in conference with the Acting-Reverend Good on a secular matter. Two aging gentlemen in suits designed for another age made haste to open wide the church doors and prepare to tend the flock as the white-robed shepherdess rushed to greet us.

Here, I thought, was a quandary worthy of Solomon. To whom would Ellen award her first hug? She was, as I well knew, a hugger. For her to smile broadly and greet us *en mass* might honor accepted protocol, but it would reflect badly on the ever gregarious and charitable Ellen Good.

To my surprise, she figuratively left the ninety and nine to celebrate with the lost sheep. In fact, I was not too surprised at *her* conduct; her family's response, however, left me in silent awe. As their daughter folded the voluminous sleeves of her robe around Simone, her parents grinned *fit to bust*, as alfalfa harvesters are wont to say. No Good was visibly puzzled, but his posture radiated a brotherly pride every bit as strong as that of his parents.

Then, the hugging order progressed exactly as one would expect; Mother was first, then Dad, and Little Brother. Yours truly was last, of course, but I expected no less. The opening salutations were mercifully brief.

"I have a few things to see to," Ellen began. "I promised Father Zukowski that I'd introduce you after service. I hope you can stand the extra few minutes before we have lunch."

Father Zukowski? I could only imagine what Ellen's parents thought. Of all the people in Keatsville to single out as a friend and confidant, a Catholic priest rated the least likely. Noah, however, was not affected. During his sojourn in my former digs, he assured me that his sister was neither impressed nor inhibited by trappings; she was naturally attracted to people of virtuous character—yours truly, of course, the exception proving the rule.

Noah had a decidedly prosaic mode of expression, but I'm confident I capture the essence of his sentiment. It struck me that my character was anything but sterling. Indeed, I did not actually meet *her*. As I recall, she perched herself next to me in a history class as if I were a homing beacon. I thought of that often; it provided me with hours of philosophic contemplation while driving alone to and from a variety of venues in two states.

"Simone and Miles," she began as she gripped each of our wrists nearest her, "We can meet in my office after dismissal."

The way Ellen said *my office* confirmed her awareness that her position was, indeed, *pro-tem*.

"If the family can be patient," she added.

The Goods would wait for her through a change of seasons. They realized their daughter accepted the duties of the job. It was part of their unbounded pride. Ellen might last a mere six weeks, but she'd not use that as an excuse to dodge the official demands of her position. Clearly, they realized, Simone and I were not in Keatsville merely as a gesture of support.

We sat together as one would expect of the Ellen Good cheering section. Noah and I had a nice chat before the service began. He was loaded down with economics and business classes, but he majored in English and American literature. It would take him a million years to earn a degree because, in addition to an impossible academic load, he had a work-study job.

"I can help my brother and his partners in the hog business," he conjectured. "I might even be able to become a consultant—like you."

I bristled. Of all the pejoratives in the world, No had discovered the one I most hated. Fortunately, I deduced that he intended his statement as a facetious remark. In that context, my ire turned to an audible chuckle.

"But—English *and* American lit?"

No Good shrugged.

"I like to read."

Radar ears caught this remark. She hijacked the conversation. Leaning forward in the pew to speak around me, Simone and No were discussing the literary merits of works as diverse as *War and Peace* and *Sartor Resartus*. Simone had yet to read the latter, but it was only a matter of time. Then, No began an exposition on his two favorite authors: Dickens and Shakespeare.

All I could do was roll my eyes. Thanks to Simone's short acquaintance with the English language, I managed to keep just one step ahead of her in our literary discussions. I'd yet to read a word of Tom, Charlie or Wild Bill. That, as I realized, would change.

Thankfully, the organ boomed, and we stood to sing the processional hymn. Otherwise I might have found myself burdened with additional authors to expound upon to keep pace with Simone's insatiable literary appetite. I loved her dearly, but her desire to discuss esoteric concepts and symbols was an intense drain on my cerebral indigence. The problem was further exacerbated by the fact that, sooner or later, I'd have to call upon my limited Romanian resources to assist me.

Scripture readings and sermons evaporate from my memory as quickly as water droplets on a hot stove. Ergo, I could not provide a single detail of Ellen's performance without aid from my faithful mother-to-be. Obviously, I preferred avoiding this. Suffice it to say that the Good Cheering Section was not the only portion of the congregation moved by the Reverend Good's oration. Keatsville Protestants—Assembly of God excluded—are notoriously reserved. Nevertheless, there was a good deal of thoughtful exchanges among the assembly on that morning. The townspeople were clearly impressed.

The Good Family decided to take advantage of the spring weather. They opted to make a lap or two of the square while they waited for their daughter to finish ministering. There were two idyllic park benches on the courthouse lawn. They assured me that they'd wait for Ellen at one of those stations if they wearied.

I held Simone's hand as we stood just inside the sanctuary's double-door entrance while waiting on Reverend Good to salute her flock as it passed into the secular world. When, at last, she bid her final farewell, Ellen returned to find us.

"Very nice sermon," I congratulated.

"Thank-you," she beamed.

Thankfully, she did not quiz me.

"Let's go to the study," she suggested.

She led us to a huge, ancient wooden roll-top desk, a matching roller chair and a modern desk lamp. There was a phone, beige area rug and two upholstered chairs stuck diagonally into the corners across from the desk. Around this were wrapped four walls so snug that opening the door presented a hazard to navigation. Not without effort did we manage to find our way to a sitting position.

Ellen swiveled her chair around and leaned the back against the heavy wooden desk. Simone and I were as comfortable in the armchairs as the broom closet allowed.

"Simone wants me to marry you," Ellen began, crossing her ankles under the chair.

"Untrue!" Simone informed. "I asked you to perform the ceremony."

It was meant as an ice breaker. It succeeded.

After our moment of levity, Ellen turned serious and spoke directly to the Romanian.

"I'm keeping this chair warm for the person to follow," she explained. "I'm not ordained, *yet*. I can't perform sacraments."

"Oh."

Simone was clearly disappointed.

"That's not to say I won't be ordained," Ellen added quickly, "but I cannot promise it will be soon."

Suddenly, Noah's cryptic remark about Simone's marital status turned ominous.

"You may not want to wait," Ellen concluded.

"We can wait," Simone responded immediately.

Ellen looked at me. I shrugged. Though eager to wed, I was prepared to defer the details to my intended. Perhaps, this is a wimpish attitude. For Simone, however, the details of our mutual *sentencing* were far more important than chronology. She impressed me as a woman who wouldn't be bothered by a wedding which included our son acting as best man and our daughter as the maid of honor. She had her heart set on a known and trusted friend presiding. That point was non-negotiable.

"We have one of my supervisors coming next Sunday. Let me speak with him about this. If there is a way, he will know of it."

Simone was satisfied. Though Ellen made no promise, her words were of comfort and relief.

Ellen quickly ran through the options concerning Simone's married name and the name of our child. She could keep her own name and the child would inherit it at birth; she could hyphenate her name as Albescu-Nelson or Nelson-Albescu as it suited her. These, in short, were trouble-free concerns.

"Suppose I keep my name, but I change my mind *after* the baby comes?" she asked. "I like the idea of being Mrs. Nelson, but—"

Ellen shrugged.

"You can change your name to anything you want, any time you want," she assured.

Simone would never suspect Ellen of saying false. However, this announcement was so bold and unexpected that she looked hard at me in case there was some linguistic slight-of-hand.

"You can change your name in a second," Ellen continued. "So long as you don't try to pass yourself off as a General or President, you can change your name to George Washington before you leave this—ah—*room*."

Simone found this an amazing revelation.

"But—ah—," she began in protest.

"Oh, there will be problems if you want a name changed on your driver's license and other documents. That's to be expected. Still, there is no legal means to keep you from changing your name whenever you want."

Simone's relief was palpable. One of her greatest concerns shrank to insignificance.

We didn't meet Father Bob that day, nor did we enjoy lunch with the Goodies. If three is a crowd, six or seven would constitute a mob. Simone managed to clear away most of her concerns by sitting in a tiny box with Ellen and finding reassurance. Even though she was not, technically speaking, a Christian, Ellen's presence and the Sunday message were a shot in her arm.

She was positively giddy as we started back. So energized was she that I insisted on driving. Simone didn't protest; she pulled over and surrendered command with a smile and a hug.

There was one shadow cast over our return. For a moment or two— but no longer—she sobered up.

"They pumped me full of something after I—*hurt* myself," she reflected. "I hope this baby doesn't have an extra arm or something."

Before I could make comment, her giddiness returned.

I was in such high spirits that I broke our journey at Wapak. I pulled into the best of the road-side hash-houses to enjoy a late lunch. The after-church crowd from Cridersville and other outlying hamlets had largely dispersed, so we needn't wait to get a freshly wiped table for two.

She ordered a tea against my coffee. The menus came with our beverages. Simone pushed her menu over to me without looking.

"Whatever you're having," she insisted.

She lifted the mug to her lips only to set it down again.

"You think tea is good for the baby?" she asked.

"When it gets a little bigger, the caffeine might cause a fuss," I mused, "but I doubt there's much danger. Ask a doctor—or Ellen."

I should not have suggested this last. There was no reason to believe that Ellen would know anything more about childbirth than Simone.

I noted that Simone didn't add any sugar to her tea.

"You'll want to call the baby John," I assumed.

She grinned but was unable to curb the redness in her face.

"If you don't mind."

I gestured my reassurance.

"John Lucian, maybe?" she continued.

Obviously, baby's name had symbolic value.

"Ion Lucian Albescu," I tried it out. "That has a pleasing sound. What if it is a girl?"

There wasn't a moment of hesitation.

"Ionanna Lucia," she assured.

She'd thought it through.

CHAPTER THREE

llen called late that evening. She wanted to drive over Tuesday afternoon to *talk*, a deliberately inexact word which did not auger well. Even Simone was on alert, but her excitement about the visit overrode reticence.

I stopped on my return from a day split in Van Wert and Lima to purchase a little—am—vegetable juice. I was disappointed but, strangely, thankful to discover the driveway empty. As I got out to open the garage door, Simone peeked through the kitchen window and frowned.

She was sitting at the table watching the driveway entrance. There was no peanut butter in sight, but, later, I discovered an empty container atop the trash bin under the sink.

I scrubbed a newly purchased glass and toweled it dry while Simone and I exchanged information about our day. She announced, unnecessarily, that she mowed the lawn. Because I made no comment, she added one of her own.

"I'm supposed to get exercise."

I let this pass. Simone was ignorant of how *not* to exercise. Pushing our power mower around and periodically dumping the grass catcher wouldn't approach her normal regimen.

When Ellen arrived in a used sedan, Simone rushed outside. She opened the driver's door and practically pulled Ellen out. Ellen received the traditional Romanian greeting, a kiss on the one cheek followed by one on the other.

Kisses? Well, not quite. It was ritualistic. A pucker during a hug was the essential feature. Presumably, Romanians don't like going around with soggy cheeks, particularly during the harsh winter months. From my vantage point, Ellen smiled and closed her eyes during the hug, so she didn't bother to pucker; Simone couldn't see.

"You give great directions," Ellen called out, seeing me holding open the kitchen entrance. "I came right to the house. No detours."

Simone took her friend by the hand and led her inside and to the couch. There they conferenced while I busied myself in the kitchen.

Ellen's journey to Cridersville was prompted, so she said, by Communion Sunday. Simone remained un-baptized. Ellen was well versed in protocol. However, not even St. Ellen expected to make a convert during an afternoon visit. Even if it were possible, there were too many bases to cover. Any missionary worth her salt knows a proper foundation must be laid before a structure can be built. Even then, it had to go up one brick and one layer at a time. This rated a project, not an evening seminar.

In truth, Ellen's visit was purely social.

"She doesn't want me in church Sunday," Simone pouted.

"She's being precious," Ellen countered. "Simone knows she's welcome. I merely explained that I am not allowed to offer communion. Strictly speaking, Simone isn't allowed to participate."

I shrugged. This matter could have been discussed in Keatsville or over the phone.

"It's hardly breaking the law," I reminded.

"Speaking as a sinner, anyone can take Communion. Speaking as a quasi-cleric, church law should be observed. There are several people who don't approach the rail. No one keeps score. If Simone attends, she'd be only one of several who don't partake."

We knew Simone. Her one great weakness was fear of appearing freakish. No one would mark her should she remain in the pew. Simone, however, would be mortified.

Simone's expression told me everything I needed to know.

"I am not going to pressure Simone," I asserted.

Ellen turned back to the Romanian and placed her hands over those of my *girlfriend*.

"Miles is right," she said. "If you are uncomfortable with this, then you do what you think best. Remember, the church is not exclusionary. You come and go as you please."

Simone forced a timid smile. By this time, I was an expert at interpreting her facial expressions. There was considerable pathos behind this one.

"I believe in you, and I believe in Miles," she replied. "To believe in anything or anyone else—it will take time."

"I understand," Ellen replied.

It appears platitudinous on the page, but Ellen doesn't do platitudes. If she said she understood, she understood.

"Ellen," I gestured with my finger, "a moment, please."

She was reluctant to leave Simone.

Once underway, I was the object of Ellen's complete attention. She was puzzled and, perhaps, concerned. What, she wondered, would require her to leave Simone alone?

I stepped back and to the side. When she came through the archway, I took her arm and escorted her to the counter. I heard her eyes popping.

"I haven't had one of those in ages," she sighed.

"Sorry, I forgot the olives, so I used what we have on hand."

"Miles, I can't drink this," she protested. "I'm driving."

"You will spend the night if I have to break your car," Simone threatened, approaching from behind.

Ellen looked at Simone and tacitly appealed to me for help. I denied it.

"I have to get up way early," she protested.

"We have two alarm clocks," I assured. "They're in working order."

She reviewed her options before picking up the martini glass.

"I can resist everything except temptation," she reported.

She didn't guzzle as she had in Kansas City. She began with a satisfied sip.

"You mix a good martini," she said.

"I'll give you the mixings to take with you in the morning," I promised. "Except for the Spanish olives. Those are my between meal snacks."

"I can't take vodka and vermouth into the Parsonage, Miles. Have you no sense of propriety?"

"Then, you'll have to drink them all up tonight," I countered.

She did not dignify such a preposterous notion with an answer.

I turned to the expectant mother.

"Once the lush finishes her drink, you two get cracking on dinner. I'm hungry."

"And what will you be doing while we're slaving in the kitchen?" Ellen demanded.

"I'll be in my room drawing mammoths on the walls."

That earned me a swat on the butt. I don't know for certain the identity of the perpetrator, but I knew swatting wasn't Simone's style. Never let it be said that I can't take a hint. Later, when I heard the kitchen stool dragging over linoleum, I knew peanut butter was in play.

Happy hour was officially open.

I retired to my bedroom computer to work on my swindle sheet, but my mind was divided. Leaving Ellen and Simone in the kitchen together set my ears ablaze. Additionally, it was my first encounter with jealousy. Simone was in congress with someone who wasn't me. Had anyone suggested I'd be jealous of Ellen, I'd have enjoyed a hearty laugh. Suddenly, it wasn't funny.

I was finishing up when summoned by Ellen's vibrant, authority-of-the-pulpit voice. The commanding tone didn't invite dalliance. I left things exactly as they were and reported to the kitchen post-haste.

Despite the lapse of several minutes, Ellen's martini was only half consumed. Pleased I was to realize that she was taking the time to enjoy it to the fullest.

"Simone tells me that they do bride-napping in her country," Ellen reported.

I was unaware of the expected response.

"I will inform the United Nations."

Ellen ignored my remark.

"Are you okay with it?"

I met Simone's dark eyes. They were ambiguous.

"What's the deal?" I asked, requiring more information than the inquisition had thus far provided.

"The bride is spirited away after the ceremony and held for ransom," Ellen said. "Payment is often made with alcohol, consumed at the reception."

"Bride for booze," I concluded. "How demeaning."

I waited for Simone to send a signal. Instead, she glared at me as if Ellen and I were discussing the life cycle of the dung beetle.

"It's a custom. We could amend it."

"Simone in return for a gross of communion wafers," I theorized.

"Details, details," Ellen sighed. "Would you object to the custom?"

Again, I looked at the suddenly enigmatic mother-to-be.

"What does Simone think?"

The question was for Ellen, but my attention was directed at the Romanian. She felt the heat of my gaze and shifted uncomfortably before clearing her throat.

"It would be a touch of home," she said meekly, "but I don't feel comfortable with strangers."

"How about Max or Noah?"

Her expression remained unchanged except for a sudden sparkle in her eyes.

"That would be—okay," she agreed.

That settled it for Ellen.

"How about music?"

"Aren't we being a little premature here?" I demanded. "We don't know when you'll be eligible."

"Let's assume soon," Ellen insisted. "If you're getting married in Keatsville, I want to get the ducks in a row."

"You don't think we can plan this out for ourselves?"

Ellen and I exchanged glances.

"I'm not taking over," she said, "but when do you two think you can get over to make the arrangements? I'll get the ball rolling."

"We appreciate your help," Simone announced timidly. "I'd like *Romanian Rhapsody, number one.*"

That settled it for me.

"*Indiana,*" I advanced immediately. "Benny Goodman if you can get."

Ellen smiled up at me.

"I'll see what I can do," she promised.

"What kind of pizza would you like?" Simone asked boldly.

Ellen shrugged.

"Whatever you want," she replied.

Simone jumped up and started for the keys. I gestured to Ellen with my head. She, in turn, looked me dead in the eye and spoke.

"Take my car. It's blocking the drive anyway."

I was miffed. This was not a time I wanted Simone out alone. Ellen ignored me as she fished in her purse for the keys. I remained where I was and simmered until I heard the motor roar to life. I turned my attention to my officious guest. It was my intention to scald her with my expression. Alas, I found her placidly holding a toothpick in her hand while she chewed on a pair of olives. To her I was the invisible man.

Try as I might, I couldn't be angry.

"You two will have to take a day off and get a license at the county clerk's office," she advised. "You must show up in person."

"I think we have an extra toothbrush," I announced. "Let's see what else we can find."

She rose and followed me at a discrete distance. Once in the medicine chest, it was child's play to find the toothbrush still encased in the original wrapping. We always kept a spare on hand, but not with overnight guests in mind.

"Miles," a nearby voice cooed. "You better come in here."

Ellen had entered the "guest room." She stood slightly inside the door; I didn't see the bed until I slid past.

It was turned down; perfectly arrayed on the pillow was a light-blue flannel night dress embroidered with petite hearts around the neck and shoulders. I'd never seen it before, nor had I seen the pair of stretchable, flexible slippers on the floor. Additionally, there was a toothbrush and a travel-sized tube of toothpaste resting serenely next to a mint candy which—once upon a time—adorned a Toledo motel bed.

"I thought it was my idea to have you stay the night," I said.

"I'm glad I relented," Ellen replied. "She might have let the air out of my tires."

I didn't doubt Simone's determination. She might well have broken Ellen's car.

Perhaps, it was unseemly of me to sit on the couch next to Ellen while my fiancé was fetching dinner. There were, however, no witnesses. Had Simone taken us by surprise, she, probably, would assume nothing amiss.

"You'll make a terrific husband," she assured. "I thought so from the first. That's why I was upset. I really thought you were going to propose to me."

"Would you have accepted?"

"In a New York minute."

What, I wondered, was I supposed to respond?

"What's a Lugen?"

That seemed safe.

"I have no idea."

"You called me a Lugen," I reminded.

Ellen laughed.

"My dad caught me swearing twice," she began. "The first time I was, maybe, ten. He took a paddle and warmed my pants something wonderful. You think I'd have learned. The next time, I was in high school. He never said a word—not a word. At supper, though, he took my chair from the table and I had to eat standing up. That may appear innocuous, but you have no idea how cruel brothers are. They still talk about it, and I still blush.

"I guarantee you, Miles, I think about that every time I'm tempted to let loose. Once at UNI, I heard somebody call somebody else a *Lugen*. Since I cannot swear like a lady, I use words that sound bad. Now, you tell me what *Hatchi* means."

"She told you about that?"

"She *wrote* me."

I should have suspected.

"I have no idea what it means," I confessed. "I thought I was being clever."

The air was cleared. Simone was out of the house. Ellen was sipping the last of her martini.

"She's incredibly homesick," Ellen announced at last.

"I doubt that," I responded.

"She wasn't a trained monkey her whole life," Ellen insisted. "Her memories were formulated as a child—before she knew what defections are. She doesn't remember events; she remembers sensations; the colors, the smells, the feelings. How can you read her poems and not realize that?"

She might as well have spoken Braille.

"What makes you think she writes poetry?" I asked innocently.

Ellen started. She sat up quickly, looked me over curiously and settled back into the couch.

"This is soooooooo interesting," she said softly.

I didn't express myself verbally, but I was starting to realize that Simone could be secretive as well as devious.

"She sends me poems often—lyric mostly. Some are pretty good. I'm going to ask Simone permission to show Noah. Something tells me, he'll validate my opinion."

The most poignant poem was a series of quatrains she wrote for Ion. I assumed it was either a copy or a recreation of a treasured document from Shawnee Mission. As Ellen couldn't read or understand Romanian, Simone altered it. What she intended as an appreciative note of affection for her dearest friend morphed into a memorial.

I felt a pulse of anger. My reaction to Ion striking a young girl was hardly one of gratitude. However, Simone considered the incident as a tangible expression of friendship. She treasured that memory.

"Sometimes, I think she's crackers," I sighed.

"I didn't understand either. They both would have been in doop-dee-dee if he hadn't—uh—spanked her. So, he smacked her where it hurt the least. Plus, he offered her a chance at instant retaliation."

"I'm glad I didn't know about this before!"

"Miles, please. Simone would take a bullet for that man. Her poem made me cry."

I sat in stunned silence. I mightn't care to read the whole thing, but I was acutely curious about Ellen's conclusion.

"She told me," I diverted, "that she never wants to go back to Romania."

"That's the Romania we all know and despise," Ellen qualified. "There is another Romania—a child's Romania; a place where every day is an adventure. That, Miles, is the cause of her homesickness."

I recalled her once telling me the area around Ft. Amanda reminded her of home.

"Thus, the wedding day kidnapping scheme," I concluded.

"It was part of her brother's wedding."

This was getting eerily uncomfortable. While I thought of many things, Ellen went into the kitchen to wash out her glass. We had no dishwasher, so she did it the hard way. Just to make certain her *t*s were crossed, she wiped it dry. The towel was thrown over her shoulder when she returned.

"Do you really love Simone, or is it an expression of sympathy?"

"That's pretty damned impudent!" I sparked.

"It's strictly rhetorical," she added quickly. "It's something to ponder."

It hurt. There must be other things to keep us occupied until the food arrived.

"Are you angry with me because I was too big a coward to propose to you?"

Ellen pulled the towel from her shoulder and twisted it before draping it around her neck. She sat with one foot under her on the opposite end of the couch. She looked pensive.

"Do you ever think about it?" she asked. "What caused you to obsess over her? What possessed you to talk to Ion that day?"

"I think about that stuff, frequently," I admitted.

"Well, there are two ways to look at it," she began. "As a believer, I consider such outlandish coincidences just another day at the office for God. However, you're skeptical. From your point of view, a lot of atoms and molecules had to join and evolve; all the stars and planets had to move just exactly right for you and Simone to get to where you are today. Your way, Miles, is way, way, way more miraculous. No matter which of these you believe, I'm not going to stand in the way. The forces, whatever their source, are too dangerous to defy."

That profundity made me very uncomfortable. I hated being put on the spot, and I hated metaphysical speculation. I, also, hated Ellen turning the Missouri bar-room tables on me.

"I'm not such a great catch," I submitted, opting out.

"I love you, Miles," she insisted, "but there are times when I want to take a baseball bat to that thick head."

"This is one of those times?"

"Yes! That woman needs to be looked after, not spied upon. You want her to be happy so much that you haven't the nerve to guide her. Do you know how much peanut butter is in that cupboard? The Golden Mean, Miles! Too much junk can't be good—particularly now."

She let it sink in. Then, she slapped my shoulder gently with the flat of her hand.

"This isn't about peanut butter, by the way. You live with her. If you see something or feel something that gives you pause, tell her. You don't have to be a tyrant or any of that, but you owe her the benefit of good judgment and experience. She's smart. You're smarter than you think. If you two team up, you'll get it right, eventually. I'd bet a lot of money on that. Just—well, just don't be afraid to talk with her."

We sat there like two Hummel figurines.

Finally, she got to her feet.

"Let me see if I can put together a salad," she mused more to herself than me.

I was left with thinking to do.

The old house creaked. There was always expansion and contraction going on, but we'd grown used to it. Our ears were skilled at discerning the difference between midnight footfalls and normal nocturnal noises.

Similarly, we were attuned to each other's sleep habits and quirks. For example, I knew when Simone was coming down with a cold or a touch of the flu just by her movements beside me. Similarly, she paid no heed to my flopping around from one side to the other as I slept. Her panic attacks were, we hoped, confined to history. Should one develop, I would be instantly alert before Simone had the opportunity to reach high dudgeon.

On the night of Ellen's stay, however, Simone was particularly queer.

The first time I was jolted into full awareness, Simone lay with her back to me, but her head was an inch or so above the pillow.

"What is it?" I whispered.

"Just listening," she whispered back.

I caught her twice more.

"Is it the baby?" I asked.

"Just listening," she repeated.

Eventually, she got out of bed stealthily. I was groggy and assumed it was her "time." When I realized the absurdity, I was out of bed and beside her.

"What's wrong?" I asked, completely flummoxed.

"Do you think she's okay in there?" she asked in return.

The relief which swept over me was, perhaps, the greatest I'd yet experienced. Just as I was on constant alert when Simone slept in the other room, so was she highly sensitive to any disturbance across the way.

My personal experience delivered me to the conclusion that nothing, short of the sun's morning rays, could assuage the concerns about events in the guest room. Any attempt on my part to reassure Simone was futile. Therefore, I kissed her on the base of her neck.

"I love you," I whispered.

Then, I padded back around the bed and climbed aboard. I left Simone to satisfy herself. She woke me, momentarily, when she rejoined me. She woke me, momentarily, when she got out of bed once more and listened at the door. She woke me, momentarily, when she cocked her head over some unexpected noise.

When Ellen's alarm clock tinged at four o'clock, Simone's feet hit the floor and she bolted for the kitchen. By the time Ellen finished her morning routine, a hot breakfast and fresh coffee were waiting. I left them to it and went back to sleep, preparatory to my eight o'clock departure.

Miraculously, my rest was complete.

CHAPTER FOUR

To avoid feeling a fool in Keatsville, Simone insisted we attend church locally. She remained ambivalent and superstitious about Christianity. Her ancestors were orthodox; her parents each attended church from time to time, but never together. The parent left at home watched the children.

Protestantism was more alien than Romanian orthodoxy. However, if it was good enough for Ellen, it was worthy of Simone's investigation. Thus, we walked around the corner and up the street to a local denomination unknown to me. We made certain communion was not on tap before settling into a pew to get an ear full about bullocks. I didn't pay much attention to the sermon. I suspect Simone didn't either.

We put the matter of the bullocks behind us and kept our newly established custom of going out for lunch after services. We agreed to try a cafeteria-style place at one of the Lima malls and found it amiable enough though we had to fight through a pile of other church-service refugees.

As we sampled bits of anything appetizing, a revolution of sorts was going on in Keatsville. There were no guns or angry words, but there was a decided change.

The properly ordained minister who stepped in to provide the sacraments was not a church grand exalted Pooh-Bah, else he would not have been ordered thither. Nevertheless, he was highly regarded, highly trusted and, most importantly, he had the ears of those in the upper echelons.

Prior to and following the service, this man learned about Ellen's work in bringing a young orphan back to life. The fact that the young scholar was a member of a rival church magnified the act of charity in the eyes of the local citizens. Likewise, Ellen's relationship with the local Padre was viewed as a welcome gesture by those old enough to remember a time when the Catholic-Protestant animus was highly toxic.

The local elders went to bat. They spoke highly of Ellen and urged a permanent assignment—to Keatsville. She was dedicated, responsible, caring and, above all, she was a shining example for the congregation and the community.

Ellen was privy to none of this. She did, however, learn of the vehement argument advanced by one of the church elders.

"We are more comfortable with the devil we know than the devil we don't know."

When she became privy to this statement, Ellen delighted in repeating it. Never did it lose the quality of making her laugh.

Whether the elder's argument carried any weight in the stratosphere of church bureaucracy, the governing powers were fully briefed on local sentiment. There was, also, the very real prospect that Keatsville was not a place for career ministers. Any of the established clergy would take up the vestments wherever sent, but Keatsville was, decidedly, a hardship posting.

On Wednesday, Ellen picked up the phone and conversed with one of the church leaders. She was asked a series of rudimentary questions: How was she doing? Did she face any daunting problems? Was she comfortable? Did she like the community? All the questions were innocuous and mundane. Then came the most amazing interrogative.

"Would you be willing to remain in Keatsville for an eighteen-month appointment?"

She was not prepared for that. Brushing aside the church's obsession with eighteen-month tours, Ellen never saw it coming. She stammered until her mind cleared.

"I'd be proud," she announced.

"Plan on it, then," she was instructed. "We'll get the ball rolling on ordination. Sit tight."

After hanging up, Ellen reclined to wrestle with her emotions. All her doubts had a merry time haunting her for the next several days. She was honored to be considered, but she didn't think she had the patience or the administrative skills.

The one great emotional pillar of this unexpected situation provided her with much needed succor. The chances were excellent that she could perform *the* wedding. There was, also, an excellent chance that the event would come prior to the baby's birth, regardless of the name it inherited.

As the following Sunday was judged *safe*, we attended services in Keatsville. Later, we enjoyed snacks and conversation with Father Bob. There was another reason—the real reason as it turned out. Ellen produced a measuring tape and tied up Simone.

"This is for a wedding present," she insisted, measuring and recording.

In typical Ellen fashion, she made no mention of her pending promotion. Similarly, she failed to mention one of Father Bob's leading parishioners was president of the local school board. One of this man's highly accomplished daughters was a leading element in the county 4-H and, save for the shoes she wore, made every stich of her school clothing. I knew Ellen boasted a blue-ribbon 4-H membership, but this informative tidbit escaped my memory. Nevertheless, Ellen and a high honor-roll student were determined to twist taffeta and become seam-stitchers for a worthy cause.

"Could we drive through Fort Recovery?" my intended asked when free of the talon-like clutches of Keatsville society.

"That's way out of the way," I objected.

"It's, maybe, a dozen extra miles if we go back through Wapak."

I was not bold enough to argue. She shaved several miles off the total, but she performed careful research before suggesting the detour.

I saw an opening.

"I'll make a deal with you," I proposed. "We'll stop at Fort Recovery *if* you ration your peanut butter."

I was prepared for a spirited debate.

"Okay," she agreed instantly.

I suspect she hadn't a first thought, never mind a second one. I was taken aback. Rather than explaining that peanut-butter overload might negatively impact on baby, I got a pass.

"Why are you such a student of history?" I asked, gathering my wits.

"Because I can be," she responded.

I let that pass, but I made a face.

"In Romania, history is easy," she informed. "Everything before Ceausescu was chaos. Everything under Ceausescu is orderly. Anyone with alternate views disappears. I want to know about where I live. It's interesting."

"And," I added, "you are not likely to disappear."

She nodded.

"I'm hungry," I complained.

"Let's be adventurous," she dared. "St. Claire and his survivors were probably starving. They made do. We shall, also."

We briefly examined a greasy spoon along the way. It looked as if no health inspector came within miles of the place. With my stomach singing a baritone aria, we continued until we found a place in Fort Recovery itself.

There was a reconstruction just outside town. After lunch, Simone examined it as if it was an estate listing and we were potential buyers. I was ready to move on after three minutes. Simone's imagination, however, would not let it go. Not without difficulty did I manage to get her strapped back in the car after nearly an hour of supplication.

I, occasionally, develop grand ideas. Had Ellen failed to light a fire under me, certain ideas might never have come to the fore.

The clocking of Simone's peanut butter ingestion was the first of several modifications I (more correctly we) put into place. I expected a battle. While I did catch her with the cupboard open and looking wistfully at the jars inside, Simone never violated our treaty. A jar had to last ten days. That remained excessive; however, compared with her previous consumption, it was a draconian reduction.

Thanks to No, Simone tried Shakespeare. Even in Romania, people knew much of this exceptional poet and playwright. One afternoon she came home from the Allen County Library with an unabridged edition of the Bard's works, I shuttered. I predicted she'd cry and moan like some junior high brat who claimed not to understand a single word. Imagine my surprise when she sat for the better part of an hour reading without complaint.

"Shakespeare invented the word *bedroom*, you know."

No, I did not know. This was but one of several million informative items about which I could have cared absolutely nothing. As previously recorded, Simone focused on details.

"What did they call it before it was a *bedroom*?"

I opened my mouth to reply only to be struck mute. This was another item of no import. Still, since Simone wanted to know, I couldn't leave her with a flippant remark. Instead, I promised to find out.

We sat together and read *Midsummer Night's Dream* aloud. I'd read a character's line and she'd read the subsequent line and so forth. Though I got many lengthy speeches, Simone got the bulk of them. When she felt the need, she'd interrupt with an observation or a question. Nevertheless, it was an enjoyable experience.

My third major modification came about because I asked about her youth. Hitherto, I avoided doing so for fear of dredging up memories she'd buried. I opened Pandora's Box, but not the one I expected.

She went on and on and on about her fishing experiences, climbing and playing in trees and the games she invented with her young friends. She didn't merely recount these experiences, she recreated them. Without exception, her narratives were fascinating!

I wanted to ask about her poetry, but I eschewed duress. However, I didn't thirst for examples. The lyric qualities of her narratives were literary gems. She and Will have much in common.

It was obvious to all that Simone is exceptionally intelligent. If there is a doubting Thomas about, listening to her autobiographical recitations would set that matter to rights.

Out of her panoplies emerged an interesting item proving both useful and slightly dangerous. Simone, at an early age, became a football addict. Anytime she came across an unattended football (*soccer ball* among heathens), Simone would dribble and shoot. This was not popular with the boys. As everyone knew, in the ancient world— that is, the world prior to c. 1975—football was a boys' game and girls weren't welcome.

Simone didn't care. She wanted to play football, and that is exactly what she'd do. She not only practiced with untended balls, she purloined them and practiced in secret. Because of her passion, her practices were intense. At the tender age of six, she realized that she must be better than the boys or they'd not allow her to play.

Shanghaied by an athletic club and forced to skate, Simone had two afternoons a week to herself. Until she was fifteen, she played soccer at every opportunity. There was one memorable day when two of the players came to blows because each wanted Simone on his team.

"Boys fought over me," she announced with pride and delight.

The day following Simone's remembrance, I brought home a soccer ball from Marion. One would have thought I'd presented a priceless gem. Up to that moment, I never saw her so animated.

I cautioned her. She could dribble and shoot all she wanted, but I didn't want her trying to take on Real Madrid in some imagined dream. She was going to have a baby. Though I judged football to be marginally safer than lawn mowing in terms of exercise, I knew from the peanut butter experience that moderation is not her strong suit.

I agreed to participate in back yard soccer. Though it did me good, I took part only as a means of supervising her.

It was the better part of a decade since Simone played. Her skills were rusty. Rusty or no, she was amazing. She dared me to guard her, to take the ball away if I could. It was as futile as tying grow a chair. Simone could stop, change direction and slither past even if I had her trapped against the garage. On our first outing, she dribbled her way toward the house with me, wearing a mask of determination, standing in her way. I charged; she drop-stepped and, by slight of foot, took the ball with her; she stepped down, and the ball popped up; she gave it a tap with her knee for elevation, bopped it with her forehead and arched it over my head. As I watched the ball travel through the afternoon calm, Simone slid around my left side, blocked me with her shoulder, met the ball behind me and was off quicker than a prom dress.

I just stood there with my teeth in my mouth and a stupid expression on my face. I'd been made an utter fool, but I was too stunned to be upset. Anger at my ineptitude, the ball or, for that matter, Simone was impossible. The delight on her face and the laughter she emitted were intoxicating.

I heard Simone laugh before. It was pleasing but reserved. It was as if she were afraid someone might ridicule her for being happy. On that day, however, and in the circumstances described, she let go with a cacophony of mirth that left me disarmed. She wasn't laughing at me, nor was she much amused by my imbecilic countenance. Simone's uninhibited laughter was an expression of unbounded joy. She'd rediscovered an old friend.

My self-appointed duties as a supervisor were put to the test that first day. As much as I was in awe with her agility, I was completely mesmerized by her delight. So addicted was I, that I nearly forgot the circumstances. Exercise might be good for mother, but baby was getting a ride; that mightn't be so good.

Ellen mentioned the Golden Mean. Alas, and confound it, I'm a subscriber.

Reluctantly, after a spirited twenty-minute workout, I called a halt.

Still giddy and smiling, Simone wiped her brow with the back of her hand and turned for the door. Automatically, I bent over to pick up the ball.

"Just leave it," she insisted.

Her smile was so broad I feared her teeth might chap. Behind her joyous expression, however, there lurked a hint of warning; she didn't want that ball inside. I read her thoughts. Wisely, I left the sphere exactly where it lay. There were few neighbor children in our vicinity to seize this opportunity.

Simone made an offering to her childhood.

The following night, we were in our Toledo home away from home. The manager ensured the same room for our twice monthly visits. It was not a deluxe room; the company would never spring for it. Nevertheless, it was clean, pleasant, and capacious. Our familiarity with the chamber made it more comfortable than it was. Simone dubbed it the *Toledo cocoon.*

The moment we entered, she snatched up the chocolate-mint candy from her side of the bed and stashed it away for home use. At some point during the evening, she'd find a way to sneak the candy away from my side of the bed. I'd smell her minty breath soon after.

"The nutrition dictator always let me have some chocolate before practice or a performance," she once told me. "She thought it gave me an energy boost. It was the highlight of any day."

She reported this with a smile on her face, but her eyes told me the truth.

On the nightstand Simone placed the Allen County Library edition of Shakespeare. When she went back to the car to fetch a bag of snack crackers she'd purchased, I decided to select our evening's reading. We'd read *Midsummer* and *All's Well* together. Simone had dispatched *Romeo* and *The Tempest* on her own. I was leaning toward *Twelfth Night.*

I lay on the bed and, being sinfully lazy, instigated a virtuoso act of clumsiness. The volume slipped through my hand and onto the floor. Out of fear that I damaged an old and worn publication, I let go with two words I never exercised in Simone's presence. I rolled over to the edge of the bed and reached for the anthology. The pages were splayed out and folded up, so I gripped each end of the binding and lifted slowly.

A scrap of paper remained on the floor. I recognized a page from a memo book we kept at home for jotting down shopping needs. Even from a distance I realized it was not a list though it bore an uncanny resemblance to one. Several words were lined through and replaced. A few amendments were lined through and amended again.

Curiosity spurred me on; I braced my back against the head-board and read.

> Born a slave
> > a drudge
> > a tool
> A life grows within
> > a votive to freedom
> > a child of the light

A chill raced up my spine.

Ellen told me Simone dabbled in lyric poems. If this sample was representative, I'd employ an alternate term.

Instinctively, I flipped the paper over and discovered a second composition. It was nearly impossible to read since there were lines and blackouts and corrections overlapping. Two lines ran vertical along the edge of the paper.

> Arid waste
> > bleak, foreboding
> Endless highway
> > black, dismal

Vanishing point
    distant, mocking
Center line
    White, broken

Should have stopped long ago!

Drive on and on and on and on
    for miles.
    for Miles.

Right on cue, the key entered the lock and the door opened. Simone closed the door behind her. The smile on her face vanished the moment she recognized the paper. A casual observer might well believe from Simone's reaction that I'd discovered evidence of murder. I was startled by the fright radiating from her visage.

"I wasn't snooping," I explained. "I dropped the book."

It was the truth and perfectly innocuous. Nevertheless, I felt as foolish as a dupe holding a smoking gun and standing over a body. Innocence stood no chance against appearances.

A myriad of alternatives was open to the Romanian expat. She could call me names for prying into her private thoughts; she could throw the plastic bag and its contents at my head; she could make up some impossible excuse for her scribbles; she could walk out on me and seek the solace of aloneness. Instead, she stood and trembled and quaked.

I was off the bed in a shot. I put one arm around her shoulders and with the other led her to the edge of the bed. I sat her down. She clutched the bag with both hands as if protecting it. She kept her eyes averted and her head bowed.

I experienced panic. Had I so upset or shocked her that the baby was in danger? No, I decided. Simone would never sit submissively if she felt her child threatened.

"Here," I offered holding out the paper.

Somehow, I thought if I could return her thoughts, she'd recover. Instead, she pushed my hand away, none too gently. That brought me to my knees in penitence.

"What is it? What have I done?"

At this juncture, I'd have confessed to waging biological warfare in Bolivia if it would elicit some human response from the mannequin seated on the bed.

She turned her head away and dabbed at her eyes with the knuckle of her right hand.

"I never meant for you to see those," she whispered.

"Why? Why do you not want me to see these?"

"They're not good!" she howled. "They are not ready! They're so—stupid."

I relaxed.

"Ellen said you send her poems," I informed. "You must intend for someone to see them."

"Not you, Miles. You're too close."

She was regaining her equilibrium.

"I—think—things I—probably—should not think. I explore the darkness and discover horrors. I write them down and send them away. I get them away, so they are—gone. When they're far away, they don't haunt me."

She gulped and labored for breath.

"In the—old, horrible days, I write things down—things I'm not allowed. I keep them hidden. When we leave the country, I leave them on busses, in closets, under beds. When we return home, my horrors are—away; I can breathe again. Then, other fears come and—I write them away."

Whatever *it was*, it was running out of steam. I realized that I'd have my hands full, but this situation was one I could address.

I sat beside her. I put my arm around her and drew her to me. She rested her head on my shoulder and relaxed.

"There is nothing you can say or write that will turn me against you," I promised. "Sometimes the load gets pretty heavy. We can share it."

"Oh, Miles! You don't know. You cannot understand what I run from."

"Try me," I dared.

She didn't reply.

After several moments, I turned her head toward me. She refused to look me in the eye, but I waited her out.

"You said you believed in me," I reminded.

She swallowed hard and nodded.

"Give me a chance," I pleaded. "If you don't want me to read your work—well, I can live with that. But, Simone, please don't go to pieces if I stumble across something."

I waved the paper at her.

"These are gone."

I went to the desk and opened the drawer. Next to Gideon were two sheets of motel stationery and matching envelopes. Returning to my distraught roommate, I begged her to watch as I slipped the memo paper into the envelope. I sealed it.

When next I saw it, the envelope lay on a café table. It remained in Toledo with our breakfast dishes.

Should have stopped long ago.
That haunted *me*.

I ached to ask about her suicide attempt. Judging by the marks on her arms, she'd no excuse to be alive. It must have been a rapid and exceedingly bloody scene. It was magnified thousands of times by my ignorance. Still, I could not demand she tell me how she survived. It was her nightmare. If she willed it, she'd share. If not, my probing would provoke her.

Simone White nee Albescu was the last person on the planet I'd antagonize.

CHAPTER FIVE

The phone rang. It was Ellen. She sounded excited and scolded me for not answering her calls the previous night. "We were in Toledo," I said, in self-defense.

"The wedding is on. Give me a date. You want inside or outside? You want formal, casual? You want a catered reception? Talk it over. Call me."

Click.

CHAPTER SIX

With no relatives and few friends, most of the details were easily ironed out. Simone and I conferenced for fewer than twenty minutes after which she lifted the phone and dialed Ellen.

We waited until the following morning to secure a week and a day off. I'd earned more than that, but Simone and I figured we'd honeymooned already. We'd be content to take it easy at home or pursue one or two of her historical interests.

I accepted verbal confirmation of my time off though, by company policy, my leave did not become official prior to written notice. There was no reason to assume that such permission would be withheld. Even if it were, I had enough sick days to cover my bet.

I called Max *way* early the following morning to invite him. The warning came too late, however, his appointment calendar overfloweth. He sent his best wishes and promised, if he sprouted a pair of wings, he'd come, but don't expect him. James was willing to take a day off work, but he doubted he could leave on short notice. He still waited table; however, he bought into the establishment and was a junior partner. He had inherited managerial duties.

Simone considered inviting a pair of former students from Wowo. In the end, she decided against it. None of my friends was likely to show, and Simone wouldn't stack the deck. Never comfortable in a crowd, her joy was inversely proportional to the guest list.

KISS: Keep it simple, Stupid. It mightn't be a Romanian maxim, but it, apparently, was a hallmark of the Albescu family.

Wednesday evening, Ellen called to check in. I was to bring two six packs each of root beer and ginger ale, a gallon of apple cider and two bottles of fruit juice—preferably cranberry cocktail.

I didn't mind, but I was nonplussed.

"That will be a ransom demand," she advised. "That and a couple bags of ice, but you can get those here."

I eyed Simone who stood next to me. She eagerly awaited her turn to speak with Reverend Good.

"Who will take Simone hostage?"

I was concerned. I didn't want my bride carted off by strangers. I didn't want a celebration to become the basis of another of her nightmares.

"Father Bob will drive the get-away car," Ellen promised. "Noah will stuff her in."

I repeated this information to Simone. After I handed the phone over, she expressed concern over the deficiency of one maid-of-honor and one best man. Ellen promised to handle the details. I was dubious. Still, Ellen could pull rabbits out of a hat.

We arrived in mid-afternoon. Ellen took us to the Hotel Good, a.k.a. the Parsonage. Simone and I would share the guest room that night with the proviso that I clear out immediately the following morning. It wouldn't take long to prepare Simone for the eleven o'clock wedding. I, therefore, assumed Ellen required time alone with the bride-to-be.

Noah arrived by bus that evening, and Ellen drove to Decatur to fetch him. He'd stay with Father Bob in the parish guest house—a bedroom and bathroom detached from but only two yards behind the *vicarage* (Ellen's diction).

As the school busses roared out of the circle drive across the street, a solitary figure approached. She was not particularly attractive but tall and immaculately dressed. Her dirty-blonde hair was alluringly disordered, her figure sleek and her legs long and sturdy. She wore light blue skirt with a knee-length hem, a matching vest and a white blouse. For a high-school student, she was impressively togged.

This was Marie Schortmann, a precocious sophomore. She possessed intelligent, penetrating green eyes; they appeared to appraise and catalogue everything. She was a four-point student, creditable athlete and a student body officer. In a larger, less familial community, people would assume that her social, varsity sports and political office were tangible results of her father's clout on the school board. Any thoughts Simone and I had along those lines vanished within minutes. Judging by her speech patterns, poise and mode of expression, I was prepared, despite her tender age, to recommend her for admission to any college or university she fancied.

Cultured and well-mannered, Marie quickly won over Simone whose natural reticence around strangers is frequently mistaken for snobbishness. She sat with us and sipped tea from a cup and saucer with all the aplomb of a finishing school graduate. Her questions about Romania were substantive and intelligent. Her comments were terse but razor sharp. Despite her social graces and intellectual perspicacity, there was not the slightest hint of self-importance.

Marie is a *lady*, struck from the mold of a previous century.

After coffee, tea and an entertaining chat, Ellen suggested that Marie produce her *magnum opus*. For the first time the young scholar's countenance reflected apprehension.

"We had to work from very small photographs," she began. "We had to guess at colors."

"Marie is too modest," Ellen injected. "She always says *we*, but I had very little to do with this. She tore around Fort Wayne for a weekend looking for fabrics and a pattern. I merely lent a hand here and there."

Marie smiled at the Reverend Good, but she effectively communicated her declination. She and Ellen were peas in a pod; neither would accept credit for cooperative efforts. The smile Marie flashed was, I am positive, a tacit continuation of previous conversations.

There were no closets in the anterior portion of the house. Thus, Marie disappeared for several seconds and returned with a gown sheathed in clear plastic. As if handling antique china, Marie turned to one side and allowed the garment to enjoy a gentle gravity assist.

Fashion illiterate though I was, I recognized that the merchandise on display was *not* taffeta. I suspected cotton. It was white with long, puffy sleeves. There was red piping about the neck and on either side of the buttons which ran down the front. There were also red, geometric designs across the bodice and over the shoulders. Predictably, the hem displayed a good two inches of the same design.

Simone gasped and buried her amazed expression behind hands pressed to her face.

"Do you like it?" Ellen asked, not able to comprehend Simone's reaction.

Simone, literally, could not speak. The tears forming in the corners of her eyes communicated volumes.

"She likes it," I assured.

Simone bounced on her toes and fanned her face with her hands.

"That's Roma—nean," she stuttered.

Only I caught the gaff. *Roma* is Romanian for *Gypsy*.

Simone was ambivalent about the ethnic group. Regardless, the Roma constituted a profound and distinctive weave in the Romanian fabric. The dress was a tangible expression of "home."

Rarely have I seen her so unabashedly emotional. When the shock wore off, she awarded both Ellen and Marie intense, heartfelt hugs.

"I can get married in this, can't I?" she asked of all assembled.

"We rather hoped you would," Ellen replied.

"Oh, Miles! It must have taken weeks! How can we ever repay you?"

"We'll think of something," Ellen assured.

Simone's response constituted complete recompense.

Simone tried it on. The seamstresses inspected closely. The dress was designed to accommodate a bulging stomach; Simone didn't (yet) fill that void. Realizing it was easier to take in than let out, the 4H conspirators plotted overnight alterations. As expected, Simone was uncomfortable with being touched and fussed over, but feelings for her benefactors squelched most of her inhibitions.

Ellen Good was a trusted friend of longstanding. Marie's admittance into her personal *Panamician* (I struggle for terms) took mere seconds. Simone rated Marie a guardian angel—if not a goddess. In the unlikely event that Marie Schortmann ever stood before a firing squad, Simone Albescu wouldn't hesitate to take her place.

Doubtless, people will classify the previous sentence as hyperbolic. Ha!

Ellen, even in her official capacity, was no stickler for formalities. Simone and I, however, would be her first matrimonial victims. She felt obligated to give a nod to custom. Noah, therefore, would stand up for me at the ceremony. Similarly, with Simone's blessing, Marie would be the emergency seamstress—just in case.

I wouldn't be so bold as to apply the terms *best man* and *maid-of-honor* for what was, essentially, the marital equivalent of a pick-up softball game. Nevertheless, the dress, a symbol of Simone's cultural heritage, touched her deeply. Despite her vow never to return to *that horrible place*, she never—for a moment—renounced her Romanian roots.

It was during the fitting of the "bridal gown" that I removed a page of memo paper from my pocket. I waited until Simone was looking before thrusting it into Ellen's hand. The bride-to-be nodded appreciatively. Her troubled verses, scribbled in an alien language, were safely removed from her Cridersville environs. She was free of them. When the next round of nightmarish thoughts arrived, she'd take up her pen anew.

I was rousted from a sound sleep and hustled out of the Parsonage early because "it's bad luck to see the bride before the ceremony."

No one in our party believed this claptrap, but I refused to buck tradition. I'd seen Simone in Innsbruck and, from my selfish vantage point, it hadn't proved the least unlucky. Ellen, however, had a secret agenda.

Noah came by and drove me in his sister's car to the café, just a short walk from Ellen's house of worship. There we joined Father Bob for breakfast. I surprised my parole officers by ordering a gut-buster.

"I'm hungry," I reported in response to their incredulous expressions.

"Aren't you nervous?" Noah asked.

It was my turn to look incredulous.

"You must be daft," I concluded.

"I'm nervous," No admitted.

It was Ellen's first time at bat with a sacrament. I didn't understand why *he* should be nervous. It would be a tiny crowd; if Ellen stumbled, there'd be few witnesses. Moreover, what could happen? The official portion of the day consisted of Simone and I signing our names to a document. It would take a dedicated genius to mess that up.

I never really had an opportunity to speak with Father Bob before. I found him affable. Over breakfast, his conversation sparkled. It was no surprise that Ellen and he were friends.

The only discouraging word was his mentioning that the Romanian Orthodox Church had its roots in the pre-schismatic Roman Church. My sarcastic bent pricked me to proclaim this intelligence as a "major news bulletin!" Perhaps, he thought I wasn't fully aware of my fiancé's heritage. Somehow, I doubted he could be so shallow.

"We're not marrying outside the faith, Father," I began, perhaps, too glibly. "Simone was not brought up in any faith. Just between you, me—and No Good here, I think Simone thirsts for a spiritual home, but her experiences retard her. She believes in the concrete— and the aesthetic. That may change, but she must find her own way."

Father Bob leaned back and momentarily showed the palms of his hands as if to say that he'd no intention of proselytizing. He'd never do such a thing behind Ellen's back, and he, certainly, wouldn't employ me as a conduit. I suspect he was easing his conscience over participating in a conspiracy that mightn't meet with his bishop's approval.

"*Among*," Noah announced.

Both Father Bob and I eyed him suspiciously.

"You said *between*," he explained. "*Between you and me* is correct. However, there are three of us sitting here, so the proper preposition is *among*, not *between*."

"This is Keatsville," my clerical friend explained. "We speak Adams County here. It's a Midwestern variant of Merican."

Noah wasn't showing off. He was part of a movement waging war against annoying grammatical errors. I sympathized. My skin crawls whenever people use the word *less* when they mean *fewer*. When attempting to correct this trespass, I often met with the same how-dare-you expressions Father Bob and I sent No's way.

"Fight the good fight, No," I advised. "I, for one, appreciate it."

Poor Noah. He was destined to be the second Good in family history to obtain a collegiate education. Such minor, seemingly inconsequential, manifestations of resentment might cause him to question the value of his studies.

In the beginning, I liked him because he was Ellen's brother, *and* he was polite. Over time, I liked him for himself. My conscience would never leave me in peace if I hurt or offended him.

The newspaper, *The Keatsville Weekly*, got wind of the pending nuptials. It was a typical small-town publication, limited to covering school activities and farm news. The bulk of the six-page paper was taken up with the court docket, police blotter and columns about who had visited whom and who was out of town or participating in county events. For weddings, there'd be a photo and feature on the bride, groom and their respective histories. Since the locals knew these things, interest was confined to ensuring one's name was correctly included in the guest list.

This wedding was different. Simone and I were from out of town and out of state. Buckeyes are not viewed favorably in Indiana.

Perhaps, the editor hoped to promote a scandal or, alternatively, to take advantage of a suspicious anomaly. Regardless, we were stuck with a photographer *and* a reporter—an honor seldom granted.

We were friends of Ellen and hardly strangers. People in Ellen's congregation knew basic salient facts about us. They knew, for example, that Simone was a refugee. One person found out about Simone's Olympic appearances. That made her a celebrity. Were Keatsville a city, and, had the city a key, Simone would have been presented it forthwith.

The upshot was that our tiny wedding party constituted the biggest event in local history since a tornado touched down and demolished Farmer Bob's (nearly empty) grain silo. That historic event occurred twenty-some years previously.

Neither Simone nor I would survive a massive turn-out of gate crashers. Fortunately, Ellen kept the time and location of our marriage a closely guarded secret; so much so that the photographer followed me about town while the reporter kept the Parsonage under surveillance. It was unnerving, so I invited the middle-aged, farmer *cum* camera-toting journalist to join our party.

It was not within his assigned duties, but the thin, sinewy, and casually dressed man was consumed with curiosity; he could not refrain from interviewing me. As he took no notes, I had no idea how much information would be reliably passed to the reporter. My bet was that all the biographical information would be mangled when the paper appeared the following Wednesday.

Frankly, Scarlet—etc.

When the time came, Father Bob drove me to the secret location.

There was a small bower in the most recent subdivision. A small but determined contingent insisted that the idyllic slice of Adams County be salvaged and converted into small city park. With the trees in fine, spring greenery and surrounded by a profusion of wildflowers, including a clump of wild strawberries, it was a worthy wedding venue.

Next to the "park," on a corner lot, sat an unfinished house. The high school carpentry class erected a new house every year. Most were simple dwellings, but this one was a massive three-bedroom home with a two-car garage. Because the local businesses discounted the cost of materials, and labor costs were minimal, the place—once finished—would go on the market for an insanely modest price. The photographer informed us that people from as far away as Wowo were interested in buying.

Mother and Father Schortmann arrived within seconds. They climbed out of their car and introduced themselves. They weren't exactly invited guests, but there were no objections to their presence. Mr. Schortmann felt his daughter was sure to be seen by all and sundry during school hours. His presence, therefore, would quash rumors that Marie was running wild.

There was a more practical reason for a school board official to be on hand. Marie's elder sister would graduate from high school in a few weeks. If she followed local custom, she'd cross the stage, accept her diploma, and get married before leaving the gym. Even though there was no son-in-law on the horizon at that moment, the Schortmann family was eager to watch Marie perfecting the skills she'd require in future.

"No flowers?" Mrs. Schortmann asked.

She was trim and attractive for her age. She made no attempt to use cosmetic weaponry against the distinguished gray amid her light brown tresses. A typical, hard-working farm wife, she'd raised a brood in her time. Still handsome, she was fetching in her light skirt and vest. Of course, she had a nice flower on her left lapel.

This woman didn't strike me as the type to criticize; *ergo*, no offense was taken.

"Everything is in Reverend Good's hands," I reported. "I just follow orders."

We engaged in convivial conversation until Ellen drove up and parked behind Father Bob's vehicle. She got out on the driver's side while Marie, in a beige suit right out of *Vogue* and with a layer of too-bold lipstick, flew from the rear door to assist the bride. Noah brought up the rear.

Wow!

That's the best I can do.

Unlike those grooms who *feel* as if they're seeing their intended for the first time when she comes up the aisle, I had no such delusion. She was the same Simone Albescu I saw in Innsbruck a dozen years before. The difference was that her smile was a regular feature of her countenance, and she wore a dress which made her—in my eyes—as beautiful in appearance as she is in character. There was evidence that she was not alone inside that dress, but one must look carefully—or suspiciously—to notice.

"There are your flowers," I informed Mrs. Schortmann.

I, on a very good day, can tell the difference between a carnation and a rose. Beyond that I remain botanically illiterate. So, Mrs. Schortmann wore a nice yellow something while Simone clutched a profusion of small somethings—a mix of three somethings to be more precise. In my eyes, of course, Simone would have looked gorgeous carrying a sack of garbage.

Ellen opted to do the service devoid of superfluous jiggerypokery. She wore a dark skirt and a mauve tunic. She, too, was beautiful.

Father Bob discretely retired to the get-away car. This was, after all, a Protestant ceremony and was better witnessed from afar. I, however, couldn't keep away from my bride. Unable to control myself, I put my hand on her arm, leaned forward and kissed her hello.

"Here, here!" Ellen playfully scolded. "None of that, now! Simone, you hussy!"

"I'm guilty," I confessed in defense of by betrothed.

Ellen then greeted the four guests—Mr. and Mrs. Schortmann, the photographer, and the reporter. After a few seconds of idle chit-chat, she asked us if we would like to stand in the shade or in the light.

"It's such a nice day," Simone observed. "The sun feels so nice."

"Well, let me stand over there," Ellen suggested, marching a dozen feet further away from the road. "I want the sun behind me."

I was in a daze. Ellen might have read form a chemistry textbook for all I knew—or cared. During the *postmortem*, Marie was gently scolded by her mother for standing practically shoulder to shoulder with Simone during the exchange of vows. I didn't notice. I doubt Simone did. For such a tiny and informal ceremony, we were as nervous and fogged up as if we were in Westminster Abby amid thousands.

We didn't say *I do*. Instead, we said, simply, *Fac.*

Perhaps, we should have warned Ellen. It didn't matter. The tone of our voices and the looks Simone and I exchanged required no interpreter.

There was one tiny glitch. I was to remove the ring from Simone's engagement finger and slide it over the wedding finger— the artery that ran from the finger directly to the heart, according to European lore. (At the risk of being pedantic, I always assumed that arteries ran *from* the heart.)

Due to Simone's condition, her fingers were swollen. Getting the ring off was a chore.

"Take your time," Ellen whispered. "We won't go on without you."

Finally, finally, I got the wedding band free without having to sever the finger. There followed a grueling several seconds during which the world stopped while I got that ring past a mountain of a knuckle.

We proceeded. We got a Protestant blessing after which I got to kiss the bride.

No kiss was ever sweeter.

"Are we done now?" Noah muttered *sotto voce*.

"Quite," Ellen replied.

In the proverbial trice, Noah was behind Simone and had his left arm loosely around her neck. Just a few months before, the woman would struggle and make a vocal row over such treatment. On our wedding day, however, she giggled.

"Noah, really!" Ellen said in exasperation.

No produced a tiny squirt gun and brandished it in his right fist.

"Don't move anyone!" he growled between gritted teeth. "I'm a desperate man!"

Only Noah, Ellen, Simone and I knew this was scripted—well, only Noah knew about the squirt gun. The poor, bemused bystanders at this farrago hadn't a clue. It might have gotten messy had Noah played his part too well.

"Okay, skirt, into the car."

Simone giggled once more and handed her bouquet to Ellen.

"Hold this, please," she said before being spirited away.

"*Ajutor!*"

She attempted a yell, but it was a supreme effort to stifle a laugh. Thus, Simone's cry for help was little more than a comedic squeak. I waved to her.

"Marie," Ellen whispered. "I'd feel better if you went along."

Marie remained nonplussed but obeyed.

"*Ajutor!*" Simone attempted once more.

"Don't shoot or I will move!" Noah warned.

"God, give me strength!" Ellen muttered between clinched teeth.

Gently, Noah opened the rear door and eased Simone into the seat. Still waving his toy, he slid in beside her.

"*Ajutor!*" Simone called, more dramatically than previously.

It would have been more effective had she yelled before buckling in.

Marie, whose trust in Father Bob was absolute, calmly got into the passenger seat and strapped herself in.

"The gun was too much," Ellen sighed. "And this—"

She held up the bridal bouquet.

"Simone did this on purpose," she concluded.

"She knows nothing of our wedding customs," I argued.

"You lie," she insisted. "I forgive you, though—I guess."

As Father Bob fled from the scene at all of twenty miles an hour, I turned to find the Schortmann contingent, a reporter, and a stunned camera man looking at us as if we had just spit on the wedding cake. As always, it was Ellen who had the presence of mind to salvage the situation.

"It's a Romanian thing," she calmly informed.

I took Ellen by the arm to lead her toward her car.

"Miles, aren't you forgetting something?"

I did my best, but I came up blank.

"Was I supposed to kiss the maid-of-honor?" I asked, hopefully.

"No, you big Lugen," she responded. "You're expected to invite these people to the reception."

I turned to find all eyes fixed upon me. I couldn't tell if they were staring at an insane man or if they waited, politely, for a ceremonial conclusion.

"Of course, you're invited," I assured.

We were at the Parsonage enjoying a delightful conversation. The phone rang forty minutes after the abduction. Apparently, Noah and Simone fell into an animated literary discussion and forgot why they were in the community hall. Ellen took the call and eyed me closely.

"The ransom demand just went up," she reported. "They want a jar of peanut butter and Noah wants a kiss."

"I'm not kissing Noah," I replied.

"He wants to kiss the bride."

I looked at Ellen.

"Simone speaks for herself," I announced. "Noah must negotiate that independently."

"Why don't we get the ice and we'll meet you at the hall?" Mr. Schortmann suggested.

"Peanut butter," I reminded.

Ellen dashed into the kitchen and came out with a jar. She tossed it to me. It was light. I unscrewed the lid and found it was only a quarter full.

"Perfect," I announced.

The Keatsville Community Hall housed a tiny kitchen, the city hall and a lending library consisting of, perhaps, five hundred volumes— nearly half of which were aimed at children and teens. It was a squat building with a flat roof to invite disaster during heavy snows. Built in the early fifties, it was perched atop a hill roughly halfway between the school and the town square. This location assured that it would catch the wind from any direction, thus, guaranteeing a perpetual chill.

Some enterprising local artist had, without promise of emoluments, created a mural on the eastern wall of the social room. Running chronologically from left to right, it featured highlights of American history from the sailing of the *Mayflower* to *Apollo XI*. It couldn't hold a candle to the Sistine Chapel, but it was a huge draw locally. Clubs and organizations, including the VFW (which had its own building) reserved the room for meetings. If any assembly became dull or cumbersome, one could admire the details contained in the mural.

Father Bob and Reverend El conspired to make a cassette of celebratory music for the so-called reception. *Romanian Rhapsody* (*No. 1*) and *Indiana* (by a Goodman quintet) were featured on each side of the tape. However, the co-conspirators realized that two tunes did not an album make. Thus, they included a smattering of their personal favorites. Father Bob opted for a slice of RimskyKorsakov's *Scheherazade* and a ditty by Schubert (no prize for identifying which one). Reverend El countered with *Leibestraum* by Liszt and—wait for it—hits of Elton John, Olivia Newton-John and The Captain and Tennille. As the walls of the library and the city hall were paper thin, the industrial-strength cassette player threatened to drive the city employees out of their gourds. During our time there, I fully expected a visit from the local SWAT team, Sherriff Andy and Deputy Barney.

Ellen made a modest sheet cake for us. Both it and the icing were created from scratch and, as with all her culinary efforts, the confection was superb. I had the honor to carry in this feast for the eyes and palate. There was a bevy of periwinkles in the upper right and lower left corners and double, overlapping hearts in the center with an arrow through and a winged Cupid flitting merrily above.

There was a cross formed by the intersection of our names, a vertical Miles and a horizontal Simone with the *M* shared.

"Isn't Cupid a pagan symbol?" I asked at the parsonage.

Ellen, occupied with something else, paid more attention to her task than to me.

"They never took out a copyright," she said off-handedly, "bad luck for them."

As we entered, the tape-player pumped out a nocturne, the instrumental prelude of Humperdinck's "Children's Prayer" from *Hansel und Gretel*. There was no difficulty in hearing the music as I entered the door and made my way down the hall past the city office. I knew not what I expected, but it wasn't what I beheld.

Marie, No and Father Bob were sitting at a table along with the city clerk and the librarian watching Simone dance. It was slow tempo; therefore, Simone's movements were slow, deliberate and polished. I recognized maneuvers from Innsbruck and Chicago. There were no skates, but a dance routine is, alas, a dance routine.

The tables were arranged in a large *U* with folding chairs arranged around the perimeter. As a result, Simone had the bulk of the tiled floor to herself. Her leaps, pirouettes and expansive arm gestures were in no way inhibited. I couldn't fail to notice the intense concentration on her face, but there was something more: she was smiling! This was not some pasted-on imitation for the benefit of scorers; this was a smile, small and delicate, radiating a warmth impossible to counterfeit.

So amazed and stunned was I that I froze in the door frame. Behind me, loaded down as she was with sodas and cider, Ellen stood patiently, without a word of protest. She was as memorized as I, though she had to peer over and around my shoulder.

Listening to the music and watching Simone dance, I imagined her gilding silently, confidently, effortlessly over the ice.

Of course, she was trained in dance. Ballet constituted an essential part of her skating. Mr. Moron, of course, would never consider such obvious facts until witnessing her stepping delicately and silently on the floor in shoes never intended for such use.

She was inhibited by the limitations of her beautiful dress. She could not, therefore, pull her foot up behind her head, or balance on one leg while the other leg and her body formed right angles—nor could she perform splits. Nevertheless, she put on a show which ended with her in a crouch. In her skating program, she concluded with a dying swan (my image since I never bothered to learn the nomenclature). She folded her legs impossibly, leaned forward with her body while extending her arms up and behind in a pose impossible for mere mortals.

I knew she'd perform this final bow. What concerned me was, given her condition, untangling herself. Alas, as in most things, Simone made it look effortless.

The applause of only five people was copious.

"Move, Miles!" Ellen hissed.

The spell was broken.

I pivoted to the side and Ellen rushed to the nearest table before she lost her grip on the large, and heavy, juice containers. Father Bob, alerted to our presence, jumped up and hurried up the hall to retrieve the remainder of the ransom. Not to be denied the opportunity to pitch in, Noah relieved me of the cake. As he admired it, Simone came over to coo.

"Who did that?" she asked, awestruck.

"Sis."

Ellen was shaking her hands vigorously to re-establish circulation.

"Marie helped," she added.

Noah was skeptical. He knew Ellen's work too well to be duped by imitations.

"Marie, probably, pre-heated the oven," he whispered to Simone.

Somehow, the cake made it onto the refreshment table. The representatives of the press entered and peppered the bride with eclectic questions. I invited the city's lady employees to join in liquid refreshment. Ellen, her arms revived, slid past the reporters to hug Simone and offer congratulations. Father Bob returned with the residuals and inquired about ice.

This was as confusing as it got. All was merriment.

When the Schortmann elders entered with two bags of ice, the party took off.

Noah demanded the payment of the remainder of the ransom. He and Simone embraced and succeeded in making me very jealous.

"That's my wife!" I reminded.

"Do you hear her complaining?" he asked.

Simone, highly embarrassed, grinned at me with face aflame.

"I don't do divorces," Ellen announced. "You're on your own."

Noah turned to Marie.

"Can I kiss the maid-of-honor?" he asked.

Marie took a step back and, also, turned scarlet.

"Not today," she said, attempting to mask her horror with laughter.

As obtuse as Mr. Moron is, I thought Marie *might* have allowed herself the liberty had her parents not been present. Regardless, I think her *not-today* response was something one might find in Freud's index.

The party grew when two elderly ladies dropped by to see why the office was unattended. After school dismissal, Marie's elder sister appeared.

Maureen was shorter than her sister by almost a head. They shared a similar physique, however, and their personalities and smiles were nearly identical. Maureen wore store-bought clothes. Still, as I watched the two together, I detected no hint of sibling rivalry. They acted like best friends.

By the time we cut the cake, we'd attracted a crowd.

Who knew who half the people were? Who cared?

Simone held up a slice of cake for me to sample. When I had enough home-made icing on my face, Father Bob and the camera-man each snapped our photo. Before I could properly smear cake over Simone, she insisted that I add a dab of peanut butter.

"Careful of the dress," she requested.

I was. I made double sure to hit only her mouth. When we got the photos a week later, Simone stood pristine and smiling next to Bozo the Clown.

It was a festive time, and, without exaggeration, I never saw Simone so happy for such a prolonged period. Heading back to Cridersville, just ahead of the setting sun, she alternated between humming and laughing at her own jokes.

There remains a single addendum to our perfect day.

Ellen trusted her brother to carry out the kidnapping with dignity and decorum. When he pulled out the water gun, however, he crossed a line. Too gracious and too aware of her official position to launch into Noah in public, Ellen could not allow the transgression to go unpunished.

During the excitement of the afternoon, I saw her lift that gun and hide it away. Perhaps, she thought she was being sneaky. As a thief, however, Ellen hadn't the skills, the furtiveness or the amorality to do it well. I let her know her nefarious actions were observed.

"What are you doing with that pistol?" I asked.

She looked about guiltily

"One day, when we're alone, I'll get him."

I have it, on the best authority, that she kept her word.

The Beginning

When men of infamy to grandeur soar
They light a torch to show their shame all the more.
Those governments which curb not evils, cause!

Edward Young (1683-1765)

Te iubesc is only slightly less vapid than *I love you*. Save for ceremonial purposes, Simone and I seldom used either; we had other ways to communicate our feelings. When she looked at me or sent me a smile, I knew exactly what she was saying. Similarly, she would take my arm, kiss my cheek or give me a hug for no reason other than the manifestation of her feelings. For my part, I'd take her arm or drape my own around her shoulders and draw her close. While seated together, I enjoyed stroking her hair; it, frequently, annoyed her, but she appreciated the sentiment.

Simone's hair is rather coarse, but it's hers. That makes it priceless. I could stroke it for hours.

In public we seldom kissed, lip to lip. Simone grew up in a culture where signs of affection can be used against both parties. Away from prying eyes, we were not inhibited.

After the wedding, I learned much more about my wife. She imparted autobiographical snippets. She was ever reluctant to share her *former* life, but I was part of her family. There are many things she'll never tell, and I respect that. The things she did relate were hair-raising enough. I daren't imagine what she kept locked away. Nevertheless, I gained understanding of certain habits and idiosyncrasies.

Simone Albescu was paranoid. One did not turn one's back on the Ceausescus. As with many tyrants, they demanded adoration, devotion and obedience. By escaping the country, Simone sentenced her family to cruel punishment. Alas, there was no way of knowing their fate. Should Simone attempt to contact her parents or to inquire about their health, it would be considered a criminal and hostile act prompting greater sanctions on those left behind. Thus, we festered.

Simone was a small fry in terms of national-celebrity status. Still, her defection constituted a finger in Ceausescu's eye. He may not have had friends, but he was feared by millions. Should he decide that an ungrateful bitch must be disciplined, who would say him *nay*?

Whenever Simone came home to an empty house, she'd fetch a kitchen knife and make a quick check of the basement. With our creaking floorboards, she never feared being taken by surprise, but she was determined to have a weapon handy if required. When in the bathroom, she locked the door behind her and exited cautiously. When she heard a car in the driveway, she made certain it was me. At this point, she'd return the knife to its drawer or slide it under a pillow or furniture until my back was turned.

Outside the home, she felt relatively safe. The *Securitate*, as she knew from experience, were horrible bullies but exceedingly craven. They'd never consider public assassination. Staying away from high places, busy streets or moving trains, made Simone reasonably safe. I did notice, however, that she got edgy near high buildings— something might *accidently* fall. Once aware of her nervousness, I made sure to avoid them when in her company.

Upon learning she was with child, she made a bizarre comment about "avoiding the penalty." I assumed she referenced the discomfort and inconvenience of her "time." Alas, she alluded to life in Romania. Any woman paid by the State was taxed when childless or un-pregnant. Since Romanian emoluments are niggardly at the best of times, punitive taxes constituted egregious hardships.

Simone once commented to Max that they didn't have breakfast in her country. We accepted this as sardonic. Later, we learned that food was scarce. People bought what they could whenever they could. Planned meals were unheard of; improvisation in the kitchen was a prized quality. Two meals a day was considered lavish by many. Between-meal snacks betrayed opulence.

The Albescu family had only one breadwinner. By mid-month, there was scarcely enough money to keep four people fed until the next cash infusion. Simone's removal to a sports school met with cheers. The Albescu daughter would get two and a half nourishing meals a day; the remainder of her family could stretch both money and food much further.

Simone made only one scathing comment about her native land during our life together. With a bitterness never previously exercised, she announced the folly of the Romanian government to insist upon striving for a population of thirty million when it could not, properly, feed two-thirds that number. When expressing this sentiment, her language was heavily garnished.

Even at the Olympics, where the athletes ate in facilities offering copious amounts of food, Simone was closely monitored. The Romanian women ate at segregated tables and were allowed only approved items—that is, food one might find in Romania itself.

"No bread," Simone announced out of the blue.

There was nothing in bread which enhanced performance, so it was denied. There were dozens of times, by Simone's conservative estimation, when her empty stomach cried out at the mere sight of a roll or a small crust of bread.

"Once upon a time," she told me while brandishing a dinner roll, "I'd kill to get this much bread."

She filled her mouth and chewed like a greedy pig.

"If you think I'm kidding," she said while gorging, "you don't know what it is to be hungry."

No, she never starved. Still, one experiences insane appetites for items denied. She confessed to crying herself to sleep because she couldn't sink a fang into some bread. A neighbor lady in Sibiu left her apartment at three in the morning to be among the first in line at the bakery. *If* there were ingredients enough to make bread, it was certain to be sold out by mid-morning.

If there were ingredients enough, Simone's mother would bake her own bread. Most days, the family went without.

Ellen and Simone were sisters in spirit if not in blood. They kept close tabs on each other, talked frequently on the phone and exchanged letters gorged with heartfelt prose, both lyric and narrative. Though anxious to perform baptism, Ellen never pressed. Often, Simone asked questions of a spiritual nature. These were responded to eagerly and at length. Nevertheless, Ellen saved preaching for the pulpit; she avoided initiating conversations of a religious nature. She figured that Simone would likely *come in* when (and only when) she was ready. To coerce her would, in Ellen's view, prove counterproductive.

Three months after presiding over our vows, the Keatsville mayor suffered a stroke and was unable to perform official duties. Though the demands of the "city" executive were minimal, they were exacting. Most local matters were addressed amicably and without lengthy debate. The mayor's main job was filling out papers and responding diplomatically to State and Federal demands. In return, the bureaucratic iron boot was kept off citizen's throats. It was an exasperating business, and no one cared to torture themselves.

Holding a special election was cost prohibitive.

What to do?

One astute city council member dusted off a copy of the municipal by-laws (*circa* 1895). In it, the council was authorized to appoint a mayor should the elected official be unable to carry out the duties of office. Such an appointment would terminate with the next regular election.

There was delight over discovering a solution for one problem, but consternation over confronting an even greater one. None of the council members wanted the job. Each was nominated, and, in turn, each declined. Thus, the city fathers (and one city mother) invoked the tried-and-true absentee rule. None of the council members absented themselves for exactly this reason. The seven private citizens in attendance, thereby, avoided nomination also. Council and citizens present formed a committee of the whole to review leading citizens *not* present and, thus, unable to decline.

In the best tradition of political conspiracy, Ellen Good was elected, by a vote of three to two, to fill the remainder of the mayor's term.

It was a lightning strike. She knew nothing of city affairs and less of politics. Immediately, she objected based upon separation of church and state.

"That ain't in no Constitution nowhere," she was reminded.

"The Church authorities won't allow it," she gasped.

"Your Church authorities have no legal say in secular matters."

"They could remove me," she reminded.

"Great! That will remove any objections to your being mayor."

She was dazed. Defeated at every turn, Ellen turned to Father Bob.

"You're a pest," he declared.

It was clear that Ellen Good was now the Good mayor of Keatsville. Even if she never set foot in City Hall (just across from the community room where Simone and I enjoyed our reception), Ellen would be responsible for city business and money dispersals.

"Will you advise me?" she asked the Catholic shepherd.

He laughed. He laughed, because the city council hadn't selected *him*. Behind his laugh, however, resided the desire to help the distressed.

"Frank Schortmann is one of mine," he reminded. "So's Senator Bob. Between them, they know State law and bureaucratic hokey pokey. They'll be happy to help you. If not, they must come to me for Confession. Often, that influences behavior."

The assurance that Ellen didn't rule alone lifted a great weight from her shoulders.

Simone and I were blissfully unaware until we came to church that Sunday. Ellen was so stunned and overwhelmed that she hadn't thought to inform us. The congregation was unusually large, and we were concerned that we might constitute two and a half people too many. It took a few moments and the cooperation of others, but we secured enough space to share a hymnal.

We heard whispered comments. Ellen was the topic of discussion, but we remained ignorant as to the reason. It wasn't until she took her place at the pulpit to deliver her sermon that we learned the source of the Keatsville buzz.

"A funny thing happened to me on my way to the church," she announced.

Polite laughter.

"I enjoyed the double distinction of being selected mayor and being cited for a parking violation on the same day."

More laughter.

"My first official act was to fire the sheriff."

More laughter. Even obtuse citizens know the mayor can't fire elected officials. Everyone accepted her announcement as a joke rather than a lie.

"Wait until Noah hears about this," I whispered. "He'll expect appointment to pig inspector."

Even the apolitical Simone knew better. Her friend, comforter and mentor would never engage in nepotism.

When our Ion arrived, Simone became ultra-paranoid. It would be just like Ceausescu to punish her by smothering a perfectly innocent infant. Therefore, she never allowed Baby John out of sight. If she put him in his crib, she remained nearby—usually, with a book. If he was asleep when I came home, she'd prepare dinner only if I stood guard.

She packed him everywhere. She trusted a select few to leave Baby John in their care but insisted they never leave him for a second.

When she accepted a job at a Lima dance studio, Simone took Baby John to work. A hireling tended to his whims and needs, but both the sitter and Ion remained in Simone's sight. The owner/ manager of the studio tolerated bizarre behavior in deference to Simone's reputation as an Olympian (and the prestige it brought the school), *and* because Simone was exceptional with pre-teens.

Psychologists tell us that children grow up to mirror their upbringing. Simone's memories of her father's comfortable lap and belated recognition of her mother's subtle acts of love set the nurturing tone for Baby John. Similarly, she treated all young people as if they were her own.

Simone's students were eager to get to their lessons. They often greeted her with a hug, even the boys, and gushed with pride whenever they did something praiseworthy. Whenever students were crushed by an inability to perform, Simone encouraged and lifted their spirits. However, she refused to coddle them. If she thought a child lacked talent or ability, she informed the parents privately. In two instances, parents continued to pay for lessons because their children so enjoyed being around Simone.

She put fun into dancing.

Simone had a modicum of training in dance. She did, however, know much about drills and techniques, particularly in ballet. She was intelligent enough to know what she did not know. On her days off, she took lessons to close the ignorance gap—always hauling Baby John along.

She enjoyed her work; she enjoyed the adoration of her young students; she enjoyed being a mother, albeit a paranoid one; and she enjoyed being a wife as much as I enjoyed being a husband. I loved coming home to her and went into a funk whenever I returned to an empty house. The moment she and Baby John returned, the world was my oyster.

Simone refused to have a baby shower prior to birth. She refused to tempt fate or risk the trauma of facing a pile of baby things should something go wrong.

The idea of being surrounded by strangers was, also, abhorrent. Having people hovering over her for two days or longer was unacceptable. Therefore, Simone insisted on a midwife. She, also, insisted on birthing at home. Alas, there are laws.

She insisted I be there. I sweated bullets with that. Of course, I *wanted* to be there. Still, there was no way to predict when her water would break. Though my road-trips were reduced from one visit every two weeks or one visit a month, my schedule remained full. There were sales appointments, training seminars and conferences. When I wasn't pitching or consulting, I attended classes and honed my skills and kept up with the avalanche of software and hardware advances. I always left a phone number with Simone. If I changed locations, I phoned her to provide another. When we broke for lunch, I'd have something delivered so I could remain near the phone.

The Valentines were still on desks, pinned to bulletin boards and taped to windows when, just after eleven o'clock in mid-February, the phone rang.

"For you, Miles," someone informed.

"Simone," I said, clutching the receiver.

"This is it," she announced calmly.

"On my way."

Everyone knew my situation. Therefore, I didn't excuse myself. My sudden disappearance was enough.

I was in Lima when the alert came—a mere thirty minutes from home. On that day, I made it in less.

We had a bag packed with essentials. There were three diapers and a blanket for baby, a cup and two lemons for Mommy.

In another twenty minutes, we were at the clinic. These were not strangers; we'd attended evening classes on site. A doctor was on call should one be required, but he remained a stranger. My greatest fear was someone, previously unknown to Simone, would appear at a critical moment. That might require sedation.

"Are you okay?" I asked, aiming the car.

"Yeah," she said cheerily, "just dandy."

Seconds later, she growled through gritted teeth.

"I—spoke—too—soon!"

I had faith in our birthing classes. Those people had seen it all. I didn't panic over her contraction. Nevertheless, it shook me up. I don't like seeing her in pain.

In a matter of moments, the seizure subsided, and we breathed again.

"Who—is it?"

She gasped mightily and croaked with a voice weak and exhausted.

"It's Ion."

Simone was huffing and puffing and gulping both spit and air. She gripped my hand until I thought my fingers would fall off. She treated me to unflattering names and comments, but they were in Romanian. I wasn't completely embarrassed.

"Give him me! Give him me!"

I realized how far gone she was. The first thing the midwife did was to plop our son on Simone's stomach. He was squalling for all he was worth which didn't amount to much. He was blue and lined with streaks of blood, but he was changing color.

"Oh!" Simone said, lifting her head with great effort. "What's that?"

Simone is the type of person to launch a comment and leave the auditor to ponder its purpose. She might be dazed enough not to identify a baby when it, literally, smacked her in the stomach. She could be joking. Either way, I admired her bravery. Twice, they offered her a needle; she shook her head vigorously. I, however, was tempted have them put *me* under!

She reached for her son with her free hand. Threatening to sever the fingers from my hand, she used the other to touch the screaming child with the gentility of an angel's kiss.

"*Buna, Ion*," she croaked. "I'm your mother."

The tears welled up in her eyes. It could be pain. It could be joy. More likely, it was both.

Three hours later, looking more pale than normal, a smiling Simone walked out of the clinic clutching me. I, in turn, held a small white bundle.

"She doesn't look like she just had a baby," a woman seated in the waiting room whispered.

No, she didn't. I thought Simone looked like someone released from four hours on the rack! I wanted her to be healthy. I wanted her to *look* healthy.

NOW!

We drove to the nearest store and stocked up on diapers, bottles, powder and other accoutrements. This done, I loaded everything in the trunk.

Because Simone was thirsty, we visited a drive-through and got a clear soda each. Then we stopped by a novelty store and purchased a helium balloon which announced, in bold white letters, IT'S A BOY.

"We'll tie it to your crib," she assured Baby John.

Only after I buy and assemble it, I thought to myself.

When I returned from my next trip, I found John and her mother resting quietly on our bed. What I did not know—thank you, God!— was that Simone had a kitchen knife hidden under a pillow. She was weak as a kitten, but if anyone attempted to visit malevolence upon helpless Ion, it would *literally* be over her lifeless form.

Three hours later, Baby John rested peacefully in his hastily assembled crib. The balloon floated placidly over his head. I lay back on the bed with my arm around Simone. She lay slightly canted with her head on my chest to watch our son sleep.

"What have we done?" she whispered.

I had no answer.

Ellen baptized John the Sunday after Baby John's fifth-week birthday.

Ion Lucian Albescu.

She pronounced every syllable precisely as Simone had coached her.

"It's your turn now," Ellen told her after the service.

"I'm not quite ready," Simone replied.

That was the proverbial *that.*

Baby John's first toy was a small, foam filled soccer ball. Of course, in a matter of days, he was showered with rattles, pacifiers, teething rings, stuffed animals and various baby knick-knacks, but these, without exception, came from neighbors and friends. Therefore, he didn't get anything from us until way late.

He was dressed in his blue jumper and strapped in his car seat/transport basket. His hair, still thin and sparse, was darkening. His intelligent blue eyes focused on the object Simone held in her hand. His mouth was slightly open and expectant.

Simone lobbed the ball and hit him in the chest. He kicked and thrashed his arms and giggled with excitement. Simone picked up the ball, lobbed it at him again and he reacted as he had before. After five identical performances, we decided that he'd had enough. Baby John didn't think so. He turned petulant. He wanted to play ball.

He refused to hold it or stick it in his capacious maw. He wanted Mommy to throw the ball at him and nothing else would do. It hurt us when he threw a tantrum, but, despite her constant presence, Simone refused to respond to his every demand. She often questioned herself. Was she being reasonable or cruel? Logic provided an answer endorsed by experts. Still, Simone's heart pumped peanut butter whenever her child was unhappy.

"Will I ever be a good mother?" she asked.

I knew how her young students adored her and how they struggled and slaved to please her. Therefore, I didn't doubt that Baby John was in good hands. Nevertheless, I'm hardly disinterested.

The revolution was not completely unexpected, but Simone refused to be moved until she saw a photo of Nicolae Ceausescu's death stare. Even then, she dared not hope. On the other side of the Curtain, leaders often advanced through assassination. There was no point in cheering Ceausescu's death if his successor was merely the obvers of the same coin.

Eventually, however, it became clear that the people of Romania rejected communist rule. Since Simone remained reluctant to contact the authorities, Ellen and I queried the State Department and the few Romanian authorities still in this country.

We expected very little and were not disappointed.

Eventually, Simone sent off a hand-written note to Sibiu asking after her family.

Nothing.

A second note was dispatched to a specific official suggested by the Romanian Embassy.

Nothing.

After several phone calls to Washington, a third note in Simone's precise, Romanian hand went on its way.

Three weeks later, we found an official envelope in our mailbox. The Sibiu authorities, such as they were, managed to locate three Albescu families. The names and addresses were provided.

Simone shook her head sadly. These people might be relatives, but she recognized no names. The addresses might as well have been Martian; the street names were unknown to her.

Since she feared the worst from the moment of her defection, she kept up a brave front. I reminded her, only once, what happened to her family was not her fault. Her attitude and demeanor in the face of adversity proved that she agreed. Had the regime been the least civil, Ion and Simone would not have fled. Had the leaders any sense of justice or compassion, they would not blame her family for Simone's actions.

Our one remaining hope was that the Albescu family rotted in some dank prison awaiting a review of their case. We never spoke of this. Simone's wistful sighs told me that she thought of this frequently.

It was Ion's second spring. I bought home some flowers. Baby John was our pride and joy. He became animated when I returned from work, and I showed my appreciation by playing with him for a few minutes before tackling any other domestic business.

There was a peanut butter sandwich on a plate on the table next to a cup of tea. There was a bite, perhaps two, taken but the tea sat cold and untouched. Baby John was seated on the linoleum just an inch or two inside the kitchen chewing his fist. The moment he saw me, he waved his arms and bounced on his bottom in his nice, yellow body suit.

"Hey, sport, how ya doin'?"

I rushed to his waiting arms and scooped him up. We did the routine huggy-huggy, kissy-kissy before I bounced him on my arm. I saw Simone sitting quietly on the couch in her normal reading spot, but she wasn't reading.

I didn't like this. Unfinished sandwich, untouched tea, silent contemplation and—horror of horrors—Baby John within inches of escaping his mother's line of sight.

"What's with Mommy?" I asked.

In response, he turned his body and pointed at her pensive figure.

Simone appreciated flowers though she seldom fussed over them. Baby John was her greatest treasure. She saw perfectly well what I brought. I hardly expected cartwheels, but, even for Simone, her enthusiasm was lacking.

As I approached, she calmly dabbed at her right eye with a knuckle.

"What's wrong?" I asked.

She motioned to the folded letter beside her and reached out for baby. He was eager to fill those open arms; I let him go. Once she had him, she accepted the flowers with quiet appreciation.

"Let's put these in water, shall we?" she asked Ion.

She got up as I settled down with the letter. It was in Romanian, but it didn't take an expert to divine the contents. The names of Simone's mother, father, brother and sister-in-law were quite legible. In the middle of the page were *Elena Ceausescu* and *Securitate* which, also, made my labored translation superfluous.

I heaved a sigh and let the letter fall back onto the couch.

We were prepared; this news did not come as a shock. Still, it was a difficult situation. My place was with my wife and child, but I was completely drained. I couldn't move.

Simone brought in the flowers in a small vase and set them on a windowsill out of baby's reach. A moment later, she gave him a dewy kiss and put him down.

"Play with your toys," she suggested.

Before she released him, he reached for a small, stuffed rabbit.

Simone and I exchanged silent expressions.

"I only met Silvia once," she confided, hardly above a whisper. "Why kill her?"

I refuse to delve into deranged minds.

"Don't give up," I advised. "Things are really confused over there. This could be one more bureaucratic screw up."

She nodded but was resigned. Ion carried the Albescu name for a reason.

From that day forward, Simone's appetite for peanut butter was erased. She associated it with devastating news.

Strangely, she never showed an open aversion to flowers or tea.

The period of mourning lasted over a week. My fears that Simone would retire inside her stoic fortress proved unfounded. Our son was the central beacon in both our lives, and she was determined that the "Last of the Albescus" would get her very best.

We continued to hope that Simone's family somehow survived Elena's vengeance. With each passing day, it became more certain that her immediate family was gone. She treasured every pleasant memory of her parents and brother, but her deepest regret was that she didn't live with them long enough to know and appreciate them as well as a daughter and sister should.

There remained a few aunts, uncles and cousins, but Simone was never close to her extended family. Simone had no desire to visit or contact them.

She looked to the future. The bulk of it rested with Baby John. If people dared suggest it might be in Ion's best interest to attend a boarding school, they'd discover how ferocious a mother tiger can be. Meanwhile, Simone relied on me more and more.

"You have done so very much for me," she announced. "Now, I want to pay back what I owe."

I objected vehemently. Simone was my wife, not some hireling

I was not acquired through the Help Wanted Pages. I often explained this simple concept to her. She refused to listen. In her view, I'd sacrificed on her behalf; she was determined to reciprocate.

"We're a team," I insisted. "The three of us."

EPILOGUE

Simone was with Ion when she applied for her green card. Because some supercilious bureaucrat struck Simone as both pompous and rude, her attitude toward American officials was equally as uncharitable as her feelings for Romanian quill-pushers. The less she dealt with them the better. She did what was required of her and no more.

I nudged her from time to time; Simone should take the test and become a citizen. She considered it. She knew much of what she'd be tested on and was smart enough to learn the rest with alacrity.

One morning over breakfast, she shared her decision.

"I'm Romanian," she announced. "It's my only link with my family and my home. I appreciate being a guest in this country, but I cannot break with my family and my heritage. I feel guilty about leaving them. That's my penance."

Perhaps, one day, Simone will reconsider. If so, she'd find her own way. Further prodding by me—or Ellen—would meet with petulance and resentment.

She kept her job because she wanted to work. She wanted to learn dance, and she wanted to teach, and she wanted to be around young, eager people. When I was away from home, she'd sit every evening with Baby John and read to him before he had the ability to comprehend. He liked the soothing sound of her voice and would enjoy sitting in her lap as she showed him pictures and explained things. Eventually, when he could understand words, he'd run for a book at every opportunity. It didn't matter that Simone had read it to him dozens of times; Mama's lap was special, and her soothing voice a Siren's song.

Ellen accepted Keatsville as a permanent assignment. Her mayoral duties were far behind her and the city council knew better than to tap her again. Fortunately, no similar emergency arose. Senator Bob tried to talk her into running for his old seat in the legislature, but Ellen declined. Her place, she insisted, was with her congregation.

Simone and I attended every first and third (communion) Sunday. The twice monthly visits allowed us to keep in touch. Ellen spoiled John shamelessly and promised to baptize our second child. She hinted mightily that she could perform a double ceremony. Simone was dubious but far more receptive. Over the months and years, she and Ellen covered acres of theological ground. Meanwhile, Simone, the voracious reader, had digested the Bible twice.

Father Bob visited a communal newcomer from near Decatur one morning to greet and invite him to Mass. Alas, the handsome young man, who bought the farm when Cowboy Bob decided he'd had all the fun he could stand, was not Catholic.

Despite Allen Overstreet's "heathenism," Father Bob introduced him to Ellen—with predictable results.

Allen and Ellen both grew up and worked on (Protestant) farms. They were instant friends. Eight months later, they were engaged.

I studied Overstreet very carefully upon our first meeting. Playing the part of an officious prig, I didn't want Ellen to wed just anybody. Always at my side, of course, was Simone and her, by now, expansive stomach. She turned John over to Ellen for safe keeping and deliberately interrupted my planned inquisition.

It was *déjà vu* all over again.

Simone approached the unsuspecting farmer from his blind side. She grabbed his hand, spun him around and pumped his arm for all she was worth.

"Nelson, Simone!"

Ellen and I exchanged knowing glances. The scene was a duplicate of an Innsbruck encounter of many years past. There was one glaring difference, however. It was the first time Simone used my name. Since then, she's used no other.

Ion warmed Simone's heart. When he began playing with the soccer ball, she became his devoted slave. Barely was he beyond the toddler stage when she began his instruction. As with her dance students, she was patient and encouraging. He enjoyed playing; she enjoyed praising him. The skills he learned were rudimentary but important.

One sunny spring day, I watched Simone and Ion taking turns dribbling around objects in the back yard.

"If he loses interest…" I began tentatively after practice.

"That's it," she replied instantly. "I think he has the aptitude to be good, but if we push, he'll learn to hate it."

"Like someone I know?" I asked.

"Yes," she replied wistfully. "Like someone *we both* know. I won't force him to endure that."

We sat at the table watching Ion finish up a bread and butter snack. Simone messaged her swollen belly with one hand. We were newly returned from the clinic with the news that this baby was female.

"Thought of any new names?" I asked, presenting my wife with a cup of steaming tea.

"Thousands. I have Ion. It's only right that you decide this time."

Without premeditation, I responded.

"Alba Iulia."

Was I trying to be funny? Even I can't say. The name just popped into my head because, in a highly metaphysical sense, that name presaged subsequent events.

Simone didn't scoff or laugh. While waiting for her tea to cool, she turned the name over in her mind.

"She's going to be teased in school," Simone announced.

By then, I concluded, she'd have acquired a nickname more suitable to her surroundings.

"Have you ever been to Alba Iulia?" I dared to ask.

"No," she replied. "I've known people from there. They speak highly of it."

Gingerly, she sipped at her drink. Finding it sufficiently cooled, she enjoyed a swallow. Moments later, the hand on her stomach ceased its caress.

"Little Alba just kicked me," she announced.

www.ingramcontent.com/pod-product-compliance
Lightning Source LLC
Chambersburg PA
CBHW061736310726
48969CB00002BA/448